Romancing Olive

HOLLY BUSH

For Eileen, Susie, Linda, Sarah and Kate. Wonderful women who were, are and will be.

Chapter One

Spencer, Ohio 1891

OLIVE WILKINS FOUND THE SHERIFF'S OFFICE AS promised, beside a busy general store. The walls were thick stone, and the bars at the windows cast striped patterns on the floor. A weary-faced man with sun-toughened skin sat behind the desk.

"Just a minute..." the sheriff said.

Olive waited dutifully as he wrote, letting her eyes wander from the cells in the corner of the room to the gun belt looped over the hook near the door to the sign proclaiming Sheriff Bentley as the law in this small Ohio town.

"What can I help you with, ma'am?" he asked as he looked up from his papers and tilted back his hat.

"My name is Olive Wilkins, and my brother James Wilkins and his wife Sophie lived here in Spencer. I am here to take his children back to my home in Philadelphia. But I am not quite sure with whom they are staying. The note from my sister-in-law's family is unclear," Olive explained as she pulled the oft-folded and unfolded letter from her bag.

The sheriff sat back in his chair and tapped his pencil stub against his mouth. "John and Mary are staying with Jacob Butler."

"How are the Butlers related to my brother's wife?" Olive asked.

"They're not," Sheriff Bentley replied.

"Then how did the children come to..."

"None of Sophie's family, the Davises, would take them in," he interrupted.

"Oh."

"Jacob Butler couldn't abide two children living on their own in that shack, so he took them home. He was your brother's closest neighbor," the sheriff explained.

"Sophie's family abandoned them?" Olive asked. Could this man be talking about James's nearest relatives? Could there be two sets of orphaned children in one small community? With the same names? No, there could not be.

"The Davis clan couldn't tell you how many children or dogs belong to them," the sheriff said. "But they sure didn't want more."

Olive frowned, certain she had misunderstood. "My brother's children lived alone on a farm? Surely Sophie's family would have never..."

"I don't right know I'd call Jimmy's place a farm," the sheriff interrupted and met Olive's bewildered eyes. "The worst part is I don't know how long the children were in the house with their mother dead and if they saw her murder."

Olive's knees threatened to buckle, and her eyes darted from the sheriff's face to her handbag to the desk. "How could that be? The Davis's letter only said that James and Sophie had died. I... I just assumed that it had been influenza or a dreadful accident of some kind."

The sheriff stood, came around the desk, and seated Olive in a chair. "Jimmy was killed when he got caught cheating at cards. He wagered the farm, and the man who killed him rode out and tried to stake his claim." He looked away and grimaced. "When I got back to town a couple of days later, I rode out to check on Sophie. It looked like she put up a hell of a fight."

Olive clutched the letter from her brother's in-laws in her hand. She pictured her only sibling in her mind's eye as a young man when she had last seen him. The pride of her mother and father, a charming and handsome boy who filled their Church Street home with laughter. At twenty years of age, he had loved Sophie Davis with such abandon; he'd left all he'd known behind to make a life with his new wife on the plains of Ohio. Sophie's kin were farmers, and she wanted no life, other than that which the soil and the tilling of it, brought. So James announced his intentions of making Ohio his new home where he would farm and raise his family.

The death of Olive's parents, only a year apart, had left her bereft, but she had cared for them through their illnesses and had seen their demise inch closer with each day. The news of James's and Sophie's deaths, however, left her grief-stricken. But her misery would certainly pale in comparison to the devastation John and Mary must feel. Without preamble, this pair of deaths had orphaned her ten-year-old niece and four-year-old nephew.

"And the children?" Olive asked.

"Couldn't find hide nor hair of them wild things. Searched everywhere. Jacob checked the house about a week later and found them living there. Mary gave him a fight. She was scared to death, even though she knew Jacob and his children. And John, that boy hasn't spoken a word since," he replied.

Tears threatened Olive's eyes. She could not decide which of all of this horrifying news was the worst. *But it could not be.* The sheriff must have some of this information wrong, otherwise... "I'll have to make sure that Mr. and Mrs. Butler understand how thankful I am someone took in Mary and John."

The sheriff propped a hip on the corner of his desk. "There is no Mrs. Butler. Jacob's a widower. His wife died a year ago giving birth to their youngest son."

"How... can you tell me how to arrange transportation to the Butlers?" Olive asked.

"I'll be going out that way tomorrow. I'll rent a wagon, unless you ride. No? Then I'll take you out there," he offered.

"That's very kind of you, Sheriff," Olive replied. The social courtesies came without thought while her heart grappled with what the sheriff had said. She pulled her cloak tightly around her and left the office feeling numb.

Olive found herself walking aimlessly through town. In her mind she played and replayed the story the sheriff had told her, and it rubbed raw all that she knew to be true of how she was raised, how James was raised, how life was to be lived. She glanced down and only then realized she still held the letter that had brought the heart-breaking news.

Sophie's family had written her that there was no one to take in the two small children after their parents' deaths, so Olive faced the greatest challenge she had ever known. She would rescue these orphans, blood of her blood, and love them and take them back to Philadelphia where she would raise them in their father's childhood home.

Olive had stared out the train window on the trip to Spencer, mile after mile, dreaming of Sunday afternoons at the ice cream parlor, helping John with his studies, and someday leading Mary into womanhood. What a wonderful continuation of the Wilkins' legacy Olive would be able to bestow. She would be firm but gentle, patient, but with high expectations of these bright shining pennies. She would read them the letters their father had written, take them to church, and love them and they would love her.

Olive made her way back to the Jenkins Hotel as night drew

closer. There was no point or need to dwell on the sheriff's grim tale. She would discover the truth on her own soon enough. She sat on the edge of the bed and surveyed the room. The wallpaper hung precariously above the bed, and a small nightstand held only a chipped washbasin and pitcher. She smelled mildew, and the oil from the kerosene lamp, now throwing shadows, revealed dark stains where the rain had run down the wall. Turning the lamp down to a soft glow, Olive undressed and dusted her skirts. Her hat she placed over the flowered pitcher. After fastening all twenty-eight pearl buttons of her nightdress, she undid her hair and let the waist-length mass pull at her scalp as she massaged her head. *Glory, does that feel good,* Olive thought while brushing her hair the required one hundred strokes.

* * *

"Good morning, Sheriff," Olive said as he escorted her down the street to the livery. "Has my brother's killer been apprehended? I failed to ask yesterday."

"Not enough men in this town willing to join a posse. Anyway, he had a three-day lead, me being out of town," the sheriff said as he tipped his hat to a young woman sweeping the sidewalk.

Olive halted mid-stride. "So nothing's to be done? Is that what you're implying?"

Sheriff Bentley stopped and turned to face her. "I sent a telegram to the sheriff in Cincinnati. And to some of the towns close by," the sheriff replied. "But I'll be honest with you. I doubt he'll ever be caught. From what Mabel said over at the saloon, he was just a drifter. She's been working there for years, and she'd never seen him before."

"So, on the word of a saloon girl, my brother's killer will go free," Olive said flatly.

The sheriff continued his brisk walk, shaking his head as he went. "This ain't Philadelphia, ma'am. There's miles of open country and not enough lawmen to go around. I'll do what I can, but I'm telling you now, chances are your brother's killer is halfway to Texas by now."

Olive sat silently beside the sheriff on the buckboard seat. This certainly was *not* Philadelphia. The idea that a man could murder two people and orphan two children on the turn of a card and ride away was astonishing. Olive wondered whom she could appeal to if the sheriff himself had given up any hope of apprehending the outlaw. But the morning was beautiful and already warm, and she undid the clasp on her cape, smoothing the black fabric of her dress. Rolling streams and meadows and an occasional man behind a plow made her imagine her brother at work in his fields.

"Will we pass James's home on the way to Mr. Butler's?" she asked.

"No. Your brother's land is a couple of miles past Jacob's," the sheriff replied. He turned to her with a smile. "Beautiful morning, don't you think, Miss Wilkins?"

Olive eyed the sheriff's smile and felt suddenly uncomfortable. Here she was, alone in the middle of God's acre with a man she met only the day before.

"Lovely," she replied and turned away, content to envision her brother's home as she had been doing on her long train trip west. Would it be brick or painted white with a picket fence? Would it look anything like their family home, her home now, on Church Street, clapboarded and lace-window trimmed? Whatever it looked like, she was certain it would be a haven for John and Mary as her home had been for her and her brother as children. That safe, comfortable home, the guardian of her precious memories and the keeper of her childhood.

It had been nearly an hour since she and the sheriff set out.

Olive was growing impatient and edgy, wondering if this man did indeed know exactly where he was going.

"You'll see Jacob's place over the next rise," the sheriff said finally, nodding ahead.

"What kind of man is Mr. Butler?" Olive inquired near the top of the hill.

The sheriff turned and stared at her. "The kind of man who couldn't let two children alone, even though they're no blood relation, and he has enough mouths to feed as is. A good one, I reckon."

Olive knew a set-down when she received it and concentrated instead on this mission of mercy she was now embarked on. She would care for John and Mary as if they were her own, as they certainly would be, just as her parents had nurtured and cared for her and James. At thirty-five, she had long abandoned dreams of a family of her own. Her job in the library and her family home was meant to be enough to sustain her. This tragic twist of events would place two young children in the care of an aunt they had never met. Olive took a deep breath to steady her nerves and scanned the landscape around her.

Fields of dark soil, turned and waiting for seed, lay before her, cut through with stripes of high grass as the morning breeze waved the hay. Olive caught sight of a cabin and a barn behind in a gentle valley at the crux of the fields. As they steered down a path to the house, Olive's eyes closed spontaneously as she drew in the rich aroma of moist fertile soil. Something so primitive, so basic about the smell of spring-turned ground.

When she opened her eyes, Olive saw a man behind a plow, and as they drew closer, she was shocked. He seemed nearly as tall as the horse he guided. His plaid shirtsleeves were rolled up and revealed enormous forearms. The man's back was to them as he coaxed and whistled to the horse. His hair hung in huge curls over his collar. Black boots to his knees and suspenders making a giant 'X' on his back held up his rough pants. The sheriff shouted, and the man turned his head. He pulled back on the reins of the plow horse, and Olive watched him unharness himself from great bands of leather attaching him to the plow.

"Sheriff," the man said as he approached the wagon.

"Hey, Jacob."

Olive looked in amazement at this Jacob Butler. He could only be twenty-five years old, and yet he managed a farm, motherless children, and John and Mary. In her mind she had envisioned a man closer to her age and certainly not a man this... rough.

"Ma'am," the man nodded.

Olive nodded back nervously, and the sheriff looked at her expectantly as he rested his elbows on his knees and pushed the brim of his hat back on his forehead. Jacob Butler stood so tall; the two men were nearly eye-to-eye, Olive noticed. She heard birds chirping and the soft tap of the sheriff's boot. She had no idea where her sensibilities had gone.

"This here is John and Mary's aunt. Jimmy's sister," the sheriff said.

"Ma'am."

"Mr. Butler, I can not thank you enough for taking in my niece and nephew," Olive finally managed to reply.

"Not a problem."

"No, really, had I known they were not being cared for by relatives, I would have come weeks and weeks ago. I will not impose on your generosity a moment longer than necessary. If the sheriff will wait, I will get the children and return to town," Olive said in a rush. Surely this very young man was struggling with all the responsibilities that parenthood entailed.

The man tilted his head and looked at her. "Suit yourself," he replied.

Olive watched as he sat down on the end of the wagon, and

the sheriff drove them on to the house. Her palms were sweating as the wagon stopped and the front door opened. A boy and a girl flew into Jacob Butler's arms.

"Daddy! Why aren't ya plowing?" the boy said through two missing front teeth.

Two more children stood in the doorway with such looks of longing it nearly broke Olive's heart. John and Mary. She watched Mary hold her younger brother back and whisper something in his ear. But John would not be stopped and found himself a place on the man's neck and latched on. Jacob Butler laughed and kissed each child and tickled the little girl's side. Olive watched the stone-faced giant cuddle the three clinging to him. He looked up to Mary, standing in the doorway.

"How is Mark this morning?" he asked.

"I can't get him to eat," the girl said with a shrug.

"Let's see if I have any better luck than Mary," Mr. Butler said as he looked at the other children in his arms.

Olive stepped down out of the wagon and followed the man as he carried the three children, hanging on at odd angles. He stopped at the door and reached to touch Mary's shoulder, but the girl slunk back and ducked into the house.

Olive noticed then the remains of a woman's touch and its decay as she stepped onto the porch and into Jacob Butler's home. The flowers near the steps were overgrown with weeds and once brightly-colored fabric, now hung limp and dirty at the windows. The sink was piled high with dishes, pots and pans and a quilt, maybe white, maybe gray, covered a rocker. Her eyes rose to a small boy tied into a high chair with a wide band of fabric. The child's head was limp, and his chin was covered with drool. Jacob Butler untied him as he cooed and a grin came to the child's face although his eyes never found his father's.

"Why won't you eat for Mary?" he asked as he kissed the infant and turned to the doorway. "This is my youngest son,

Mark. And those two are Luke and Peg."

Olive latched onto the stares of the two remaining children. "And they are Mary and John?"

"How does she know our names?" Mary asked.

John saw his sister's scowl and ran behind Jacob Butler's legs.

"This is your aunt," Mr. Butler said.

"Which Davis are you?" Mary said with fists clenched.

"I'm not a Davis. I'm your father's sister. My name is Olive Wilkins," she replied.

"Well, there's no money left, if that's what you're here for," Mary said.

Olive shook her head. "I... I don't know anything about any money. I came to take you back to my home in Philadelphia."

John clung to Jacob Butler's leg, crying, and Olive saw fear grow in his eyes. And, conversely, hatred in Mary's. The Butler children, sensing Mary and John's distress, began to wail as well, and Olive thought her eardrums would burst. Mr. Butler carried Mark, while Luke and Peg clung to his arm, and he dragged John, firmly latched to his leg, to the rocker at the window. When he had finally settled into the chair with four children in his lap, he rocked slowly and talked softly until the wails began to subside.

"Miss Wilkins?" the sheriff said. "I've got to get going. Are you coming?"

Olive looked from the sheriff's sympathetic face to Mary's seething one and onto Jacob Butler's comforting smile for the children as he rocked.

"Mary," Olive said, "I know you've had some difficult times, but I have a home with a yard and a lovely school nearby. It's where your father grew up. He'd want you to be there. I want you to be there."

"How would you know what Pa wanted?" the girl said.

"Well, we grew up together, had a wonderful childhood,

and I just know that James..."

"If it was so wonderful and you two were so close, how come I never met you before? I don't want nothing to do with Mama's family, but at least I knew who they are. Where you been?" Mary asked.

Olive was stung by the scorn in her niece's voice. "Mary, we've just met but, I will not stand for disrespect from you."

"Miss Wilkins?" the sheriff said.

"If you could please give me a few more minutes, Sheriff," Olive replied.

"Going to take longer than that," the sheriff said as he walked out the door.

"Mary, listen to me. I have the finances to provide you with a good education and clothes, and in my home there is a bedroom for each of you. A yard to play in and..." Olive stopped as she saw Jacob Butler's mouth turn into a grim line. "Oh, Mr. Butler, I didn't mean to imply that your home is less than..."

"If it's all right with Jacob, we'll stay here," the girl said.

"But he's not family, Mary," Olive replied and took a step towards her niece.

Mary moved to within a foot of Jacob Butler and he watched as she did.

"He come and got John and I and buried Mama. He'll do."

"Came and got," Olive said.

"What?" Mary asked.

"The correct grammar is 'he came and got John and me,'" Olive said as she wiped her forehead. "Never mind." The sullen state of the children, their tattered clothes and dirty hair, were shocking. Their anger and fear, palpable with every word Mary spoke, was horrifying. How could this Jacob Butler, even as a widower, allow these children to fall to such a state?

"Mary, will you hold Mark for me?" Mr. Butler said as he rose.

Jacob Butler went out the door without a glance to Olive. She followed his broad back, and when he stepped down from the porch, he turned to her.

"Miss Wilkins, may I make a suggestion?" he asked.

"Certainly," Olive replied.

"Why don't you stick around here for a while and let John and Mary get to know you?"

"I could tell the sheriff to have someone come back for me this evening, I suppose," Olive said and shaded her eyes with her hand.

"No. Not one day. I mean for a while," Mr. Butler said.

Olive brooded a bit, mumbling to herself. "I imagine it would be easier on the children if I did. I can't imagine staying much longer at the Jenkin's Hotel, though. Is there a reputable boarding house in Spencer?"

"There's nothing reputable in Spencer. And anyway I don't mean an hour away in town. I mean here."

Olive's face tightened, and her mouth flew open in shock. "Mr. Butler, to suggest such a thing!"

"Look, all I'm saying is that you don't get to know children or anyone for that matter til you've lived with them," Mr. Butler replied.

"Miss Wilkins!" the sheriff called.

"Fiddle dee dee! Can't you see I need a moment?" Olive said and began to pace the narrow porch. "Sheriff?" she said when she looked up.

"Yes, Miss Wilkins?" he replied.

"Couldn't I stay at my brother's farm? Would anyone object?" Olive asked.

"I don't think that's a good idea," the sheriff replied, shaking his head.

"That would solve everything," Olive said. "The children would be back in their own home, and we could get to know each other. In time I could convince them to move back to my home in Philadelphia."

"Before you talk to John and Mary, I think you should go see you brother's place," Mr. Butler said.

"Yes, I suppose you're right. I may have to go back to town for supplies. Sheriff, can I trouble you?" Olive asked.

"Sorry, no, Miss Wilkins. Got to get going," the sheriff said with a shake of his head.

Olive looked to Mr. Butler, and he turned and went into the house. When he came out, he motioned her to follow, and they walked to the barn.

"What are we doing, Mr. Butler?" Olive asked.

"Going to your brother's place," he said as he began hitching a wagon.

"Who will stay with the children?" Olive wondered.

"Mary can handle them for an hour or two. It's not far, and if there's trouble, I taught her to fire the gun," he said as he harnessed the horse.

"Mary is going to defend herself and four children?"

"No, she'll fire into the air, and I'll come," Mr. Butler said and climbed up on to the seat.

Olive pulled herself into the wagon on her own, scuffing her shoe and nearly putting a hole in her stocking. "Humph," she said and turned to face this giant beside her.

The man lifted the reins lightly to the horse's back. Olive was anxious to see her brother's home and make it ready for the children. She may be scrubbing floors and beating rugs for days to come, but she knew John and Mary were worth the effort. Olive made a mental list of supplies and groaned when she could not remember the name of the soap that Millie, her mother's housekeeper, had used to make the furniture and floors shine. She felt Mr. Butler's eyes on hers, and she turned to look at this stranger who was so intimately entwined in her life without her permission and without her regard.

Jacob Butler's chest was huge, and his arms barely fit through the rolled up cuffs of his shirt. The gentlemen of her acquaintance, business associates of her father or patrons of the library, were smallish men who made their way with their heads not their hands. They were gentle men and learned men. Olive caught a whiff of earth and lard soap as she stared and raised her brows in question.

* * *

Jacob looked at this spinsterish woman riding beside him. He could hardly believe this frightened, mousy thing was Jimmy Wilkins's sister. Not a hair was out of place under her dark bonnet. Schoolmarm glasses, a brown cape and a black dress. Was she dressed for mourning? The only hint of color on the otherwise drab woman was a pair of clear blue eyes. Her skin was pale, but she obviously enjoyed the feel of the sun on her face

"What was the grunt for?" he asked.

"Ladies do not grunt, sir. I did not grunt," she replied.

"Yes you did, ma'am," Jacob said. They rode on silently for a few minutes.

"I can't seem to remember the name of the soap our housekeeper used. And I was wondering if it would be available in Spencer," she said finally.

"Soap?"

"Yes, Mr. Butler. I can't think of the name. But it certainly did work. Mother wouldn't let our housekeeper use anything but it on our furniture and floors and banisters. I can smell it as I sit here." She turned and looked at him from under the wide brim of her bonnet. "What, Mr. Butler? Have you never been unable to remember something? It's on the tip of my tongue."

Jacob could only tilt his head and shake it in amazement at

this woman. She had no idea of what she was going to see when they came to Jimmy's farm. It might be fun watching this proper know-it-all when she realized there were no floors to polish, just dirt to be swept. He could have revealed a thousand indignities surrounding the home of Jimmy and Sophie, but he decided this woman needed to see it with her own eyes.

* * *

Humph, Olive thought. *Does he think I'm so old, I'll forget my name like Mrs. Patterson?* That poor soul didn't know a spoon from a fork and needed round the clock attention from her daughter Theda. Poor Theda. She would never experience anything like this and couldn't wait for Olive's return with her niece and nephew. Theda and Olive had discussed at length this mission of mercy that she was now embarked on. Olive was counting on Theda's help with John and Mary, knowing her lifelong friend would love these children nearly as much as she.

Mr. Butler turned the wagon onto a rutted lane, and Olive was nearly knocked from her seat by the jostling. The holes were filled with dark, slimy water, and Olive felt a fine spray of moisture hit her face as the horse trotted down the road. She grunted as the wagon pitched and, noticing a spot of dirt on her brown coat, picked away the droplet of mud. Olive saw Jacob Butler didn't shift at all in his seat. Just braced one long leg on the buckboard as Olive hung onto her glasses.

"Is there another road we can take to get to James's home?" Olive asked.

"We're on Jimmy's land now. No other way to get to the house."

Olive sat up at his announcement. This was James's farm. Her head twisted and turned, but she saw only barren ground with an occasional boulder here and there. A huge, dead tree lay on its side, partially pulled from the ground, some roots still holding. Grass grew from a hole in the side of the trunk and contrasted the gray of the bark. A fence began on her right only to abruptly stop at a stack of rotting rails near the end, weeds growing up and around them. A rusting saw straddled the wood, and the sun caught the edge of the metal, forcing Olive to shield her eyes. James must have been very busy with his home and crops to leave the entrance in such disrepair. *But Rome wasn't built in a day*, she reminded herself.

Olive sat up straight as they crested a hill. The sun shone brightly, and Olive squinted to get her first look. "Where's the house?"

"Right there," Jacob Butler said and nodded ahead.

"All I see is a shed of sorts, Mr. Butler," Olive said as she shifted in her seat.

"That's the house, Miss Wilkins."

Realization dawned on Olive, and she turned to the man beside her. "No, I'm sure you're mistaken."

Mr. Butler stared straight ahead. No reply. Olive turned and focused on the grim scene before her. She saw a clothesline strung from a tree to the house. A line of birds sat on it and sang and chirped beautifully. Olive wondered if Sophie could see them from her kitchen window in the morning. But as Olive let her gaze roam, she was overcome with despair. The house was big enough for one room, listing a bit, with shingles, tumbling off. The plank siding was brown and weathered. No yard really, just a stretch of mud broken by an overturned bucket.

Olive stepped down from the wagon and watched Mr. Butler wrestle the door to the house off its hinges. He ducked through the opening and came back outside.

"Seen enough?" he asked as he approached.

Olive's hand was a fist around a wooden slat on the wagon. She glared at him as she marched by. He grabbed her arm, stopping her abruptly.

"No need to go in the house," he said.

She shook off his hand with a huff and turned a determined face his way.

Mr. Butler looked skyward and dropped his hold.

Olive walked slowly to the doorway. She heard buzzing from within and stepped into the dark interior, unable to see, but overwhelmed by a powerful stench. When her vision adjusted, she found the source of the noise. Thousands of flies and maggots swarmed over a dark blotch on the dirt floor. The sight and smell was so horrid she turned and ran outside.

"The bugs? Why are there so many bugs in the house, Mr. Butler?" Olive asked through pale lips. He barely met her eye yet Olive could see the pity on his face and felt the blood drain from hers.

"Miss Wilkins, why don't we head back to..."

"Tell me Mr. Butler."

"Look, there's nothing to be done."

"Tell me," Olive screamed.

"Sophie was cut up pretty bad, and by the time I got her buried, she had pretty much bled out all over the dirt," he said.

"And?"

"When I lifted her, the bugs and maggots were already nesting in her face," Mr. Butler said, his voice rising. "That's what happens when there's blood spilled."

Olive straightened, horrified with the picture he painted, yet certain he told the grim truth. She found herself at the side of the house emptying her stomach on the bare earth.

"It's clean," Mr. Butler said.

"Thank you." Olive replied as she accepted the folded bandana from his hand.

"Like I said before, let's go back to my place and try and sort this out."

Olive did not understand any of what she had seen or heard. She desperately needed to know the whole story. She held the hanky to her nose, walked back to the house and inside.

Piles of rags were heaped in a corner, near an unswept fireplace. The table was piled with filth, its chairs over-turned. Olive saw scurrying movement under a blanket covering straw. She picked up a pair of glasses from the mantel with a shaking hand. Olive closed her eyes and held her brother's spectacles to her breast.

"As if killing their parents wasn't enough," she whispered as Jacob Butler came through the doorway.

"Pardon?" he asked.

Olive swept her hand around the squalid room. "Wasn't it enough that this outlaw killed Mary and John's parents? What possessed him to destroy their home as well?"

"You think the man that killed Sophie did this to the house?" Mr. Butler asked.

"So vicious," Olive hissed, staring wide-eyed around the room.

Jacob Butler closed the gap between them in two strides. He turned her roughly to face him. "For the love of God, woman. Don't you get it? Your brother was a cheating, lazy gambler and his wife a drunk."

Olive's mouth opened in shock. "It can not be. James married a woman who drank alcohol?" Mr. Butler's hands fell away from her shoulders.

"Drank alcohol? She could drink most men under the table, and when she did," Mr. Butler replied, "she spread her legs for any man in the room."

Olive's hand flew to her mouth, and she whispered, "Poor James."

"Poor James?" he shouted. "He knew what she was. He didn't care. He gambled with the money she made and drank the

18

whiskey that was left when she passed out."

"She made money? James couldn't provide for his family?"

"She was a whore, Miss Wilkins," Jacob Butler said quietly. "It kept food on the table. Jimmy never could figure out why his crops wouldn't grow, while he spent his days in the saloon at the poker table."

"So you are saying that Sophie and James's home always looked like this?" Olive asked.

Jacob Butler nodded his reply.

Olive's eyes rounded in horror. "John and Mary lived like this."

"Let's go," Jacob Butler said and reached to cup her elbow in his hand.

Olive pulled away and turned to the rough wooden trough overflowing with dishes and dirt and looked out the solitary window to an elm tree. There, standing clean and pure, were two white crosses in the ground. An involuntary gasp escaped her and tears threatened again. Outside, Olive knelt on the hard earth, between the graves and picked up wilted wild flowers.

"You buried them," Olive said without turning.

Jacob Butler knelt down on his haunches, hat in hand. "It gives me comfort to go to my wife Margaret's grave. I knew the children would want to know where their parents were buried."

Oddly, tears would not come as Olive stared at the hard earth. Her shoulders shook, but not a single drop escaped. Sordid visions flew through her head and countless questions begged an answer, but she could do nothing but softly ask, "Why?"

* * *

Jacob watched the woman's tall, slight form shake, and he regretted his anticipation of seeing her surprise. Her complete and utter shock was so genuine and heartfelt that he could feel nothing but guilt for letting her see her brother's dismal existence. Jacob knew what it was like when your world began to crumble before your eyes, and he knew this woman, right now, was watching all that she believed and held dear, filter through her hand like so much August dirt. Jacob watched her rise, stumble over a root and right herself before he had time to reach out. She climbed into the wagon and folded her hands in front of her.

Jacob pulled himself into the wagon and clucked the horse to turn. He regarded Olive Wilkins in a new light. Clearly shaken, but not broken. To this sheltered woman's credit she had held her head high and demanded to understand the ugliness surrounding her brother's demise.

"Thank you, Mr. Butler," she said.

"Miss Wilkins, I should have never brought you out here."

"No, Mr. Butler, I would have never believed you if you had merely tried to tell me. I needed... I needed to see it for myself," she said.

He nodded, and they bumped along towards the morning sun.

"My God, Mr. Butler. What did Mary see go on inside those four walls? How will she ever get over it?"

"Children are stronger than we give them credit for. I don't think Jimmy ever let one of Sophie's ah... friends near Mary. Not that I'm sure they didn't try."

"Is that why Mary shrinks away from you when you reach to her?"

Jacob nodded. "I think so. I was pretty surprised she stood as close to me today when you were talking about moving back to Philadelphia. She doesn't usually get within ten feet of me."

"There must not be a soul on this earth she trusts," Miss Wilkins whispered.

"No, I don't think there is."

The long ride home was quiet. Jacob stole glances at Olive Wilkins and watched her swallow and purse her lips.

"Mr. Butler? When you asked me to... when you mentioned my staying on... were you, are you still...?"

"You're welcome to stay, Miss Wilkins. I'll bunk in the barn."

* * *

His quick response brought Olive to tears faster than the horrid sights she had just seen. She buried her face in her hands and wept. The tears poured, unheeded for her brother and his wife and for John and Mary. For herself and her shattered daydreams.

Mr. Butler's arm crept around her, and she turned and clung to him. His flannel shirt was soft and warm and caught Olive's tears. She was sobbing uncontrollably on the chest of man she had met that morning, but it felt right, was right. As if there were no other humanity left on the earth but this man. Two strangers, stranded in a tragedy they had not written. Olive sniffed, righted herself and focused on the unwilling victims of this play. Convention be damned, she thought. If she must live on Jacob Butler's farm until John and Mary could be coaxed back to civilization, then so be it.

"Don't let the children see your tears, Miss Wilkins," he said.

Olive realized they were pulling up in front of the Butler house. She quickly dried her face and stood up in the wagon. This weathered house, with its patterns of crops, looked clean and new and righteous. What she had dismissed as shabby earlier in the day was in a dire need of scrubbing, yes, but held a family, and held it with love. No wonder Mary did not want to leave. This was a castle and this man, Jacob Butler, a prince, compared to what Mary had known.

Chapter Two

OLIVE FOLLOWED JACOB BUTLER INTO THE HOUSE, and children came running from all directions.

"Daddy," Peg and Luke screeched as John jumped up and down. Mr. Butler kissed every head but Mary's. He nodded in her direction, and she looked away.

"Children," Mr. Butler said. They silenced immediately and turned to face him. "Miss Wilkins, John and Mary's aunt, is going to stay here with us on the farm for awhile."

Luke and Peg took a step closer to Olive. Luke grinned a toothless smile, and Peg held her hands together at her chest. John seemed confused and turned his questioning gaze to his sister. Mary's mouth was a grim line, and Olive could feel her anger from across the room.

"I'll sleep in the barn with Luke and John," Mr. Butler said.

The two boys looked at each other and exchanged questions without words. "Why do we have to sleep in the barn, Daddy?" Luke asked.

"Well," Mr. Butler said as he crouched down, "ladies need some privacy. We men will be fine in the barn."

Luke and John stood tall, and John nodded as Luke repeated, "The ladies need some privacy."

"Mary, you and Peg can share and give your aunt my bed. Mark will stay in his crib. Have you thought about what we'll be eating for supper, Mary?" Mr. Butler said.

"What am I? Your slave?" Mary shouted and ran out the door.

"I'm sorry about Mary's outburst. It was uncalled for," Olive said.

"No need to apologize, Miss Wilkins. Mary's mad at everybody," he replied.

"Mr. Butler, may I use your wagon to go to town?" Olive asked surprising even herself.

Olive would not be beholden to this man for more than she already was and intended to stock the larder. Her head swam with her decision to stay, living with a strange man, as well as the deplorable state the children were in. She would see the banker in town, go to the general store, fetch her bags and purchase fabric for clothes for the children. All the change, all the agony and uncertainty of the day rebounded through her head, and the only thing she was completely positive of was her ability to make clothing for her niece and nephew. It was a small surety, but of that skill she was confident, and she clung to it.

"Sure. Ever drive a wagon?" he asked.

John, Peg and Luke screamed and scrambled for shoes. "Hurry up, Peg, we're going to town," Luke said.

"Now children," Olive began. Three excited, smiling faces looked up to her as she said, "I'll take you another day, children. I have many things to do."

Luke blew air where his teeth should have been and lost his smile. Peg's lip trembled, and John's face was a symphony of disappointment. Olive tied her bonnet, picked up her purse and tried not to look at the three faces. She climbed into the wagon, and Mr. Butler explained where the break was while she picked up the reins. As she thanked him, she couldn't miss the three broken hearts lined up in the doorway. Maybe company wouldn't be so bad on her solo expedition behind a horse. Peg lifted her hand to wave, and Olive gave in.

"Alright children, you may..." she started but was not heard over the roars and whoops.

They climbed in the wagon, still shrieking when Jacob Butler gave them a look. The air was thankfully quiet.

"Mr. Butler, I'll be getting some things from town. Is there anything you...we need?" Olive asked.

"Bacon, Daddy," Luke whispered. "You said next time we go to town, we could get bacon."

"When I finish that plowing job, we'll get bacon," Mr. Butler said.

"We don't have no pigs," little Peg said quietly to Olive.

"Any pigs, Peg," Olive corrected.

"Without no pigs, we don't get no bacon," the little girl said as she swung her head side to side.

Olive's eye twitched with the double negative. She climbed down from the wagon and headed back to the house.

"What's she doing, Daddy?" Luke asked and squirmed in his seat.

"Not a clue, son," Jacob Butler replied.

Olive walked out of the house and climbed up into the wagon, muttering as she went. Shaking her head, she fixed Jacob Butler with a taut smile and slapped the horse into motion.

"Ya forget something?'" Luke asked finally as the wagon rumbled down the road.

"No, but your father certainly did," Olive huffed.

Olive would have enjoyed the nearly one hour ride if the children had not jumped and shouted as if they were on the greatest adventure of their lives. Thankfully, the lane was straight and dry, and the horse needed little encouragement. When they arrived in town, the children were near giddy with excitement.

"Now, I have some business to conduct in the bank, and I expect you all to be mindful of your manners," Olive said to the children as they climbed down from the wagon. They stood straight like little soldiers and marched behind her as she opened the heavy door.

"Good afternoon, sir. I need to have monies transferred from my bank in Philadelphia. Can you accommodate me?" Olive asked at the barred window.

"Yes, ma'am, certainly," the clerk replied.

Olive looked down at the children as she conducted her business and found Luke and Peg fascinated with the shoe string ties on the next customer. But John was hiding in her volumes of skirts.

"Luke, Peg, stand up beside me, please. Yes, that's better," Olive said as Peg reached up to hold her hand.

Olive uncovered John's face and found him staring wide-eyed at a man at the next window. The cowboy was dirty, and his shirt, sweat-stained as he peered around Olive to John's face.

"Hey, ain't you Sophie's kid?" the cowboy asked.

John turned into Olive's skirts and Luke and Peg inched back to her.

"Hey, I'm talking to ya. Ain't you Sophie's boy?" he asked again.

John quivered and Olive laid her hand on his shoulder. "This young man is my brother James and his wife Sophie's child. I am his aunt."

"Well," the cowboy said and hooked his thumbs in his suspenders. "I knows it's Sophie's boy, but folk wondered if Jimmy was his Pa."

The other customers and the tellers let out chuckles, and Olive heard whispers. She turned her head slowly and met each smiling face til it sobered and then faced the cowboy. "This is my brother James's son. My nephew. State your business, sir."

The cowboy shrugged, and Olive turned back to the window and completed her transaction. By the time she gathered her purse and the children's hands, she was shaking and furious. Olive nearly dragged the children down the street, and when she looked down at them, she saw fear and in John's face, shame. She knelt down on the dusty sidewalk as she had seen Jacob Butler do and addressed them.

"Do not let anyone's words shame or frighten you. Words can not hurt you." They nodded together, solemnly, but John would not meet her eye.

Olive stopped at the hotel to fetch her bags before going to the general store. She placed her valise under the seat of the wagon and looked up to find John staring at a man across the street. The disreputable-looking character was staring back, his hands on his hips. The stranger pushed back his hat and leaned forward as if to get a better look at her nephew. John's face was white, as were his lips, and his bottom lip trembled. Olive had not time nor the inclination to deal with another bold, rude person like the cowboy in the bank. She took John's hand and led him to the general store.

"Afternoon, ma'am," a round man wearing a white apron said.

"Good afternoon, sir. I have a letter of credit from my bank in Philadelphia. I would like to open an account until my money is transferred," Olive said. The children turned slowly around, eying all the goods in the store, while the man read her letter from her bank.

"Yes, ma'am, that'll do," he said. "What can I get for you today?"

Olive pulled a long list from her purse and the clerk hurried to keep up with her demands. Sugar, flour, salt, vanilla, paper, pencils and the list went on, and on and the children's mouths dropped.

"And now, sir, I need you to show me what you have in the way of fabrics," Olive said.

The storekeeper pulled a stool over to reach the bolts, and Olive fingered each one as he laid them on the counter. John and Mary's clothing was so worn and threadbare that she was surprised they were still in one piece. She unrolled heavy chambray and held it up to John's body. She twisted and pulled the fabric and counted in her head. John stood, arms out, as Olive measured. Luke and Peg were quiet as they watched John being twirled, plaid fabrics across his arms, denims down his legs. Olive indicated the yardage on each bolt and picked two bright ginghams for Mary. She turned and smiled, done with the task, to the children and watched as Luke and Peg looked down at the floor.

An arrow pierced Olive's heart as she realized her blunder. "Double the order of denim and flannels, sir. Now, Peg, which cloth would suit you?"

Peg stepped forward, eyes glistening, and peaked over the counter to touch the fabric. Her lips were pursed as her hand went back and forth between two flowered prints. She looked up to Olive and her lip trembled.

"I don't know," she said.

"Well, Peg, the dress you're wearing is blue. What colors are your other dresses?" Olive asked.

Peg yanked hard on Olive's skirts and she bent down as the girl whispered in her ear. "This is the only one I got."

Olive's face flushed, and she turned to the clerk. "Sir, will you kindly tell me my balance so far?"

The clerk tallied with a nubbed pencil and looked over his glasses. "Eighteen dollars and sixty three cents."

"Very reasonable and in that case, sir, you will need to cut additional pieces of the gingham and six yards each of these flowered designs. Is that ribbon I see by the bolt, sir? Yes, the blue. I'll take six yards of that as well."

Olive watched the children glance from one to the other, with questions in their faces. "Come along, children," she said, and they followed her out of the store to watch the shopkeeper and a young boy fill the wagon to overflowing. Olive thanked the man and asked him to watch the wagon for an hour.

"Where we going now?" Luke asked as he trailed along behind her down the sidewalk.

"It will be a good hour-ride home, and I believe we'll all be too hungry by that time. We're going to Hannah's for our supper," Olive said.

Luke's eyes widened, and his little jaw fell. "To a place that gives you vittles?"

"Yes, Luke. A restaurant. Now, again I must remind you all to be mindful of your manners."

The three children sat still as stones once seated at Hannah's. Olive ordered ham dinners for them all. Luke pushed his hair from his face, and Olive watched Peg pick up the cue, straightening her dress. Olive heard the girl's crossed ankles tap on the chair rung as they swung loosely. John refused to lift his head until Olive instructed them to unfold their napkins and place them on their laps. When the food arrived, Luke and Peg struggled with the silverware, but managed slowly to devour the round, pared potatoes, swimming in butter. John wasted no time with utensils while he guarded his plate.

"John, please wipe your hands and pick up your fork," Olive said. His head swung defiantly, and his limp, filthy hair hung in his eyes. "John, pick up your fork and knife. Cut your meat like this," she instructed.

Olive could have sworn she heard a faint growl when she reached across to help John with his food. The utensils slipped from his hand, slimy from butter and grease. As the fork clattered to the floor, John saw the stares of other diners, and the boy slunk back in his seat. Olive wiped the children's faces and piled the leftover ham onto bread. Peg yawned, and her eyes threatened to close while Olive hurried to get the children to the wagon. The sun was setting, and she tucked Peg into a soft spot between a bag of flour and the new fabric. Peg's tiny hand, found its way under her cheek, and her eyes closed before Olive snapped the reins. Olive was exhausted herself as she clucked the horses and struggled to keep the two boys against her.

* * *

Where in the hell was that old crow, Jacob scowled. Out with the children, my children, no damn idea where she was going, he thought, as he turned his mare onto the road leading into town. When he saw the wagon approach, not a half-mile from home, he let out an involuntary sigh of gratitude. His horse, Bessie, thankfully, would know her way home in a blizzard, and as he stepped down from his own mount, he smiled at the picture he beheld. John was in Miss Wilkins lap, snoring, and Luke jostled in his slumber against her arm as she held the reins.

"Where's Peg?" he asked.

"Oh, Mr. Butler," Miss Wilkins said.

"Where's Peg?" he asked again and pulled Luke into his arms.

Miss Wilkins gestured to the back of the wagon. Jacob turned his head and saw the sleeping angel amidst a mountainous pile of supplies.

"If I am to stay awhile at your farm, it is only fair that I contribute to the coffers. You mustn't have realized your cupboard was nearly bare. I made a list this afternoon," Miss Wilkins said.

"I can feed my family," he replied.

"But you're not expected to feed mine as well," she said. "I think we had best get the children home now. Don't you?"

"We'll talk about this later, Miss Wilkins."

* * *

Olive's eyebrow rose in a salute to the thrown gauntlet as she urged the horse quietly to home. She lifted the slumbering Peg, as Mr. Butler carried the boys to the barn. Peg's breath was warm and wet against her neck as she laid the child down on the small bed. The little pink mouth lay open, and Peg let out a sigh of contentment as she curled into a ball. Olive eased the worn shoes from Peg's feet and unbuttoned her dress. The petticoat underneath was filthy and barely covered the child's round backside. Olive pulled a worn blanket over Peg's shoulders, and she snuggled down as her thumb came to her mouth.

Olive found her two valises on the porch and the horse and wagon, gone. She should have guessed Jacob Butler was a proud man, and he would not view her purchases as a contribution but rather a gift. *Pride goeth before the fall*, she quoted silently.

Olive poured water into a basin and took the pins from her hair. She washed off the dust and dirt from her trip to Spencer, but she could not cleanse from her mind the look on John's face when the cowboy spoke to him in the bank. The twenty-eight pearl buttons on her nightgown buttoned, she shook her head and rubbed her scalp as she sat down at the kitchen table. It was then she noticed Mary curled in front of the fireplace on a blanket. Olive knelt beside the girl and lifted a stray strand of hair from her cheek. *What goes through this child's head when night falls and dreams stir?* Olive wondered. She leaned down and kissed her, and Mary scuttled further under the blanket. Olive settled back onto the hard chair to brush her hair the required strokes.

In bed shortly, her head hit the pillow, and Olive succumbed to the tiring events of the day. Her eyes were barely open when she turned her itchy nose into the rough fabric of the sheets. Her lids rose, and she caught the scent of a man, Jacob Butler. The smell was intoxicating. Earthy and masculine. Olive gave into the guilty pleasure and reassurance the aroma brought and refused to think about the implications of sleeping in a strange man's bed.

* * *

Jacob stood at the window and watched through the grimy glass as Olive Wilkins kissed Mary and sat down. Her nightgown was buttoned to her neck, but as she stretched and rolled her head, Jacob found himself mesmerized with her slow, calculated movements. The brush pulled through volumes of thick hair, reddish in the firelight. It swayed and moved of its own accord, and Jacob watched her face. This is her forbidden pleasure, he realized, as he watched her move through the strokes. She sighed, and her eyes dropped to half-mast. When she pushed her chair back abruptly, Jacob jumped from his voyeur's position into the shadow of the porch. He peered in again to watch this strange woman climb into his bed.

* * *

Morning came all too soon for Olive, but she rose and moved her neck to work out the kinks. Peg slept the sleep of the innocent, mouth parted, strands of hair bathing her face. Olive opened the door, bucket in hand and found a full bucket on the porch in the gray light just before dawn. Mr. Butler must rise early, she thought, as she rinsed her face and hands and dressed. The firewood nearly beat her in a test of wills, but Olive managed to fill the stove and get a blaze going.

Jacob Butler materialized in the doorway, and Olive jumped

as she felt him approach.

"Good morning," she whispered. "Where is the bacon, and are there eggs to be had?"

He motioned to a small bucket filled with hay on the table. Large brown eggs were nestled amidst the straw.

"I keep the bacon and milk in the fruit cellar under the house. I'll get it," he said.

Olive was rooting through dirty pans and filled a pot with the water from her washing when Jacob Butler returned to the kitchen. She filled a second pot with water and turned to the table with a knife to slice the bacon.

"Don't cut more bacon than Mary and John and you will eat. I'll make mush for me and the others," he said.

Olive straightened and stared at him. "You would have Mary and John eat bacon in front of Luke and Peg while they eat mush?"

"I told you yesterday. I can take care of my family," he growled in a whisper.

"Your pantry was nearly bare. I know you are very busy, Mr. Butler. And a trip to town is an inconvenience, but I don't know how you planned on feeding these children and yourself. A jar of beets and beef jerky will only go so far."

"I have a plowing job for a neighbor. It'll be finished soon. When I get paid, I'll go to town for supplies," he said, his voicing raising.

"And what, pray tell," Olive whispered and sat her fists on her hips, "will you and the children be eating until then?"

Jacob Butler sputtered and narrowed his eyes, and Olive was sure he was about to let out a roar when they looked down to find John and Luke, clinging to the table edge. Moments passed, and Luke yanked on his father's sleeve.

"Miss Wilkins bought bacon yesterday, Daddy. We can have that for breakfast," the little boy said.

Olive looked up to Jacob Butler's taut face.

"None for me, Miss Wilkins," he said.

"Mark's awake," Mary said as she came from behind the curtain dividing the kitchen from the beds.

Jacob Butler rushed to the crib, and Olive's face reddened as she realized she had forgotten completely about the infant. The man picked up his son and crooned in the babe's ear, but the child began to moan in an odd fashion.

"Mark needs his diaper changed first thing in the morning. He has a rash," Mr. Butler said.

Olive watched Jacob Butler's large tan hands unpin the sopping fabric. The child's head seemed abnormally large for his body. Mark's strange cries and inability to meet anyone's eyes made her wonder if he was blind.

"What is his condition?" Olive asked.

"His diaper's wet," Mr. Butler replied as he wiped the baby's behind.

Olive sensed his reluctance, but she could not still her tongue. "I know that, Mr. Butler. He seems to have some other problems as well," she said quietly.

Olive took an involuntary step back when she met Jacob Butler's stare. His eyes were dark and glittering and when he spoke the tone made Olive flinch.

"Mark is fine."

Olive swallowed, knowing she had tread on some sacred subject. "I have wash water on the stove. Leave his diaper off, and I'll bathe him." She reached down to touch an angry looking rash on the child's legs and privates. "Do you have any cornstarch?"

"I don't know. Look in the panty," Mr. Butler said.

"Mary, would you begin to fry the bacon? Luke, John, come here and rinse your face and hands in this water. Good morning, Peg," Olive said and returned from the pantry with a small cloth bag, marked, cornstarch.

Olive had no idea why she had volunteered to bathe the infant. She had never done it before, never seen it done and was still flushed from seeing her first miniature view of a male's privates. The keening wail, though, had touched Olive's heart. Peg stood beside her at the crib, tousled and rubbing the night from her eyes.

"Would you like to help?" Olive asked and looked down at the girl.

Peg nodded and yawned and held the dry cloth, while Olive washed Mark with a warm rag. The infant's head tossed back and forth, and he seemed to be calming. Olive heard the sizzle of bacon hit the black, iron skillet. She made a paste of cornstarch and water as she had seen Theda do for her mother. The woman wore diapers that Theda and Olive had sewn, but Theda confided that her mother had a constant rash. The baby's cries subsided completely as Olive smeared the paste on the boy. He began to gurgle and drool, and Peg looked up at her.

"He's happy now," the little girl said.

"How do you know?" Olive asked.

Peg's head tilted, and her palms came up at her sides as her shoulders lifted in a shrug. Olive found a set of miniature one-piece drawers and struggled to get the baby's legs in the hole before an arm popped out of its spot. Peg giggled and Olive's hair began to inch its way out of the pins.

"Miss Wilkins?" the girl said.

"Just a moment, Peg. Mark is making this a bit difficult," Olive said.

"Miss Wilkins?" she asked again.

"One moment, Peg."

Olive was barely hanging on to her patience with Peg's interruptions and Mark's squirming, but as she held up the infant in triumph with the last button hooked, she turned to Peg. "Yes, dear?"

"You forgetted his nappie."

Olive's head snapped back to the dangling child as his union suit slowly became wet.

Mary did a fine job with eggs and bacon, which Olive was thankful for since she had to begin again with Mark's clothes. She instructed Luke and John to wipe the table and found six reasonably clean dishes. Jacob Butler tied Mark in the high chair, and his children looked up at him expectantly.

"Bless this food we are about to receive. Amen."

Olive raised her head and found Mary already eating and John picking up his egg with his hands. "Please wait until the blessing is complete to begin eating, Mary. John, use your fork, please."

Mary scowled at her, and Olive watched Jacob Butler feed the infant the soft yoke of his egg. There was no bacon on his plate, and as their eyes met, he challenged her with his stare. When he spoke, Olive was not sure if he addressed her or the children.

"I'm going to the Baxter's farm to finish the plowing. I won't be home until sunset. Will you watch Mark? He gets fussy out that long in the sun," Mr. Butler asked.

"Certainly," Olive replied.

"Get your shoes, Luke, Peg," he commanded.

"You're taking them with you?" Olive asked.

"Always did. Had to. I won't ask you to watch my children," he replied.

"I had hoped they could stay here and help me with chores."

Olive could only imagine how difficult plowing was, let alone with Luke and Peg to watch. She had no intention of revealing her plan to make some new clothes for his family to this proud man. The children's eyes swung back and forth, waiting for the verdict.

Jacob Butler's eyes darted, and she knew he struggled accepting her help, even though she couched the idea into a plea for additional hands.

"Fine. I probably won't be as long if I don't have the children to watch. Thank you," he said.

"I ain't doing no chores," Mary said.

"Any chores, Mary. I am not doing any chores," Olive said as she stood.

"That's what I said. I ain't doing no chores."

Olive turned around quickly, and the younger children's mouths opened at the look on her face. "Let's be perfectly clear, Mary. Everyone will help. That includes you."

Mary's face was awash with defiance, but Olive knew instinctively she must hold her ground. Mary needed love, obviously, but guidance she was desperate for. The tension in the air was thick, and Olive turned to the man heading out the door.

"Wait, Mr. Butler. John didn't finish his ham at the restaurant yesterday. Take it with you for your dinner."

* * *

Jacob's breath caught in his throat, as she handed him the bread with the ham between. How long had it been since someone, anyone, had thought of him? How long had it been since a woman handed him much needed food to break his hunger in the middle of the day? A year, Jacob thought. He hadn't realized how sorely he missed the small give-and-take between man and wife that made grinding out his existence bearable.

But this was not his petite, dark-haired Margaret with a light laugh and strong hands. No, this woman didn't have the heart-shaped lips she had. Nor the full breasts he buried his face in when they made love. Jacob had loved Margaret since he was twelve-years-old, and she him. He grabbed the wrapped food sternly, blaming this meddling woman for making him feel. Feel anything. *That part of my life and heart is gone. I buried it with Margaret*, he thought. Easier to deny the need than to face it. Easier to blame this old maid for the tightening in his chest than face the wrenching hole that Margaret's death had left.

* * *

Olive watched the play of emotions that blew through Jacob Butler's eyes and wondered what he was thinking. She watched him kiss the children and nod to Mary and walk out the door, those massive shoulders lower than usual.

"What do we have to do?" Luke asked.

"Well, children, we are going to begin with cleaning up this house. Mary, get the dirty dishes out of the sink. The rest of you can bring the breakfast dishes over," Olive said.

Mary scowled, and Olive ignored her. Olive carried the hot water from the stove and dumped it in the pan. She rolled up the sleeves of the brown dress and handed Mary a dry rag. Mary looked down at the rag in confusion.

"What do you want me to do with this? There's already a rag in the sink," Mary said.

"I'll wash; you dry, Mary," Olive said.

"I know how to scrub dishes."

"I'm sure you do," Olive said and looked down at the girl.

"I can earn John's and my keep," Mary said as she grabbed the sopping rag.

"Mary," Olive said puzzled, "what is this about? I wash. You dry. It's not that complicated."

Mary took a step back, and Olive saw tears form in the girl's eyes.

"My ma told me I had to earn my keep. I know I hafta. I could make it on my own, but there's John. I hafta earn my keep ta feed John. I know. Now gimme the rag."

Olive's voice caught on a hitch of emotion, and she hated the look of helplessness and fear on her niece's face. Olive walked to the table, sat down and held her head. How would she ever explain to this girl that her love is unconditional? How would she erase a lifetime of anger? At that moment Olive hated her brother. Not for the squalor or the gambling or the disrepair of his home but for the pain he allowed his wife to inflict on his own child. *Why, James, why did you allow it?*

"Mary, come here and sit down." Olive watched as she turned from the sink, and she saw suspicion rise on Mary's face. "Please," Olive added. "Mary, look at me. When I told Mr. Butler I needed help with chores, I didn't mean I wanted you to do them. I meant we would all work together. You are not my servant, Mary. Nor do you have to earn your keep."

"If John and me are goin' to eat, then I have to do my chores," Mary said.

"I may be disappointed you choose not to help, but I would never deny you food because of it. My love for you and John is not based on how much work you do," Olive said softly.

Mary rolled her eyes, and Peg stepped close to Olive. "You love John and Mary?" Olive nodded at the little wide-eyed girl, and she continued, "My mama loved us. She told us every night when we said our good nights to God."

Olive pulled Peg onto her lap and squeezed her tight. "Of course your mama loved you. How could she not?"

"Daddy says she watches us from heaven, and she still loves us," Luke said as he laid his hand on Olive's arm. John inched close to Luke.

The grief and wanting was so clear on the four faces before her that Olive struggled to speak. Instead, she gathered John and Luke onto her lap with Peg and kissed all three heads.

"A mother's love doesn't stop because she's not here."

Olive looked up to Mary and continued, "We don't always know why things happen the way they do, but we can always be sure that our mothers loved us."

Mary turned back to the sink, and Olive watched with resignation. "And," Olive said, "if we get the chores done quickly, we can begin making some new clothes for everyone."

The little ones on her lap cheered and hugged, and their eyes lit up with anticipation. Olive directed each of them in a task, and although it took twice as long Olive was sure, she had each small hand busy with something. Mary handed Mark a tin cup, and he proceeded to pound it on the table. Olive looked at Mary over the din of the children's voices and constant drumming from Mark's cup.

"He stays quiet when he has his cup to bang," Mary said and shrugged.

Olive laughed. "This is quiet?"

The corners of Mary's mouth began to turn up. She quickly turned her attention back to sweeping the floor in front of the hearth.

"Alright children. Let's cut this fabric, so I can begin on some new clothes," Olive said as she unrolled the first piece. "Now, this denim, we'll make into pants for Luke and John. Mary, Peg picked the ginghams and prints. Do you like any of them? I think with your blue eyes this rose-colored flower design will look lovely on you."

Peg's head barely reached over the table and she rested her chin on the edge. Mary and John's eyes darted between each other, and John went to his sister. Mary's face was white, and Olive could see John squeezing her hand.

"What do I have to do?" Mary asked grimly.

"Pick a fabric, Mary. That's all," Olive said.

"Ma said ya never get something for nothin'," Mary said, and John looked up at Olive.

"Your mother was wrong in this case. I bought this fabric to make some new clothes. I was just hoping I could teach you to sew."

Mary edged closer to the table and felt the cloth. Her head did not lift when she asked, "Ya think the pink one would look good on me?"

"I do."

Olive spent the rest of the day cutting and sewing and trying to keep eight dirty hands off the new fabric. Mary sat down to sew a long straight seam, and Olive watched the girl struggle.

"Oh, dear," Olive said as she lay Mark down in his crib for a nap. "I didn't start anything for supper."

Mary followed Olive into the pantry, and the girl's eyes widened at the new stores on the shelves. "We could make ham and beans with a piece of the bacon," the girl said as she picked up the dry goods.

"Perfect," Olive said. "What do I do?"

Mary looked up at her aunt. "Why don't I get it started?"

The day rolled on, the house full of clutter and the smell of bacon and beans simmering on the stove. Olive straightened from the table, pleased with what she had accomplished but exhausted from the task. She pressed her fingertips into the small of her back and arched, stretching and relieving the ache. John and Luke wore new denim pants, and Peg was twirling in a simple new dress. Other than knowing the exact location of every book in the library back home, sewing was Olive's skill, and her crafts revealed her passion. Peg's gingham dress was trimmed with a white collar. Olive combed the child's hair as Peg sat still on her lap and reverently touched the folds where her skirt settled over her legs. The hair was knotted, and the combing nearly brought Peg to tears. But she bravely faced the pain for the prospect of a matching bow in her hair.

Mary worked at her stitches slowly, and Olive felt she was

stubbornly determined to complete the dress. Olive was pleased and hoped the sewing would give them some common ground. John's flannel shirt was cut, and Olive pinned the seams and sat down at the table to stitch.

"Daddy's home," Luke cried. He, John, and Peg ran out the door to greet the wagon.

* * *

Jacob kissed the children as they smiled and clung to him, and he noticed Peg's hair was different. It was combed and plaited and tied with a ribbon that matched... a new dress. That's why she was gibbering and touching the fabric. Jacob stood in the doorway, finding Miss Wilkins and her niece hunched over needles.

"What's this?" Jacob said.

"Hello, Mr. Butler." Miss Wilkins greeted him with barely a glance.

"What's this?" he repeated.

"Pardon?" she said and looked up.

"Miss Wilkins? Can I talk to you outside?" The children looked into Jacob's eyes as they clung to him and slowly shimmied down his arms and legs.

"Yes?" Olive Wilkins said as they stepped off the porch and away from the house.

"What is Peg wearing?"

"I bought fabric for clothes for John and Mary, and I noticed that your children needed some new garments as well. We've had a very productive and pleasant day. Thankfully, Mary started beans for..."

"My children don't need new clothes," Jacob interrupted.

* * *

In the span one sunset brought, Olive knew from the tone of his voice that Jacob Butler was angry. But she had not expected this growling voice to come out of twitching lips. He stood, hands on his hips, feet spread, obviously expecting a reply. If he had been upset about the bacon she imagined he was furious now.

"Yes, Mr. Butler, your children do need new clothing. Peg's petticoat barely covers her bottom, and the holes are bigger than what's left." Olive watched the man's face contort, and his tension escalate. "Luke's pants come to his knee, and Mark's diapers are threadbare."

"I know what my children's clothes look like, Miss Wilkins."

Olive pursed her lips at the outrage in his whisper. "Fiddlee dee dee, Mr. Butler. It's just a new dress and pants. What's the uproar?"

"I don't have the money for the cloth, and I won't accept charity. The clothes will be returned to you," he said.

Olive's eyes rounded in horror at the thought of taking the cherished dress from little Peg. Her eyes narrowed to slits, and she removed her wire-rim glasses. "Pride, Mr. Butler, is a sin. And to think you would turn your sin to hurt that child. Well..."

"My sin. My children," he shouted.

Olive inelegantly stamped her foot, surprising herself, and her finger came within an inch of Jacob Butler's face. She shook it and shouted a lame threat, "If you so much as dare to take that dress from Peg, I'll... I'll leave... and I won't come back."

Mr. Butler harrumphed, and a smile curled one side of his mouth. "Don't let the door hit you in the ass."

Olive fiddled trying hurriedly to rehook her glasses over her ears, snorting and blustering. She ran straight into Jacob Butler's broad back. Olive stumbled backwards, readjusted her skirts and flew to the giant's side as he stared at his doorway. There, Peg and Luke stood staring back at their father, and the looks on their faces must surely been the reason he stopped quickly.

"Is Miss Wilkins goin' ta leave?" Luke asked.

"Daddy?" Peg sobbed. "Do I have ta give back my dress?"

"Yes, Peg," he said.

Peg's eyes glistened with tears.

"Mr. Butler, please," Olive began, "don't make her give the dress back."

* * *

Jacob watched the children run to Olive Wilkins and huddle in her skirts. He felt his heart breaking as he listened to their sobs. He stepped into the kitchen and found Mary holding Mark in her arms with a look of pure hatred on her face.

"It's plain mean to take that dress from Peg. You don't know what it's like when folks stare and point at ya. Whether it's 'cause your dress is three years too small or your pants come up to yer knees or... maybe 'cause of who yer ma was." Mary's voice quivered in anger, and she shoved Mark into his arms. "Here, he's all peed through."

Jacob sat the infant in his crib and lowered himself into the rocker as the cries on the porch wound down. Peg's old dress lay in a heap on the floor in front of him, and he supposed this is the spot she had stood when she pulled the new dress over her head, stepping out of the old one and letting it fall to the floor. Jacob picked up the threadbare garment and rested his elbows on his knees as he looked at the faded print and stains on the fabric. His head dropped in shame. He had not noticed or tried not to notice how small and worn it was. But there was no extra money and certainly no money for fabric. Jacob barely had enough for the mortgage and food. He scowled thinking of the wagon piled high with supplies that Miss Wilkins had bought. *I don't want help*, Jacob thought, *I don't need help*. A small hand, Luke's hand, rested on Jacob's shoulder, and he turned to his son standing beside him. Luke had put on his old pants and fought valiantly to smile.

"It's alright, Daddy. This year's crop will be better. Miss Wilkins said that we don't always know why things turn out like they do, but we can always be sure of one thing. That our Mama loved us, and I know you love us, too."

Jacob's head hung and he hated that his son bore the grief of his failures. He looked down at the boy's legs and saw bony white knees sticking out of patched pants. Jacob grabbed Luke and squeezed, and Luke hugged him back with all his might.

"Does Miss Wilkins have to leave?" Luke whispered into his father's ear.

"Why, son? Do you want her to leave?" Jacob asked looking into Luke's eyes.

The slim shoulders shrugged and he tilted his head. Jacob wondered what was going through his boy's mind.

"She's nothing like Ma," the child replied.

"No, she's not."

"But," Luke began and looked down at his hands as they twisted in his father's shirt, "but it was kind of nice having her here today. We sang songs, and she cut cloth and showed us the slates she bought each of us to learn our letters."

Jacob knew guilt gripped the boy, admitting that he had warmed to the woman, not his mother. How lonely are these young ones for the feminine touch that even spindly old Miss Wilkins had in her hands? He pictured Peg's face as she ran to the woman's arms. Bony arms without a doubt, but gentle arms reeled his daughter in with a hug. And Jacob recalled the little things Margaret had done for the children that he would have never thought of. Things that would have never occurred to him. Kissing every skinned knee. Smiling with encouragement at the smallest victory. The things mothers do without conscious thought. The reasons that God in his wisdom had made women, mothers. Mary's rebuke stung the most, though. The girl barely spoke, half afraid she'd lose her bed and board. She must have felt the children's shame in the pit of her being to gather the courage to lash out so at Jacob. He stood, holding Luke in his arms and went to the porch. He watched their faces turn to him, and he took a deep breath.

"Miss Wilkins?"

"Yes, Mr. Butler?"

Jacob looked out over the horizon and back to the huddled group. Without meeting an eye, he whispered, "You can keep the clothes, children."

"What did you say, Mr. Butler? We can't hear you," Miss Wilkins said.

Jacob's shoulders rose and lowered slowly, and he sucked air through his front teeth. This dag-blamed woman wasn't going to make this easy, he saw.

"The children can keep the clothes."

Peg's face lit up, and she started to her father, but Miss Wilkins's hand stilled her. "Do you have anything else to say, Mr. Butler?"

"Alright, I was wrong, Miss Wilkins. And... well, thank you."

"Apology accepted, Mr. Butler." She sent the children to clean up and held her head stiffly, staring at him. She broke the gaze and walked primly past him. "Wash up for dinner, Mr. Butler. Cleanliness is next to Godliness."

Jacob scowled, kicked the dirt, and mocked her words back to her. *The old biddy*, he thought.

Chapter Three

"**M**ARY, PLEASE DO NOT BEGIN EATING UNTIL the prayer is complete. John, please use your fork," Miss Wilkins said.

Jacob looked up at her as he released his children's hands from prayer and watched her evenly repeat her instructions. Her voice did not rise, nor did her eyes as she quietly reminded the children of their manners. The meal was hot and filling, and Jacob watched Miss Wilkins neatly dab her mouth.

"Mr. Butler, I would like to begin instructing John and Mary, and I hope you will allow me to include your children. Have they had any formal education?" she asked.

Jacob clenched the metal of his fork between his teeth as she inquired after his children's schooling. He evenly met her gaze and slowly pulled the utensil from his mouth.

"Their mother taught them."

"Fine. Good. We will have a starting place then. Mary, what grade are you in?" Miss Wilkins asked and smiled at her niece.

"Hardly went to school," the girl said.

"Why?" Miss Wilkins asked as she lay down her utensils.

Mary sopped bean drippings with her biscuit. "Ma said it was too far to haul me every day."

"What did your father say?"

"He took me a couple a times, but then I had to walk home. I told Ma I didn't want to go back," she added.

"You walked from town?" Miss Wilkins asked.

Mary nodded and stared at her plate. "Pa taught me some, though."

* * *

Olive regarded Mary and wondered if it would ever sound natural to hear her brother James referred to as "Pa". It was hard as well to hear that her brother had done little to educate his children. "Your father was quite the scholar when he was young. I'm sure you'll pick up your studies quickly. John," Olive said and turned to the boy, "would you like to know how to write your name?"

The child's eyes widened, and the hair Olive promised herself to wash hung in his face. His head slowly swung from side to side. She wondered about her brother's youngest child. He had yet to speak and although clearly frightened at the bank when the cowboy had spoken to him, he seemed happy when in Jacob's home. He followed Luke as if attached by an invisible thread to the boy. Otherwise, John was glued to his sister's side. But Olive had not heard a word uttered. She vowed to speak to Mary and find out what the girl knew of her brother's silence. Olive's hand went slowly to her temple as she contemplated all the problems she faced in order to get these children back to her home in Philadelphia.

"Mr. Butler? Do you have a bath tub?" Olive asked.

"Yes."

"Good. Mary will you begin doing the dishes? I have water boiling, and I would like to start with some haircuts before you take your baths, children." Olive said.

* * *

Jacob had watched the worry grow on Olive Wilkins's face when she addressed her nephew. He felt for the boy as well. The day Jacob found the children in their home after their mother's death, John was huddled in a corner, staring blankly at some far and away spot. Mary had screamed and fought him, but John limply allowed himself to be carried to the wagon.

Jacob looked at Olive Wilkins now while the children howled, and she turned a deaf ear. She went from subject to subject, issue to issue, so quickly, Jacob wondered how she kept it straight in her head. Jacob agreed that Luke indeed did need a trim and sat the squirming boy on the table. Miss Wilkins produced a small pair of sewing scissors and cut away. She revealed her concentration by sticking her tongue in her cheek and holding it there while she studied the boy's hair. Snip, snip, Jacob heard while he watched Luke and listened to the protests and moans. When she was finished, Jacob thought a different boy sat on the stool than his own son, Luke.

"Now, John," Miss Wilkins said and turned to her nephew, smiling.

John's eyes were wide and fearful, and he cried until Jacob held him in his arms so his aunt could cut his hair. She stood close to Jacob and tilted her head, wondering, he supposed, where to begin. The soft summer scent of lilacs hit Jacob's nose, and he was transported back to his childhood home and the smell the breeze brought through that kitchen window. Olive Wilkins's dress was unwrinkled, the collar still stiff, and he wondered how she managed to look so neat amidst the chaos of his house. As she trimmed and smiled, Jacob watched her hands as they moved through the task. Long, lean fingers, nearly white, and he studied the veins of blood that moved through them. Loving hands, lovingly wading through dirty, dark hair, touching the child's face as she went. Convincing the boy, with her touch that he had nothing to fear. As she bent close to trim the hair around John's ear, Jacob found his face inches from her hair. And he could not stop the image of her brushing that hair as he spied through the window the day of her arrival.

"All done," Miss Wilkins declared.

John touched his ears, as if wondering if they were still attached.

"Mary, why don't you let me trim the back of your hair, too," Miss Wilkins asked.

"Why?" the girl said.

"I don't know, Mary," Miss Wilkins said as she sighed, "maybe just because it would look nice, and we could pull the top back with a ribbon for church on Sunday."

"We're goin ta church?" Luke asked.

"Well, of course, children," Miss Wilkins stated in the no-nonsense fashion Jacob was getting accustomed to.

"You can trim my hairs," Peg said quietly.

"Sit down, then, little miss," she said.

Peg's eyes darted, but she smiled a smile that Jacob knew meant she loved the undivided attention she was receiving. Miss Wilkins trimmed an uneven inch or two and looked up to Mary.

"Come, sit down. Please, Mary," she said.

The girl shrugged, and her aunt trimmed her long hair as well.

"What about Daddy? His hair's long, too," Luke asked.

"Oh, no, children," Jacob said and shook his head.

Miss Wilkins studied him. "You could really use a trim, too."

"I cut my own hair, thank you."

* * *

Olive shrugged, turned from Jacob Butler and asked, "Mary, is the water boiling?"

The girl nodded, and Olive sent Mr. Butler and the boys to the barn. Peg stripped and Olive lifted her into the tub. She scrubbed hair and ears, elbows and knees and when Olive pulled the dripping, shining child from the water she turned to Mary. "You're next."

"I ain't bathin'."

"I'm not bathing," Olive corrected. "And yes, you are bathing."

Olive watched Mary look at the tub and then string a blanket between the water and the door.

"I'm terribly sorry, Mary. You are old enough to want some privacy. I'll comb Peg's hair on the bed while you bathe," Olive said.

Mary stepped behind the blanket as she eyed the window and doors. Olive heard the girl's clothes come off and the splash of water as she stepped in the tub. A half an hour passed, Peg's hair was drying, and still Mary had not gotten out of the water.

"Mary, you're skin will be wrinkled if you don't get out soon," Olive called out.

Mary emerged wrapped in a blanket, and Olive marveled at how beautiful her niece was. Olive dug down deep in her still-unpacked bag and produced a small tin with holes on the top. "Would you like to use some of my talc?"

"It feels so good," Peg whispered and rubbed her arms where the powder lay.

Olive stepped behind the blanket, added hot water to the tub, stripped and sank in. Oh, God, she thought, I never realized how good a bath could feel. When the water grew cold she stood, and dressed and called out the door to Jacob Butler.

* * *

Jacob stepped into the steamy room and looked at his little Peg, clean and fresh and her hair, shining. Mary's hair was wavy and the girl looked amazingly relaxed and well... pretty. He had never noticed, he supposed through the grime and the scowls.

"Can you empty the tub, please? I want to get the boys bathed," Miss Wilkins asked.

Jacob dumped the tub, and Miss Wilkins refilled it as Luke and John looked on in horror. "Off with those clothes," she said.

"Do I hafta, Daddy?" Luke whined.

"Yes, you do, Luke. And you too, John," Jacob said.

The protests died into a water battle, and Jacob listened while Miss Wilkins fought six hands, with Mark in the water too, and the kitchen floor became a sopping mess. When she finally produced three wet, howling boys, Jacob dried them and dressed them.

Jacob studied this woman, so full of contradictions. She seemed so timid and quiet, and yet she commanded these troops with a firm hand. She had to be exhausted, he thought, both mentally and physically, and he gave her credit for being made of sterner stuff than he had first thought. Miss Wilkins's hair hung to her waist, and even though long, it waved and curled at the ends. As she dried her glasses, he noticed the resemblance to her brother and his children. And she, too, with her hair down and damp and no glasses, was pretty. *I wonder why she never married*, Jacob thought.

"Now, everyone at the table, please," Miss Wilkins instructed. Peg ran to take a seat. The woman produced primers and slates and soon had each child copying their name from the letters she had drawn at the top of the board. Mary harrumphed and slouched, but Miss Wilkins coaxed the girl into reading a story.

"Mr. Butler? May I speak to you outside?" Miss Wilkins asked as she pushed John's chair closer to the table.

Jacob closed the door in wonder as the children listened to Mary read and compared slates and the smell left in his nose was clean and innocent. The smell of a child bathed.

"Yes, Miss Wilkins?" he asked.

"Why do you think John doesn't speak?" she asked from the shadows the dim light threw from the cabin window.

Jacob shrugged his shoulders and guided her down the porch step. "Truthfully, I never noticed if the boy spoke much before, but he sure isn't talking now. No, I don't know why."

"Is there a doctor in town?"

"Yeah," Jacob said. "Doc Hunter."

"I'm going to take John to see him then on Monday. Maybe there's a physical reason. I should ask Mary, I suppose," she said as she tilted her head to the sky.

"Don't be hard on yourself, Miss Wilkins. You can't fix a lifetime of problems in two days."

Jacob watched her drying hair curl around her face as she studied the darkening landscape. She looked down then and sighed.

"I just never, ever, in my wildest dreams imagined the conditions they lived under. The pain. The... the... I would've have come if I'd known. The letters from James painted an idyllic picture of a quaint farm and a happy family."

Jacob saw misery and guilt and worry line her face as the shadows of night descended, and she shook her head. "It wasn't your doing. And it's not your fault," he said.

Miss Wilkins met his eyes and declared softly, "Whose fault is it then? Who more than their blood relatives? I failed them."

Jacob watched a shiver run through her. "Are you chilled?" he asked.

"No, Mr. Butler, I'm not chilled. I'm angry."

"Anger doesn't solve things. Sometimes nothing does. Except time."

"But I could have come sooner," Olive Wilkins said and stepped back from him, fists clenched. "Why didn't I, Mr. Butler? I'll tell you why. I've lived my life, my whole thirty-five years, reading books and watching other people live their lives. And now, here, those children bear the brunt of it. I buried my nose in a book and my house and my cat and failed them miserably. I made quilts for charities and ignored the questions and the doubts I had. I painted a picture of domestic tranquility and never dreamt these children were living, do you hear me, Mr. Butler, living a Dickens tale."

Jacob's head inched back with her near hysteria, as she asked and answered her own questions, and he knew there was nothing to convince her otherwise. He watched as she calmed herself, righted her dress, and shook her head.

"All you can do now, Miss Wilkins, is love them, and maybe the past will right its self," he said.

"Yes, of course, you're right. I'm terribly sorry you witnessed my outburst." Olive Wilkins turned and walked to the porch.

Jacob pulled the tobacco from his pocket, rolled a quick cigarette, and leaned against the tree, suddenly grateful for two minutes alone without the demands of children and the farm. Olive Wilkins was a puzzle, that was for certain. Hot and cold, she blows from ranting and raving to apologizing. He figured he'd never before met such a moral, upright individual. Other than his own mother, perhaps. Miss Wilkins was stiff-looking sometimes and judgmental sounding too, all done up in black, until she smiled at one of the children. That smile transformed her into an attractive-looking woman. And after her speech, just a few moments ago, Jacob knew her harshest judgments she reserved for herself.

When he entered the house, he was amazed at the picture before him. Miss Wilkins sat with the children at her feet, except

Mary, and read aloud from a book. The children listened, and Mary pretended she didn't as she leaned against the fireplace. Not a sound could be heard but the melodic tones of Olive Wilkins's voice as she made characters come alive through another's words. Soon Peg's head was nodding, and Miss Wilkins closed the book.

Luke's eyes were barely open as he begged to hear more.

"Tomorrow, children," she said softly and carried Mark to his crib. Jacob nodded to Miss Wilkins as he picked up the boys and carried them to the loft in the barn.

* * *

Sunday morning arrived, and Miss Wilkins had the children ready for church; Jacob was proud as he looked over the reasonably clean and well-dressed group. Jacob had trimmed his hair and bathed and was in his best shirt. He had not been to church since Margaret's death, but when he quietly told Miss Wilkins that he would wait in the wagon, her eyebrows raised, and she pursed her lips. Without an ounce of remorse, he imagined, she threatened to tell the children he wouldn't be joining them. Luke, John and Peg were so excited about the outing, laughing and talking, and Mary kept touching her hair where Miss Wilkins had pulled it back with a ribbon. Jacob grumbled but followed as the little ducks clamored for Miss Wilkins's hand on the church steps. Mary was visibly nervous as she saw a group of children her age turn and stare, and Jacob caught her eye.

"You look fine, Mary," he said.

She blew out a nervous breath and went into the church as Jacob held the door. They were seated in a pew, and Jacob watched as heads turned and whispers escalated before the reverend stepped into the pulpit. Miss Wilkins held her head high, smiling and nodding and cooing to Mark.

Jacob saw some of his friends, other farmers, and heard them whisper and look as services ended and the congregation waited between pews to leave the church.

Jack Steele spoke up. "So, Jacob, first time I've seen you in church for awhile." Bill Williams elbowed Jack but grinned in encouragement. "You know what they say, when a woman gets a man to church, the altar's not far away."

Jacob knew his face colored that his boyhood friends would think that he had set his cap to the dowdy and older Miss Wilkins.

"She's Jimmy Wilkins's sister. Here to take her niece and nephew back to Philadelphia."

"Oh," Bill Williams said and hooked his thumbs in his suspenders. "Where's she staying?"

Clearly, Bill knew Olive Wilkins was staying at his farm. News in a small town traveled with lightning speed, and Jacob was sure he and Miss Wilkins were the focus of much speculation. "With me."

Jack Steele cocked his head. "Get's mighty lonesome sometimes. I'm sure you appreciate the company."

* * *

The minister had droned on, and Olive was sure she knew the Scriptures better than he. Reverend McGrath confused the Old Testament with the New, and he seemed to create disciples' names as the sermon required. His bulbous red nose may have been the result of illness or liquor, Olive concluded. At the end of the service, she and the children patiently waited in line to greet the minister when she heard a man ask Mr. Butler where she was staying. Olive watched as the men's wives pinched their husbands' arms and shook their heads.

"Mr. Butler has kindly allowed me to stay at his home to

allow me time to get to know my niece and nephew," Olive said.

Olive hated their knowing stares, and worse yet, she was embarrassed that Mr. Butler was so obviously uncomfortable with the implication of a romance. Olive was well aware of her looks and her age, but it did nothing to lessen the pain that Jacob Butler would die a slow death before courting her. She had seen this before in the eyes of men when caught talking to her at a social. They scurried away before anyone tied them to the spinsterish Miss Wilkins.

Mr. Butler introduced Olive to the men and their wives. Beth Steele and Florence Williams both smiled at Olive, and she was jealous suddenly of their age and marital status. The thought of marriage hadn't crossed Olive's mind for fifteen years, but she found herself staring at the gold rings on the women's hands.

"Nice to meet you," the pretty, plump Beth Steele said.

"We're glad you're here for those children," Florence Williams said.

Olive realized she desperately missed conversation with another woman. "Thank you. They have some difficulties to overcome."

"I would think so after how they lived," the Florence said. But then the woman's eyes widened. "I'm sorry. I didn't mean to say... I... oh, never mind."

"No insult taken, Mrs. Williams. Unfortunately, I was unaware of the circumstances of their home." Olive noticed the younger children wander past the line of adults to the porch steps. She watched as they met up with other children. "Mary, will you look after them for me?"

Mary's shoulders slumped, and she faced the open church door as if it were a chasm that she could not cross. She looked up to Olive and hesitantly walked outside.

"The church social's next Saturday, and we have a quilting bee and a potluck supper and then dancing. Will you be coming,

Miss Wilkins?" Beth Steele asked.

Olive leaped at the chance to talk to other adults, be useful, and introduce her niece and nephew to what society Spencer had. "That sounds wonderful," she replied.

Suddenly she heard John's wails and adults shouting. Olive rushed past the minister and the others in line, and her eyes widened at what she beheld. Mary was fighting, fist fighting, a boy near her own age.

"Mary, what are you doing?" Olive shouted and saw that Mary's hair had come undone, and her new dress was dirty and torn. Mr. Butler pulled Mary away from the boy.

"Nothin'," the girl said as she looked up at Olive.

The boy's mother flew into the milieu and slammed chubby arms onto wide hips. "Bertram, what are you doing?"

"Fighting will solve nothing. And in front of the church on Sunday morning. Explain yourselves," Olive said.

Bertram's mother had a vice-like hold on her son's ear, and she shouted shrilly, "What happened?"

"Nothing. I was just talking to her and she," Bertram said and nodded with malice to Mary, "started shoving me."

Olive heard the distinct sound of hand-hitting-cheek as Bertram's mother shook his shoulder with her other arm. The woman's fat cheeks jiggled, and her girlish twists of curls bounced with her tremors.

"If I've told you once, I've told you a thousand times, stay away from that white trash," the woman shouted.

Olive's eyes widened and her chin dropped and she stood in awe of the woman's reasoning. "Pardon me?"

The woman swirled in a fury. "Everyone knows the Wilkinses are trash. Low-born and common. I don't want my Bertram near them even if he was giving her the thrashing she deserved."

"Now, wait a second, Luella. This girl's been living with me, and I don't take kindly to anyone talking that way about her," Jacob Butler said. "That's all I'm going to allow on that subject."

He held Mary by the arms tight against him, and Olive watched as the girl turned her head into his stomach. The giant arms encircled her and rubbed Mary's back in an unconscious motion.

"Mary, tell me what happened," Olive asked.

The girl's eyes would not rise from the ground, and she slowly shook her head.

Bill Williams turned to Luella. "It's all over now. Sometimes youngsters fight. Let's forget it and go home."

Luella looked around Bill Williams to Jacob Butler. "And to think you brought this wild thing to church and made good Christian folk sit beside her."

"That's enough, Luella," Jacob said. "I said once I won't allow anymore talk like that, and I mean it."

Olive's heart was pounding in her chest, and she felt angry tears building behind her eyes. "This 'wild thing' is my niece and 'good Christian folk' don't cast the first stone," she said.

"Humph," Luella replied and hauled her son down the walk by the ear.

Olive noticed Luke and Peg buried in her skirts on one side and John trembling and crying on the other.

"Let's go," Mr. Butler said as he put his arm around Mary to lead her to the wagon.

Florence Williams laid her hand on Olive's arm. "Luella Grimm is a loud-mouth gossip. Don't pay her no mind."

Olive's head swung around on the notion of dismissing the woman's cruel words, but Beth Steele joined in. "Florence is right. Everyone knows how Luella is."

Olive excused herself and followed Mr. Butler to the wagon. John climbed in the back and snuggled up close to his sister. Olive didn't recall the ride home, only the silence in the wagon. Mark began to cry in her arms, and she realized she was holding him too tightly. She loosened her grip and rocked the child, swaying in her seat. Luella's words, "low-born and common" rang through her head, and for once Olive was glad her parents were gone. To hear her family name referred to as "trash" would have been more than her parents could have borne. Once home, Mary jumped from the wagon and ran to the fields. Olive called to her, but Mr. Butler shook his head.

"Let her be a bit," he said.

Olive slumped at the kitchen table and recalled the dreadful scene at church. She had no experience in teaching a young woman that fist-fighting was inappropriate. Where would she have leaned that lesson, Olive thought, with a grim smile. She and Theda would have no more engaged in fisticuffs than danced naked in the streets. The only redeeming moment on the steps of the church that morning came when Jacob Butler defended Mary to that odious woman.

What a picture he made, standing tall, holding Mary close and comforting her, while setting the boundaries for his make-shift family. He was, without a doubt, the most handsome man she'd ever met. And, more importantly, she believed Jacob Butler was as loving a father as her own father had been. Olive prepared dinner and scowled and talked under her breath until she noticed the children staring.

"We didn't do anything wrong," Luke said softly.

Olive's shoulders dropped. "I know children. I'm sorry. I am not angry at you."

Olive sat down, and the three children approached her cautiously.

"Mary let him have it," Luke said nodding, wide eyed.

Olive noticed John's head drop. "What started the argument, children?" she asked.

Luke and Peg looked first at each other and then to John's

bowed head. Luke shook his head softly at his sister, but Peg turned to Olive anyway. "He said something mean."

"Who said something mean, Peg?" Olive asked.

"That boy," she whispered and scrunched her face into a scowl.

"Bertram?"

John ran to the door, and Luke made a face at his sister and followed. Peg's shoulders dropped, and she looked up to Olive obviously battling where her loyalties lay. Her eyes darted and she eventually ran to the door to follow the boys. Olive wondered what Bertram had said to throw Mary into such a fit. But knowing the attitude of Bertram's mother made Olive cringe at what offense the boy may have offered.

* * *

That evening as Olive continued the story she had begun to read the night before, Mary crept into the house. Olive started to stand, but a look from Mr. Butler sat her back in her chair. She finished reading early, amidst protests of the children, but she found she could not concentrate on the story as she watched Mary curl into a ball in front of the fire. Olive lay in her bed, staring at the ceiling and listened to the quiet of the house and her heart beating as she replayed the scene in front of the church in her head. She jumped as she felt the blanket lift, and Peg snuggled close to her. The child pushed Olive's hair away, and she felt Peg's warm breath on her ear.

"That boy called John a bad name," the little girl said.

Olive turned her head in the dark and whispered, "What did he say, Peg?"

"That boy says John don't talk on account of he's a dummy. That John's an Indian."

Olive narrowed her eyes. "An Indian?"

"Yeah, that John's caught something from Mark to make him an Indian."

Olive whispered softly, "An idiot? Did Bertram call John an idiot?" Olive watched the shadow of Peg's head nod. "John is not an idiot, Peg. Do you understand?"

Peg nodded again in the dark and lay her head on Olive's shoulder. When Olive thought the child slept, she heard Peg's terrified words. "Am I goin' to catched something from Mark?"

Olive's eyes closed, and she pulled Peg tight against her. "No, Peg. Mark's problems are not something one catches. He is not an idiot, and neither is John."

Peg yawned softly and relaxed. But Olive could not. Mary fought to defend herself and her brother and Mark. Tears of regret formed in Olive's eyes as she thought of her foregone conclusions concerning her niece. I condemned her as well. Olive had never faced the kind of viciousness that Mary had, and she found herself wishing she had gotten a shot in at the boy as Mr. Butler's friend held him. What an unOlive-like thought. Words were how disagreements were settled in her world. But here, faced with harshness, what words would she have to solve the prejudice and hate spilling out of Bertram's mouth.

* * *

"Good morning, Mary," Olive said and smiled as the morning sun poured through the windows. Mary looked grim and wiped her face with a rag. "Where is the dress you wore to church yesterday? We need to wash and repair it."

Mary eyed Olive's cheerful face and pulled the dress from the pile it lay in. She threw it on the table and looked dubiously to her aunt.

Olive picked up the dress and smoothed it flat. She retrieved her sewing supplies and began to thread a needle.

"I ain't sayin' I'm sorry," Mary said.

"I'm not saying I'm sorry."

Mary ran her tongue over her teeth and fidgeted as she stood. "Well, I ain't"

"Mary, can you get me the small piece of white fabric lying there? I think it will be enough to fix the hole in the collar," Olive asked.

Mary handed Olive the cloth. They sat in silence with just the soft snores of Peg and Mark breaking the spell. Olive watched from the corner of her eye as Mary began to speak and stopped. Olive waited patiently and hoped and prayed her niece would confide in her.

"I don't care what folks say about me, but I won't let them talk about John or Mark," Mary said finally.

"I'm sure you wouldn't," Olive said and continued her stitch.

"It ain't right."

"No, it's not, Mary," Olive agreed, lifting her head to meet her niece's stern face.

Mary stroked the edge of her dress, looking into her lap and out the window.

"Mary? Do you know why John won't speak? I'm going to take him to the doctor today, and I thought you may be able to give me some information before I do," Olive said and laid her stitching in her lap. "Or maybe your grandparents already took John to see the doctor?"

"My grandparents? You mean Ma's Pa and Ma? Fat chance of that happening. They don't do nothing for nobody if'n it don't get them something," Mary said.

"Mary," Olive said. "That's disrespectful. I'm sure your mother's parents love you and John and want the best for you. They wrote to me, didn't they? I gathered from their letter they just didn't have the room for you at their home."

"Yeah, right," Mary said with a scowl. "Just didn't want to bother is all it was. They'll be wanting us back come harvest."

"Hardly, Mary," Olive said as she stretched out Mary's dress and straightened the torn hem. "I've been meaning to call on them. It's only proper, and I've put it off too long already. Would you like to ride along when I go?"

Mary jumped from her chair in a hurry. "Don't do it, Olive. Don't make me go. I won't go. I'm telling you, I won't. And I won't let you take John neither."

If Mary's expression were to be believed, she was mortally afraid to visit her grandparents. The girl was wide-eyed and panicked. "You don't have to go if you don't want, Mary. I'll not make you," Olive said in a calm voice.

Mary sat down and stared out the window, her foot tapping on the floor.

"Maybe when I get home from taking John to the doctor, we can begin on another dress for you," Olive said and looked out the window where Mary was staring. "It's near time Mr. Butler was up."

Mary swallowed, stood and hurried to the sink to begin the makings of coffee. Without turning from the stove she asked, "Do you want hot water for tea?"

Olive smiled at the girl's back and replied, "Yes, Mary, that would be nice. Will you have some with me?"

* * *

Before noon, Olive asked Jacob to hitch the wagon and if he needed anything from town. He gave her a look she knew meant that she was to bring nothing more in the way of supplies.

"I'm going to take John to see the doctor. Peg told me last night that Bertram called John and Mark idiots. That's why Mary was fighting," Olive said. Mr. Butler's face grew crimson, and he swore. "I can't blame the girl now for her reasoning, although, I did."

While Jacob hitched the wagon, Olive called to John. He came meekly, and Olive smiled at him. "Come on, John. I have some things to do in town today, and I would like you to help me." Olive watched as he glanced to Luke and slowly began to climb into the wagon.

Olive checked her purse and straightened her dress once seated. The boy sat quietly beside her, and she let herself enjoy the ride to town. The sun was shining, and the world looked new. She touched her bag again to check on the letter she had written to Theda. She smiled to herself as she imagined Theda reading the contents. Her dearest friend would be shocked at the state she had found Mary and John in, but Olive feared the woman would faint dead away when Olive revealed she was living with Jacob Butler and that she had driven a wagon to a town an hour away. What a different perception a week had brought her.

Olive herself, days ago, would not have believed what she had seen and done. She was nearly a different person than the woman who came on the train that short time ago. And Olive knew in her heart of hearts that she would never, ever, be that woman again. She had wept at her brother's grave, wept for her brother's children and put aside all she knew to be right and proper to care for those children. Olive glanced down at the stern, worried face of her nephew. Her throat tightened and she knew that she would do all in her power to see this miniature of her brother past whatever demons haunted him. And Olive felt more alive, more focused, than she had ever before in her life. To hide on Church Street seemed foreign to Olive. Because that's what she had done these past thirty-five years. Hide from life and its problems and, therefore, condemn herself to never feel triumph. No, she would never allow herself to hide again.

Olive held John's hand as they began down the street past the sheriff's office.

"Miss Wilkins?" she heard from behind.

"Oh, good morning, Sheriff Bentley," Olive said as she turned.

"Morning, ma'am. John," the sheriff said. "May I speak to you in my office?"

"Certainly," she said and followed him into the small, cool building. John stopped to stare at large wooden case with a glass front holding guns of all sizes. The sheriff took her by the elbow and led her near the jail cells.

"Miss Wilkins. Jeb Davis was making some ugly noise about these children and you in the saloon last night," the sheriff whispered.

"Jeb Davis? I don't believe I'm acquainted with a Jeb Davis," Olive replied.

"He's Sophie's pa," the sheriff explained.

"What could Sophie's father possibly have to say in regard to me? I've yet to meet him. As a matter of fact, I was just telling Mary we'd best soon make a social call on the Davises," Olive said.

"You don't want to do that, Miss Wilkins," the sheriff said and shook his head.

Olive paused. "What kind of things was he saying?"

"Things not fit for a lady's ears. But with his last daughter running off with a traveling salesmen, he's going to be looking to get Mary back to the farm to do the stepping and fetching. Keep your eyes open, ma'am," the sheriff said.

"I'll do that, Sheriff, but I hardly see what rights Mr. Davis feels he has with these children. He did, after all, ask me to take them in. I still have his letter," Olive replied.

Olive led John up the steps to the doctor's office as the sheriff had instructed her as she was leaving his office. These accounts of Sophie's family from the sheriff and Mary made her wonder how James had married into such a family. Surely a decision such as the guardianship of orphaned children would have never made lightly. But in his profession, the sheriff must regard even liquor talk with a skeptical eye. As for Mary's account of her grandparents, Olive was convinced recent traumas had certainly colored her vision somewhat. The sheriff had implored her again to stay clear of the Davis farm. He had also asked her to save him a dance at the church social. Olive had rolled her eyes. Save him a dance, she thought and snorted as she opened the door on the landing.

"May I help you?" a wizened man in a black vest asked.

"Are you Doctor Hunter?"

"Yes," he replied.

"I'm Olive Wilkins. This is my nephew, John Wilkins. May we speak in private?"

The doctor scratched his head and pointed to an open door. John's grip dug into Olive's hand, and she smiled to reassure him.

"Doctor Hunter, John has not spoken for some time, and I would like to know if you can ascertain the reason?" Olive asked.

White bushy eyebrows rose, and the doctor looked down at John and back at Olive. "Well, let's take a look see," he replied. Olive lifted John onto a table, and the doctor looked kindly to the boy. "Do you think I could look down your throat, son? It won't hurt. All you have to do is open your mouth. Yes, that's right, boy."

The doctor looked down John's throat and in his ears and felt his neck. Finally, the man opened a drawer and withdrew a well-worn slingshot. He looked up to Olive and shrugged. John's eyes widened, and the doctor laughed.

"This thing is nearly as old as me, and that's mighty old. My pa made it for me when I was your age. Do you know what it is?" Doctor Hunter asked. John nodded. "Can you tell me what it is?"

John looked away, trance-like, as Olive had seen him do before when some one addressed him directly.

"Here, boy, look out the window and tell me if you think you can hit the smithy's sign if you had the right-sized rock," the doctor said and led John to the open window. He led Olive to the other side of the room as John examined the toy. "Miss Wilkins? Do you know the circumstances surrounding your brother's wife's death?" he asked softly.

"Yes, Doctor, I do."

"Well, I'm just a country doctor, but I'll tell you I think that boy suffers from a hysteria of sorts. Seeing what he saw happen, being unable to stop it." The doctor paused. "Living in the house with his mother's corpse rotting before him. I don't think John's problems are physical."

Olive bowed her head. "I wasn't sure. I didn't want to guess. But I do admit, I wondered if John is able to talk but just... unwilling."

"Sometimes folks get through this kind of thing. Sometimes they don't. You'll have to wait and see. Keep talking to him, Miss Wilkins. Someday he might surprise you and talk back."

Olive nodded, and they both looked at John as he stared out the window. "Doctor Hunter? I know it's not my business, and you may be unwilling to answer, but do you have any idea why Mark Butler is the way he is."

"I heard you were living out there," the doctor responded. Olive started to speak, and Doctor Hunter held up his hand to silence her. "Don't go getting all riled. I've seen enough in this lifetime to know it's not my place to judge."

"Yes, I am living at Jacob Butler's farm," Olive said.

"Well, then I'm guessing you have some questions." Olive

nodded. "Unlike John here, Mark Butler will never get better. His mother died trying to deliver him and truthfully, I'm shocked the boy lived," the doctor said.

Olive tried to conceal her curiosity, but failed. "What happened?"

"The child was too long in the birth canal, without air, and I believe the lack of oxygen and the pressure of the contractions damaged his brain. Permanently."

The doctor wiped his hand through his hair, obviously remembering and distressed from it. "I never saw a woman struggle against death so long and so hard to save her child. It was out of my hands and in God's, but she fought for every breath, losing blood by the bucketful to deliver him. Some things you'll never forget, and I won't ever forget the sound of Margaret's voice begging me to save her son."

Olive felt a chill wiggle down her back with the doctor's words. She watched the man's Adam's apple bob. "And Mr. Butler took his wife's death very hard," she said.

The doctor snorted a reply. "Took it hard? My God, I never saw a man grieve and cry the way he did. I worried he'd not be fit to take care of the other children. I found him outside beating the trunk of a tree until his hands were bloody."

Olive pictured the tall, proud Jacob Butler and could not imagine him losing control so completely. "Is there anything I can do for Mark?"

The doctor eyed her wearily. "No, but Jacob is determined to treat him as though he has no problems. I'd say you should follow his lead."

Olive thanked the doctor, gathered John's hand and led him outside. She found the post office, mailed the letter to Theda and headed home. John sat close on the ride home, and Olive bent down to kiss the silent boy's head.

Chapter Four

OLIVE FOUND HER DAYS MELTING ONE INTO the other. Hard work, uncertainty about her effect on the children and the profound change of habits made Olive wonder and pray as she wearily lay down each night. Only then did she give into the anger eating at her heart. How could James lose sight of everything he'd been taught? Did her father know how James's family had lived? Would his killer ever be brought to justice? Would these children ever escape the horrors they'd seen? She saw subtle changes in the them, though, and was convinced routine had brought them. Olive would be the steadying influence in their lives from now on. She would make the decisions, set the example and raise them.

Saturday arrived before Olive realized, and she was glad she remembered how to make her mother's peach cobbler as an offering to the picnic. The simplest of recipes was often the best, but Olive wished she had her mother's painted crockery to hold the dessert. Olive struggled and hurried with the children and looked down at herself as she picked a spot of crust from the front of her brown dress. What a mess I must be, she thought. Olive opened the second valise, still unpacked and withdrew a chestnut-colored dress. Although plain, the fabric was fine and stiffly shining and revealed a pattern in its weaving. A slightly scooped neck, more appropriate for evening than day, puzzled Olive, but she harrumphed and wondered if any one in this town would notice. Probably not. Very little respect for propriety, Olive thought, considering whom she had met thus far. Peg and Mary watched Olive pull the dress over her head, and Peg touched the fabric and oohed.

"It's so pretty," Peg said and watched Olive pull her hair back into its tight bun. "Wear your hair like mine," Peg added with a smile.

"I'm far too old to wear a pony tail, Peg,"

"Yeah, but it would be pretty pulled up with your black ribbon," Mary said and twisted the silk in her hand.

"Do you think it would look nice, Mary?" Olive asked.

"I could fix it," Mary said.

Olive smiled and Mary shrugged. She conceded to the girls' ministrations and could have fallen asleep as they brushed through her hair. Mary pulled the top back and braided a thick knot with Olive's hair. Peg ran to do Mary's bidding, fetching combs and ties, and the two girls seemed to enjoy themselves so much, Olive knew she would have worn a bee hive on her head to make them this happy. When she looked in her small mirror, it was all Olive could do to not groan audibly. She looked like a woman she knew back in Philadelphia, long past her prime, always wearing young fashions and styles, and to she and Theda's opinion, made herself look ridiculous in the process. Mary had pulled her hair loosely back, and the rest lay in curly heaps on her shoulders and arms.

"You look beautiful," Peg said, hands clasped below her chin.

"Thank you, Peg, Mary. You've both done a fine job," Olive said with a smile.

Olive gathered her bag and heard the door open. "Come

on," Luke cried. "We're goin' to be late."

When she turned, Olive met Mr. Butler's eyes. He was staring at her in the strangest fashion, and it brought goose bumps to Olive's neck. She rolled her eyes uncomfortably, wondering if he thought her a dolt in an evening dress and her hair down.

"Are we late?" she asked.

"You look so pretty," Luke said and smiled his father's rarely seen smile.

John walked slowly to her and took her hand to escort her from the kitchen.

Olive could not resist glowing in the attention, even though her admirers wore short pants. She accepted John's hand and held her head high as she passed Mr. Butler.

"Doesn't Aunt Olive look pretty, Daddy?" Peg asked.

"Miss Wilkins looks nice," Mr. Butler replied.

Olive raised a brow, as her hopes oddly had, that he would think she looked pretty or beautiful or attractive, but not just nice. And she fought a lump in her throat and wondered if and when her own niece and nephew would ever call her Aunt. They all climbed in the creaky wagon and set off. Near the picnic grove, Jacob Butler slowed the animals and turned in his seat.

"Now remember what I told you." The children nodded. He addressed them all but held Mary's gaze. "Stay out of trouble, don't go far without each other and if anyone gives you lip, like Bertram did, you get me."

The children nodded their assent, and Olive stood in the wagon to view the gathering. Tables were covered with gingham checks to hold food, and blankets were spread on the ground for picnicking. Olive smiled and turned to the children, telling them she had never really eaten a meal outside.

"What?" Luke cried. "Never been on a picnic?"

"No," Olive laughed. Peg shook her head and bit her lip

and John offered his hand to Olive.

"I'll help your aunt down, John," Jacob Butler said.

Olive's eyes opened wide as she for the first time was offered help from the wagon, or a chair or anything by the stone-faced giant. She laid her hand in his and lifted her skirts an inch or two to see where she was stepping. Once on the ground, she looked up to his face and blinked. They stood inches apart, and his eyes were boring into hers. She could smell his shaving soap and see where he had cut himself that morning. It was dreadfully intimate. And unnerving. "Thank you, Mr. Butler," she said finally.

* * *

Jesus, Mary, and Joseph. Who would have thought this woman had all this beautiful hair? Pulled back, soft, not severe like usual, and lying thick and rich across her shoulders. Even those silly spectacles of hers don't look so bad, Jacob thought. And a dress to match that hair, scooped just enough to reveal soft valleys above what Jacob supposed was a good handful of bosom.

"You may release my hand," Olive Wilkins said.

Jacob jumped and realized he had been drifting. He turned quickly and reached to take Mark from Mary as the girl climbed down. From the minute he and John and Luke had walked in the door of the house, Luke screaming about being late, Jacob had not been able to clear his head. Olive Wilkins wasn't pretty. When she smiled at John as he escorted her to the wagon, Jacob realized something he'd just as well not thought of. Olive Wilkins was beautiful.

* * *

Olive carried her dessert to the table and cringed when she saw all the fine dishes the women had prepared. "We must look a bit weak in the cooking department," she whispered to Mary. The girl nodded but eyed all the goodies before her. Olive watched as Beth Steele and Florence Williams approached.

"Olive, so happy you came. What did you make?" Beth asked.

Olive and Mary exchanged glances. "The peach cobbler."

The two women turned to the table and Florence asked, "Did Jacob still have peaches put up?"

"No, I bought them canned at the mercantile," Olive replied.

Florence's eyes widened. "You bought canned peaches? They must have been dear."

Olive shrugged.

"If you're still here in the fall you come over to my house, and we'll do our canning together."

Olive smiled but said nothing.

"Have you ever canned before?" Florence tilted her head and asked.

"Well... no... I never did, and I wouldn't have the foggiest idea where to begin," Olive said and laughed.

The two women regarded her, wide-eyed, and then laughed as well. They led Olive to a well-worn quilt and sat down to chat and observe the party. Mary stood shyly against the tree near the blanket.

Florence looked up. "Come sit down, Mary. You're old enough to sit with the women. Come on." Florence patted an empty space, and Mary gingerly sat down. "When my Sue comes back, you can wander around with her for awhile."

Olive was grateful to the women for readily accepting Mary, and they talked until Florence's daughter joined them.

"Sue, this is Mary. Why don't you two go see what games they have set up for the youngins'?" Florence said.

Sue chattered a mile a minute, and soon Mary was following her. Olive listened to the fast friends as they talked women talk. Children, husbands, work, worries. Olive knew her face colored as Florence described her husband Bill chasing her around the kitchen table once the children were asleep. Beth giggled and covered her mouth.

"Oh my," Florence said suddenly. "I didn't mean to make you uneasy, Olive. You not being married and all."

A rousing round of male laughter brought the three women's heads around and Olive saw Mr. Butler talking to the women's husbands while he held Mark.

"Hmm," sighed Beth. "That man is mighty good-looking, even if he doesn't smile so much anymore."

"I'm thinking he has all his parts and some to spare," Florence added and stared.

Olive let her gaze dip uncharacteristically to Jacob's crotch. One would certainly think he did have all those parts, Olive mused. He also had a magnetism that was hard to deny. Jacob Butler was the embodiment of masculinity. "What was his wife Margaret like?" she asked.

Beth Steele's head dropped. "She was my best friend growing up. I still miss her."

Florence patted Beth's hand. "Beautiful is the first thing to come to mind, I'd say. Dark-haired and small and a good wife and mother."

Beth lifted her head. "Everyone I know, including me, was after Jacob, and who could blame them? But I can't say I was jealous. Margaret and Jacob were a perfect match. Just perfect."

"Everyone thought Jacob would take a wife soon after Margaret died, three children and all, but Beth and I both think that man will never find anyone he loves as much. Or could love him as much as Margaret did," Florence said.

The women sat silently for a while watching the men until

Florence spoke up again. "If my Bill's any measure, that man's got to be mighty itchy by now."

"Itchy?" Olive asked.

Beth frowned and Florence shrugged. "Oh, don't look at me like that Beth Sinclair Steele. How long would Jack last without some loving?"

Beth pursed her lips, but then a smile slowly lit her face. "He usually doesn't last till bed. I swear that man gets itchier by the day."

Florence laughed, and Olive was shocked by the conversation. What happened between men and women was never, ever, brought up in conversation. It was private. Sacred. And these women, Olive could swear, acted as if a wife's duty was... well, enjoyable. Since she had not married, Olive's mother, to her obvious relief, had completely ignored the subject.

Jacob approached the blanket holding a sleeping Mark, and Olive knew her face colored.

"Can I lay him down here for a nap?" Jacob asked.

"Yes, of course."

"Are you having a nice time, Olive?"

She nodded and realized that this was the first time Jacob Butler had ever addressed her by her first name. "And I think the children are having a grand time."

"They sure do look nice in the new outfits you made." Jacob knelt down on his haunches. "Did I ever thank you?"

"You made those outfits? I declare. You sew a fine stitch. I thought Peg and Mary's dresses were store-bought," Florence said.

"I can never get a piece of ruffle to lay like that. Will you teach me?" Beth asked.

"I'd love to," Olive said and smiled.

"Jacob, we told Olive we'd show her how to can in the fall, but what if she's not here in the fall," Florence said. "Talk her into staying and then she can teach us to sew."

Olive was embarrassed and stared at her hands folded in the lap of her dress. She looked up to find Jacob regarding her.

"She can stay as long as she likes or needs to. I already told her that," he said.

Their eyes met and held, for a moment only, but Olive thought the skin would peel from her arms from the brief connection between them. "That's very kind of you, Mr. Butler. Jacob. I am hoping though, I can convince Mary and John to return with me soon. We've imposed too long."

"Luke and Peg will miss them. But I think Peg, especially, will miss you more," he said.

The thought, up until now, of leaving Peg and Luke and Mark had not occurred to Olive. She looked down to the sleeping boy and wondered how in so few days, had these children wormed their way into her heart. Leaving them would hurt for a long, long while.

"I will miss them desperately," Olive said.

Jacob nodded grimly and stood to return to the men.

"That's more than that man's said in six months," Beth commented to Florence's nods.

* * *

"So how is life with the Spinster Wilkins, Jacob?" Bill Williams asked.

His friend's indirect insult stung. "Miss Wilkins is doing fine. She loves those children of Jimmy's, and she's been working like a mule," Jacob said.

"Working like a mule, huh. Anywhere's near your bed?" Bill asked.

Jacob knew he meant no offense, not really. Just the way men talked about women. But he narrowed his eyes all the same and gave Bill a glare that instantly drew quiet.

"Miss Wilkins is a lady. And I treat her like one. Best not to imply anything else."

"We didn't mean nothing," Jack said quickly.

The men turned then to look at their wives and Olive. "She sure does look different with her hair down. Kind of pretty," Bill said.

It bothered Jacob to no end that he had felt the same. She looked beautiful today. And he wasn't in the mind to hear the men make comments about her. She deserved respect. She had earned it. Olive deserved a home, children, and the return of the love she lavishly gave. He hoped for her sake that she found it. But he wondered about whom the stern, moral, thirty-five-year-old woman could find who would appreciate her intelligence and compassion. Jacob shook his head to clear his mind of such thoughts. Worrying about another person would accomplish nothing and he had his own long row to hoe, as did Olive.

* * *

Late afternoon, found Olive, Beth and Florence with sleepy children making pillows on their laps and legs. The days were not yet long though, and as the sun began to drop, Olive felt a chill. The dance would be in the Cooper barn behind the church, and the men came to sit with the still drowsy children while the women moved the food and drinks.

Olive stood in the barn with Mary and John by her side and watched as the fiddler began and the dancing started. John had followed Luke most of the day, but he now seemed content to lean against Olive's leg and twist her skirt in his fingers.

"Did you enjoy yourself today, Mary?" Olive asked.

Mary lifted her shoulders slowly, to drop them and tilt her head. "Pa brung me to a picnic once," she said.

It was on the tip of Olive's tongue to correct the girl, but Mary's wistful tone stopped her. She looked at her niece, but the girl would not meet her eye. "I miss my mother and father every day," Olive said.

Mary nodded. "They was wrong about lots of things, but ya know, they were still my Ma and Pa."

Olive knew it cost the girl to admit her parents shortcomings. And Olive thought of their faults and hers as well and how much it had affected Mary in her short ten years.

"We all make mistakes, Mary. Not one of us who walks this earth is perfect. I'm sure there are good things to remember," Olive said.

"Yeah, some."

"Good evening, Miss Wilkins," the sheriff said.

"Oh, good evening, Sheriff," Olive replied.

"Miss Mary, John. You look mighty fetching tonight, Miss Wilkins," Sheriff Bentley said.

Olive silently compared Jacob's "nice" to the sheriff's "fetching." The man's hair was slicked and parted in the middle, and his vest buttons squirmed from their holes with every breath he took. But his jacket was clean and his nails trimmed, and Olive thought he made a very presentable appearance. Male attention of this nature was a short list for Olive, and she decided then and there to enjoy it.

"You look very nice this evening as well. The picnic was wonderful. Don't you think?" Olive asked as she watched the dancers line up.

"I let the deputy go to the picnic so I could be here for the dance," the sheriff said.

Olive smiled. "Should we be expecting trouble or something unusual to happen this evening?"

"Truth be known, I was hoping you would honor me with a dance," he said.

The casual humor fled Olive's eyes immediately as she remembered his words the day she took John to see Doctor Hunter. "Oh, Sheriff Bentley, I'm sure there are others with whom you would prefer dancing."

The sheriff eyed her seriously, and the children's heads followed the conversation. "No. I can't think of a one."

Olive looked from his outstretched hand to the other dancers. To be asked in such a fashion was new for Olive. Those occasional partners in the past had felt obligations. A friend's brother or father, shoved in her direction. No regrets, Olive thought, *I am done watching life go by.*

"I would be honored, sir," she replied.

* * *

Jacob carried Mark with Peg and Luke trailing him to John and Mary as they watched Olive and the sheriff dance. Olive held herself primly, but when the sheriff spoke she laughed and smiled at the man.

"What's she dancing with that fool for?" Jacob said as much to himself as to anyone near by.

Mary looked up to him and the slightest of smiles graced her lips. "I think the sheriff's sweet on her."

"Well, she looks silly out there, dancing and laughing like that," Jacob said.

"But Aunt Olive looks so pretty today," Peg said. "Mary and I fixed her hair."

"Yes she does look nice today, Peg. But a woman her age shouldn't be acting like that," Jacob said. His reaction to Olive earlier in the day had scared him sorely. He had been plain old flabbergasted. Jacob would admit he liked and respected Olive but to be attracted to her was a whole different thing. And as if to confound his thoughts further for some reason it was bothering him beyond belief that she was dancing with Bentley.

"The sheriff said she looked fetching," Mary added.

"She's not too old to dance, Daddy. See, they swing around the corners just fine," Luke said.

Jacob grimaced and knew he would not win this argument. Nor did he understand what had prompted him to comment at all. He handed Mark to Mary and led Peg onto the dance floor. He swung his daughter around as he held her, and she giggled and kissed his face softly. And for one breath-taking moment she looked as her mother did when Jacob first met Margaret. Jacob had been twelve and she eleven, the first time he spotted the dark-haired beauty. He had fallen in love that day and never looked back. Margaret had been his destiny, and now his future was raising a bewitching miniature of her, a solemn son, and the child that, through his birth, had taken Jacob's mate and his heart. He squeezed Peg roughly as if to either cling to this future or condemn the past.

Jacob led Peg back to Mary, Luke, John and Olive who had just come off the dance floor. "Mary, would you like to take a turn?" he asked.

* * *

Olive watched Mary's indecision and desire, and she nearly hugged Jacob for the gift he was giving Mary. To be included and wanted was so evident on the girl's face that Olive wanted to shout yes in her stead. Jacob held out his hand, and Mary looked up to Olive as if searching for approval. Olive smiled her response, and Mary laid her hand in Jacob's. He led the girl slowly through the steps, and when they were finally turning corners with ease and speed, Olive saw what she thought she might never see. Mary was smiling and glancing right to left as if to be assured that all saw her. Dancing. Olive clapped, and the children called to Mary as she spun by in Jacob's arms.

And Olive knew, as if time had stopped, that this man would be the only man in her lifetime to reach this far into her heart. She would be able to say, when going to face her God that she had loved. Maybe not love in the romantic sense, the intimate sense, but that still clearly, she had loved. The thought gave her pause and brought calmness to her soul that was unequaled. The fact that Jacob would not return that love did not in the least diminish the light in Olive's heart. And Olive understood with new clarity that to love was a far greater gift than to be loved.

Jacob guided Mary through the crowd of dancers. Olive smiled her gratitude and a smile grew on Jacob's face as he looked at her over the tops of the children's heads. "Mary, you looked as though you had been dancing all your life," Olive said as she turned to the girl.

Mary's cheeks were flushed, and she held her head tall when she responded. "Its not as hard as it looks."

"Jack Steele said a storm's blowing our way. Best be getting home," Jacob said.

Olive looked around the barn, one last time, recalling what a wonderful day it had been. They said their goodbyes and loaded the children into the wagon. The wind began to whip up, and Olive squinted her eyes into the dust.

"Could be a bad one," Jacob said. "Climb in the back and cover yourself and the children with the canvas. The rain will be following."

Olive stood in the back of the wagon and swayed with the wind. The air grew cold, and Olive fought to spread the heavy fabric out and not lose it to the storm. The rain fell in sheets, and the children were soon soaked and frightened. Olive was growing afraid as well with the constant streaks of lightning etching the skies and the roar of thunder following closely. Mary held John, and Peg and Luke huddled on either side of Olive while she held Mark tightly against her. When the wagon stopped, Olive peered out from the thin shelter the canvas gave. Jacob had climbed down from the wagon and was leading the terrified, neighing horse forward. The wagon started again with a lurch, and Olive said a silent prayer that they would get home.

After what seemed like an eternity, the wagon stopped again, and Jacob lifted the canvas. "We're home," he shouted.

The rain was still falling hard, but the wind had died down, and Olive heard the rumble of thunder at a distance. The children dashed to the house, soaked, and Jacob led the horse to the barn. Olive lit lamps while Mary started a fire and the children began to peel out of wet things. Jacob stepped into the house, boots squishing, water pouring off his hat.

"The boys will have to stay in here tonight. The wind tore some of the barn roof off, and our bedding's soaked," he said.

"That's fine, Jacob. I confess, I left the shutters above the bed open this morning. It was so beautiful out when we left. Our bed is soaked as well. I just told the children we'll sleep in front of the fireplace," Olive said.

Jacob kissed the heads of the children and turned from the puddle he stood in.

"Where are you going?" Olive asked. Her teeth chattered as she looked up at him. "You said your bed is soaked. We'll make room."

"Wouldn't be proper, Olive."

Olive looked up as she helped Peg into her nightgown. "Oh, fiddlee dee dee, who's to know. And anyway," Olive said and stared into Jacob's eyes, "we wouldn't have made it home if you hadn't guided that horse for the last hour. You've got to be tired, and I know you're wet to the bone."

Luke and John were frightened and clinging to Olive. Mark had fallen asleep as soon as Olive changed him and laid him in his crib. Mary looked nervously out the window, and John held her hand.

"Please stay, Daddy," Peg cried. "It was scary in the wagon."

"What if the storm comes back?" Luke asked.

"Go get some dry clothes, while Mary and I change. Bring the milk when you come. I bought cocoa at the general store, and we'll have a treat before bedtime," Olive said addressing Jacob and the children.

* * *

Jacob fought the rain on his way to the barn and thought about the day. When he led Mary from the dance floor, he'd seen Olive watching him. Her eyes, soft and warm, peered into his with intensity and gratitude. He had made Mary happy, and Jacob knew that this woman ached for any triumph with her niece and nephew. She was barking out orders now and seemed determined that he stay in the house.

Jacob conceded he didn't really want to sleep in a stall with the horse, and the children did earnestly look afraid. *Why am I,* he thought? Sounds too close to a family, gathered together at bed, that's why.

When Jacob returned to the house, Olive was propped up against some firewood with a blanket thrown over it and another over her legs, reading from a book, aloud. Jacob had changed into dry clothes on the porch and carried the pitcher of milk. Olive rose, heated the milk, and instructed Mary to continue the reading. Mary stumbled but worked her way through the words while Olive handed each child a mug. Their eyes widened as they sipped the sweet, hot concoction, and soon eyelids began to droop.

Jacob sat on the chair and watched as Peg curled under

Olive's arm and lay her head on the woman's breast. The boys were snuggled together, and Mary sat holding her knees, listening to the story. Olive's hair was loose; Jacob figured, to dry in the warmth of the fire, and her glasses sat at the end of her nose. Her white nightgown was buttoned to her neck, and tiny pleats were sewn in the fabric to her waist. Jacob supposed Olive had sewn it, and he wondered if anyone had seen if before. He was sure not, and he wondered why she would stitch so many details and make it so becoming if she was to be the only one to see it.

* * *

Olive stood as the last eyes closed, and she helped Mary lie down. She kissed the foreheads and wiped sticky cocoa from chins and mouths before finally turning to Jacob.

"I'm tired as well, if you don't mind. I think I'll lower the lamps."

Olive sat down near the children, spread out like a spindle in the heat of the fire. Jacob picked up the blanket on the table and laid it out on the floor. The slowing rain on the roof pattered, and in the dim light Olive began brushing through her hair.

"Do you always brush your hair this much before bed?" Jacob asked.

"One hundred strokes."

"Why?" he asked.

Olive shrugged. "I suppose because my mother always did. Seems silly now. I wear it back mostly, but I guess its just habit."

"It looked beautiful today," Jacob said.

Olive's head snapped around in the shadows, and she was glad she could not see Jacob's face. If he was jesting with her, then the darkness didn't reveal it, and she could imagine the sentiment as true. "Thank you."

The room was quiet, except for the soft rhythmic breathing of the children until Olive folded her glasses and sat them with a clink on the stone mantle. She stretched out and sighed and the blankets snapped as she pulled them over herself.

"Jacob? Are you asleep?" she said softly.

"No, Olive."

"I want to thank you for this day. I had a wonderful time, and so did the children and especially for dancing with Mary. She glowed in the attention, and I have had little success with her. It meant a great deal to Mary and to me."

"I'm glad you enjoyed yourself. And dancing with Mary was no big thing. She and all the children looked nice today, and I was proud of them. The clothes and all I mean," Jacob whispered.

"It was a big thing. Mary was nearly bursting, and I know you did it to make her happy. It was a kind gesture." Olive chuckled. "And even the Spinster Wilkins had a dance partner today. My, oh my."

"Don't call yourself that," Jacob said.

"Well, I am a spinster. I don't even mind. It allows me to be eccentric and throw caution to the wind. My father's sister was a spinster, and my mother said that was why she talked to herself. I'm named after her you know." Olive laughed softly into the still air. "Mary and John will soon giggle at me like James and I did at our Aunt Olive."

"Why did you dance with the sheriff?" Jacob asked. The room was still except for the soft pattering of rain on the roof.

"Because he asked," she finally replied.

Olive lay awake for a while until the regular breathing of the children lulled her in its monotony to sleep. The last conscious thought in her head was the actual distance between her and Jacob Butler. Was it three feet or four? *It may be a mile to Jacob*, Olive thought, but it was pleasantly reassuring and somehow sensual to be sleeping so close to a living, breathing, handsome, kind man. She closed her eyes and curled the blanket near her chin, smiling.

* * *

Olive awoke from a strange dream with no idea where she was. As consciousness slowly overtook sleep she focused as well as she could without her glasses on the coals glowing softly in the hearth. She was toasty warm, front to back, and her cheek cradled by flannel. Front to back, she repeated in her head as she became aware of her surroundings. There was a huge male arm draped over her waist, and her eyes opened so fully they crossed. Olive was now wide-awake and painfully aware of her position. Jacob had somehow ended up behind her. She turned her head ever so slowly as if the slightest movement would send her off a sheer cliff. Jacob's mouth was open, and her hair was a tangle over the stubble of his beard. He breathed softly into her ear and then shifted and buried his nose in her hair. *Good God*, she thought, *what am I to do now?*

Hoping to extricate herself subtly, she shifted and began to sit up. The arm around her tightened, and a deep, male hum of contentment reverberated through her head. She lay stiffly in his grip without a notion as to what to do next. His hips pushed softly into her backside and if possible, Olive's eyes opened wider. Jacob nudged repeatedly, escalating in speed and tempo. Bizarrely, all she could coax from her sleep-muddled mind was the word "itchy." Jacob mumbled and groaned, and to Olive's opinion, if he grew any louder, he would surely wake the children.

"Mr. Butler!" she whispered as loudly as she dared.

He chewed on her ear in response.

"Mr. Butler, please," she said again.

"Hmm, what?" he responded, dreamily.

"Mr. Butler, somehow you have managed to roll my way," Olive said.

* * *

Jacob had closed his eyes with a vision of Olive dancing with the sheriff. Only to be replaced by a picture of Peg asleep on her breast. The wistful resignation in Olive's voice when he asked her why she had danced whirled through his head before he dropped off to sleep.

Now there was a woman in his arms in the steamy dream floating through Jacob's head. She was nearly as long as he stretched out, and rounded and soft in all the good spots. His hips were pounding into female flesh, and his mind drifted to the place of semi-consciousness that overtook him when he was near completion. But a voice broke through the sexual haze, and when recognition occurred, he stopped instantly.

"Mr. Butler!"

Jacob jumped back on his elbows and feet like a great crab on the sand. He flew back, arms and legs flying until his head hit the table and he knocked over a chair.

Mary sat up, her face sleepy and tousled. "What's the matter?" she asked.

"Nothing, Mary, go back to sleep. Mr. Butler ah... ah had a nightmare," Olive said.

Thankfully, Olive's vision was poor enough that she was unable to see his revulsion. She looked at him and blinked, and he stared back. Jacob stood, righted the chair, and opened the door, allowing for his escape and the cool night air to run along Olive's back. She lay awake, watching the dawn arise. Her heart, so happy as she fell asleep, was torn from her chest in the rays of the new day. Olive was certain her feelings for Jacob had not emerged to intimacy or romance. *Whatever intimacy feels like*, she thought. But nor was the emotion so shallow that she did not feel his reaction to the depths of her soul.

Chapter Five

JACOB DID NOT GO INTO THE HOUSE FOR breakfast or dinner. He stared into the rounded backside of his plow horse and fought the images in his dreams. He was embarrassed, confused, frightened, repulsed and attracted all at the same time. *How in God's name did I end up rubbing on her backside like that?* She was bossy and even manipulative on occasion. Certainly not qualities a man looked for in a woman. But yet she was gentle and kind and thoughtful with the children and soothed them in a way, which he knew he never could. *But I'm not looking for a woman or a wife,* Jacob thought and shook his head. She's too tall, too thin, too Olive for his tastes, as well. Her hair was nice, he admitted to himself, and when she was not dressed like a schoolmarm, very pretty. Olive was a lady, that Jacob knew for sure, and he dreaded facing her at supper.

* * *

Every time a porch step creaked or the children shouted, Olive's stomach rolled. She would calm herself by talking her way through the previous night's episode. Close quarters naturally made her available. Oh, no, available, sounds as though

I'm waiting by a saloon door. Not available, within reach. Well, her sewing basket had been in reach as well. Jacob was surely mortified that he had reached for her of all women to scratch the itch. Scratch the itch. *Now there's a strange thought,* she mused, as she stirred Mary's stew. Florence had used the phrase at the church social when she had been talking about her husband Bill. And, in retrospect, Olive understood the expression much better. One would have thought a swarm of bees had nested in Jacobs's pants the way he gyrated. The door flew open, and the children shouted and ran to their father.

"Miss Wilkins."

"Mr. Butler."

They both nodded and made brief eye contact. Olive's face grew warm, and her eyes lowered down Jacob's body and to the crotch of his pants. *Yee Gads,* she thought and turned away quickly, imagining his hips in motion.

"Mary made stew for dinner. We're ready to eat." Olive said. She had just begun to relax when Luke asked if she would be able to read that evening. John was nodding and smiling as he stuffed his face.

"Can we sleep in front of the fire again?" Peg asked.

"Will you make hot chocolate again?" Luke asked.

Mary stood to carry her plate to the dry sink. "Well, I don't want to sleep on the floor again. It's too hard."

Peg giggled. "My bum hurt today, but I don't care. I want to sleep there again."

"We won't be sleeping on the floor tonight, Peg," Olive said.

The little girl looked at her quizzically. "Does your bum hurt, too, Aunt Olive?"

Olive looked at Peg. She heard Jacob cough. "That is inappropriate language for the supper table, Peg."

"What should she say?" Mary asked. "My Pa said 'ass.'"

"Or 'butt'," Luke said and he and John huddled together and giggled.

"That's enough, children," Jacob said.

"Mary, would you begin the dishes? I want everyone else to work on his or her primers. Mr. Butler, would you step outside with me a moment?" Olive said.

Jacob nodded and followed her out the door. Olive squared her shoulders and opened her mouth, only to stop and pinch her lips. She snorted, twitched her nose, and faced him.

"About last night, Mr. Butler," Olive began and looked into his eyes. *What long lashes he has*, she thought, and shook her head. "About last night. I understand... I have been told that, well, men, occasionally have... needs, that left untended, may well grow, may build," Olive stopped. *So far, so good*, she thought. "And that sometimes whatever, oh, excuse me, whoever might be there may be mistakenly..." Olive stopped again and looked at Jacob, and she saw that he was fighting a smile. "Really, Mr. Butler, I see nothing humorous in this situation."

"I'm sorry, Olive, I don't mean to laugh. It's not a laughing matter, but listening to you try to talk about it is."

"In any case," Olive continued, "whoever may be, what word shall I use, handy, might be the mistaken object of your affection. Considering you were sleeping." There, she had said what she needed to say.

* * *

Olive has no idea how beguiling, how bewitching she is right now, Jacob thought. Stumbling and snorting and trying to talk about something she had no idea of.

"If that was the case, Olive, I'd hardly ever leave my mare alone when I slept in the barn," Jacob said.

Olive's eyes widened. "Well, hopefully, you can tell the

difference between me and your horse. Either that, or you're a lot itchier than Florence said."

"Itchy?" Jacob said.

Olive's face colored to Jacob even in the dim twilight.

"Well, yes, that was the word that Beth and Florence used. Even though I rarely approve of slang, I find that the word is, well, appropriate." Olive finished and looked away.

"The three of you were discussing me? And the word used was 'itchy'?" Jacob asked.

Olive nodded once.

Jacob sat his hands on his hips. "In the first place, women aren't supposed to talk about that sort of thing. And in the second place, well in the second place, I can tell the difference between you and the mare," Jacob finished with a shout.

Olive's mouth dropped. "Well, you would have never known it the way you nearly tore the house apart trying to get away from me."

"Is that what you think, Olive? That I was trying to get away from you?" Jacob said.

Olive granted him a thin smile. "Well, I didn't see your mare in front of the

fireplace," she said.

Jacob shook his head and let a rueful laugh. "Olive, you don't know what you're talking about."

"In any case, Mr. Butler, I think we can both continue on in a mature fashion and dismiss the entire episode."

Jacob grabbed her shoulders, turning her to him. "Wait a second, Olive. Remember what you thought about your brother Jimmy and his farm. You didn't know anything about that and you couldn't have been more wrong in your silly notions. You sat in your house in Philadelphia, you said so yourself, and made up some fancy story about the life your brother was living. Well, that should have taught you something."

"What do my misconceptions regarding James have to do with this?" Olive asked.

"You don't know anything about what goes on between men and women. Don't pretend that you do. Sometimes the want is so strong that nothing can stop it."

"That is a fine conclusion in general terms but has nothing to do with the specifics of our case," Olive said sharply. "There is no 'want.' There was an awkward moment, a mistake. I am not the kind of woman, or the age for that matter, who inspires 'want.'"

She was so sure, so certain that she was uninspiring. But yet as he held her and listened to her argue and watched fire grow in her eyes, he knew she could not have been more wrong. For whatever reason, he could not resist looking at her lips as she bit out her last words. And it was his undoing.

* * *

Olive watched as Jacob brought his face closer and closer to her. She swallowed and awkwardly looked away. His hand released her shoulder, and he gently touched her chin, pulling her face back to his. He spoke, she knew, but as his eyelids lowered, and she felt his breath on her face, she was mesmerized, not with his words but with his look and touch.

"This is *want*, Olive," he whispered.

Jacob's lips touched Olive's, and her eyes fluttered closed. His growl into her mouth tightened her throat and made her heart skip a beat. Jacob's large, rough hand trembled as he cupped her face. That fascinating smell of his filled her head, and her shoulders drooped as her head tilted back.

When she awoke, her lips were still lightly touching Jacob's. His eyes were closed, and he was panting softly. Olive's thoughts were a shambles. Embarrassment, confusion, and if she were honest with herself, pleasure. She shook her head, wiggled from Jacob's hold, and ran into the house.

* * *

Jacob drew in a breath as the door slammed and wondered aloud what he had been thinking. When Olive swayed into him, Jacob wound his fingers into her tight mass of hair and heard pins hit the porch. His tongue snaked its way into her mouth, and he pulled her roughly, tightly against him. No thoughts of right or wrong, spinster or widow, had entered his head. Only that woman, with skin as white and soft as corn silk and hair heavy enough for him to drown in.

I kissed her, and I would kiss her again. What had happened the night before could be explained away with a hundred excuses. But he was not sleeping or dreaming on his porch right now. How did her apology or explanation end up in a kiss? She was not Margaret. But yet when he kissed her, he felt for the first time in a year, with certainty, he was home. *Damn her*, he thought. Even wrapped up, chin to shoes in black fabric, hair pulled tight, she was meant to be kissing him and it felt right, was right. Jacob's mouth pulled into a grim line, knowing and hating himself for it, that he would remember and replay that kiss as clearly as the first time he had kissed Margaret.

* * *

The rest of Olive's evening was a blur as her mind reviewed every word she and Jacob had spoken. She helped Peg dress for bed and wondered if something she had said or done had misled Jacob. Mary eyed her quizzically, and she turned from the girls regard. Did he think I wanted him to kiss me? Does he know I've never been kissed, not really kissed? Did he think I had some grand design or scheme coming west for these children that included him?

Olive dropped down on the bed and stared out the window at the full moon. *But how could I have known he was waiting at the end of my journey? Well, maybe not waiting,* Olive thought, *but here all the same. This is heartache,* she said to herself. *I will file this sensation away with all the new and wondrous and troublesome feelings I've had since coming to Spencer.*

And perhaps it was time to go. Perhaps the children were ready. Perhaps if she didn't see Jacob Butler every day, she wouldn't dwell on what she had purposefully missed. Her mind cleared, and she relaxed, squirreling away these thoughts for future review. But soon her eyes closed, and she felt Jacob's breath on her face, and the light touch of his lips on hers. This is "want" as well, Olive admitted, and brushed her hair one hundred and twenty strokes.

* * *

Jacob announced at breakfast that he would begin planting that day. "Luke and John, I'd like you to help me." The children nodded, and Jacob caught Olive's eye for the first time that morning.

"I've been lax in attending the laundry, Mr. Butler. Do you have a large wash tub?" Olive asked.

"I'll start a fire on the side of the house so you can wash outside. There's a spot set up for a kettle," Jacob said. "I was thinking I might turn over a small piece of ground out back. Maybe get a vegetable garden started. Then we'd have something to can in the fall."

Olive looked away quickly, picking up dishes and turning to the sink. Jacob wondered why, and when he began to think of a future and the time in between now and a harvest that included

Olive.

"That would be nice, Mr. Butler. I don't imagine John and Mary and I will be here for the canning, but I'd be happy to help get your garden started," Olive said.

So this is how it will be, Jacob thought. Just as well that the Spinster Wilkins leaves soon. Jacob rose, thanked Olive for the meal and motioned the boys to follow.

* * *

"When's the fall?" Peg asked.

"What do you mean, Peg?" Olive asked.

The girl's lip trembled. "Is that when you're leaving us? And taking John and Mary, too?"

"Oh, Peg," Olive said. "We can't live here forever. This is your home. Mary and John are my responsibilities. My home and theirs, too, is back in Philadelphia."

Olive sat down and pulled Peg into her lap. The little girl cuddled against her, and Olive continued, "Your father, someday, will meet a nice woman and fall in love. A young woman, and then maybe you'll have more brothers and sisters."

Peg's eyes darted. "But I don't want more brothers. I want you and Mary."

Olive rocked Peg slowly. "Well, enough of this. We've got lots of laundry, and since I don't have any idea of what to do, you'll have to help me."

"Ya never done washin'?" Mary asked.

"No, Mary. I sent my soiled clothes to a woman down the street, and she returned them clean."

Mary and Olive carried the dirty clothes outside and filled the kettle with water.

"What if me and John want to stay with Jacob?" the girl asked.

"John and I," Olive replied

Mary huffed and asked again. "What if John and I want to stay with Jacob?"

Olive stirred the clothes in the hot, soapy water. "I'm hoping that soon, very soon actually, you'll want to return with me to Philadelphia."

Mary was quiet as she dumped more dirty clothes in the water and retrieved clean ones from the pot. "Why can't you stay here with Jacob? He doesn't beat you or nothing."

"It isn't proper or right, Mary, for us to remain together unmarried. Mr. Butler has been kind allowing me to stay this long," Olive said.

"Marry him then," Mary said.

"I can't just marry him. Marriage is sacred and requires both parties to love and be committed to each other. Mr. Butler and I don't love each other," Olive said.

Mary stared at Olive openly. "I saw him kissing you last night. My ma kissed lots of men, but she only kissed my pa like you was kissing Jacob."

Olive's face fell and turned three shades of red. "Mary! I... I... that's not...you shouldn't have been . . it was a mistake... I..."

Olive's fluttering fell silent as Peg pointed to a man on horseback approaching the farm.

Olive squinted as the man came closer, and Mary edged up to her. Olive looked down to Mary's face and saw wide eyes and fear. "Do you know this man?"

Mary nodded, and the rider dismounted. Olive watched him limp, and the filthy clothes he wore shed dust. His battered hat shaded his face, and Olive swallowed nervously at the grim, despicable picture he made.

"Good morning, sir," Olive said.

The man eyed Olive from under the brim of his hat, rolled a lump of tobacco from one cheek to the other and spit a long stream of juice.

"Ya look just like that lying, cheatin' lazy piece of crap that Sophie got herself hitched to." The man turned his regard from Olive to Mary. "Come on, girl, git yer brother. There's crops to be brung in, and your grandma needs help with the cookin' and such."

So this was the man the sheriff had warned her about. The same man, Olive realized now, that had stared so menacingly at John the day they had gone to town for supplies. Olive reached her arm around Mary and could feel the terror emanating from the child. Peg was wrapped in Olive's skirts, and her dark eyes were as round as saucers. "Just a moment. She's not going anywhere," Olive said.

"That so," he said and spit again.

Olive eyed the wet spot on the ground where he had spit inches from her skirt. She had no idea what she would do if this man decided to take Mary by force.

"I'm Sophie's daddy, and I needs the youngins'. So git the boy and do it fast. I ain't in the mood for no lip from some schoolmarm," Jeb Davis said.

"You said in your letter there was no one to care for these children. I'm her aunt, and I intend to raise her and her brother. Mary, take Peg and go in to the house," Olive said.

Mary looked up at Olive and back to her grandfather. Her face was white. "I ain't getting my stuff. I won't go with him. I'll run away."

Olive smiled confidently although her stomach churned. "Of course not, Mary. You and John are not going anywhere. Go into the house." Olive said again to Mary, but her eyes did not leave Sophie's father's face.

Olive felt Mary back up and Peg turn out of her skirts. The two inched backward til their legs hit the landing and they turned and scurried across the porch. Thankfully, Olive heard the bar drop across the door.

"That weren't too smart. Them kids is my girl, Sophie's. I told ya I need the help. They're mine, by rights. Not git outa the road," he said.

Olive stepped between him and the porch. "Those children don't belong to anyone. Not you or me or anyone. And certainly they were not meant to be your plow horses. Now, get off this property."

Olive never saw the fist coming. Only knew when she hit the ground that he had punched her. Her ears rung, and her glasses flew, and she felt blood trickling from her mouth. She pulled herself up on all fours and felt blindly for her glasses.

The man stood above her, laughing, as Olive ran her hands through the dirt. He pulled his leg back and stopped when a voice came from inside the house.

"Better not," Mary shouted.

The man chuckled an evil sound and recocked his leg. The booted blow to Olive's midsection would have knocked her senseless had it not been followed by a blast of shot into the dirt. Olive yelped with fear, and the man clenched his fists.

"I'll kill you, ya little bitch, git out here," he shouted.

"Stay in the house. Lock the doors," Olive screamed. Another shot reverberated in the air, and Olive rolled on the ground. She heard steps on the porch and could vaguely see Mary standing feet spread with the shotgun pointed at her grandfather.

"That guns a shaking so bad girl, you'll never hit me. Now put it down and git your things fore I git mad enough to beat some sense into ya."

"I'm not going with you, ever. And neither is John. And I know that if you're on the wrong end of a shotgun, especially within spittin' distance, you don't stand a chance," Mary said.

The man eyed the girl, and the woman on the ground.

"We'll see about that." He spit again and turned to mount up. Olive heard and felt the pounding of horse hooves and turned to find Peg holding her glasses.

When the rider was out of sight, Mary dropped the gun and ran to Olive and Peg. Tears streamed down her face, and she fell to the ground on her knees, shaking. "Aunt Olive, are you all right? Don't die. Please don't die."

The last conscious thought Olive had, before tumbling into darkness, was that Mary had called her "aunt."

* * *

Jacob heard the shotgun blast and stood straight looking back across the fields. Another. Mary would've never fired that gun twice if there hadn't been real trouble. He left the horse standing and began to run through the muddy, plowed ground. The boys followed, and he could hear John's wailing and Luke's encouragement. By the time he could see the house, Jacob was sweating and winded. He was still running full tilt when Peg spotted him and began to run to him, crying. The child flew into his arms, and he stopped a moment to catch his breath and soothe his terrified daughter.

"What happened, Peg? Is everyone alright?" he asked.

"Aunt Olive," the child cried, and he looked up to see Mary trying to lift and drag Olive across the porch.

"My God, Mary, what happened?" he said as he put Peg down and ran to the steps. Olive's face was bloody, and bruises were already forming.

Mary wrung her hands, and Jacob could see she was nearly hysterical.

"My grandpa come for John and me. He beat up Aunt Olive. Don't make us go, Jacob. I'm sorry," Mary said.

The girl continued gibbering and apologizing when Jacob

opened his arms to her. Mary blew a breath hard through her mouth, looking at Jacob's outstretched hands. Fear, he supposed launched her into his arms, and she clung to him, quivering. She sobbed, and Jacob rubbed her hair and back and shushed her.

"Nobody's leaving, Mary. Not if they don't want to. Now help me with Olive," he said.

Jacob bent to pick Olive up from the twisted heap she lay in. Her head fell back over his arm as he carried her into the house and laid her on the bed. Mary went for water and rags, and the boys ran through the door.

"What happened?" Luke cried.

John ran to his sister, and she hugged him. He walked slowly to Olive lying stretched out on the bed and watched her chest rise and fall. Jacob saw the boy's terror grow and he pulled the child close to him.

"She's going to be fine, John. Rub her hand so she'll wake up," Jacob said.

The boy, white-faced, nodded grimly and knelt beside Olive.

"Now tell me what happened, Mary," Jacob said as he washed the dirt from Olive's face. Her lip was split, and her mouth already a swollen mess. Mary recounted her grandfather's visit, and Peg held her hand as she did. When Mary told Jacob that the man had kicked Olive, he felt the blow in his side as if he had received it. In his mind, he saw Olive facing the danger alone to protect Peg and Mary. When she was done talking and shaking wildly now from the retelling, he stood up from Olive's side and went to Mary and put his hands on her shoulders.

"You did the right thing," he said.

Mary nodded and bit her lip. Jacob turned back to Olive and touched the angry cut on her mouth. She groaned, and Jacob called to her.

Olive awoke with a start and shouted, "Mary, Peg, where

are you?"

"They're here, Olive. They're fine. What hurts?" Jacob asked.

Olive laid her head back and closed her eyes. "Everything. My side the most. Mary's grandfather..."

"I know. Mary told me the whole thing. I wished you would have gone in the house as soon as you saw a stranger," Jacob said.

"So do I," Olive said grimly. She opened her eyes and saw John by her side. His lip trembled, and she held up a limp hand to his face. "I'll be fine, John."

"My God," Olive said and nearly sat straight up. "Where's Mark?"

"He's here, Aunt Olive. Slept through the whole thing." Mary said.

Olive looked at her niece and tears came to her eyes. "You saved my life, Mary." Mary's lip trembled. She smiled tentatively, and Olive held her hand out to the girl. Mary stepped closer.

"And all along, I thought I was here to save you," Olive said.

All heads turned as they heard hoofbeats coming hard. Jacob grabbed the shotgun and went out the door. When Olive heard Jack Steele's voice, she breathed a sigh of relief. The two men talked softly on the porch until Jacob came back inside. "Jack heard the shots, and he's going to get Beth to see to you, Olive."

* * *

Olive awoke from a fitful dream to find Beth Steele's gentle hand on her face. "Sit up for me if you can, Olive. I want to wrap your ribs and put your nightgown on you."

"Where are the children and Jacob?" Olive asked.

"Out in the barn."

Olive touched her chin lightly and grimaced in pain. She looked up as the other woman stared at her kindly. Olive's lip began to tremble, and she gave in, away from all other eyes but this woman, to the fear still trapped in her throat. As she sobbed, Beth held her and rocked.

"The bruises will heal, Olive. You'll be as good as new in a week."

"That's not it, Beth," Olive admitted. "My appearance has never meant much to me. It's just..."

There was silence in the small cabin until Beth asked, "Just what, Olive?"

"I was terrified," Olive said as she looked Beth in the eye. "Not for myself, but if he had taken or hurt Mary or Peg or Mark, I don't know what I would have done. I've never been so afraid in my life," Olive finished in a whisper.

Beth's eyes softened. "Mothers will do anything, anything for their children. Including laying down their life. I know. I have two children of my own."

Olive lay back on the bed and stared at the ceiling. "Peg and Mark aren't my children. Even Mary and John aren't mine. But even still," Olive ended quietly and turned to face Beth.

Beth tilted her head. "You're more a mother than Mary and John ever had. And you can't tell me that Peg and Luke haven't warmed to you. I saw it at the picnic. I see it in their eyes today. They're worried about you. They love you."

Olive's vision of Beth suddenly swam, and her lip trembled, yet again. "Oh, God, Beth, how will I leave them? I love them, too. I never knew, never expected, things to turn out the way they have."

"Jacob will miss you as well," Beth said.

Olive turned her head. "I don't think so." She looked at her hanky and smiled ruefully. "I would have never dreamed when I arrived, I'd end up living here. Getting to know Jacob and his children. But we're adults, with responsibilities and certainly different ways. The age difference alone has made things awkward. He has been kind, though."

"Oh, Olive," Beth said. "A man being kind doesn't need held back from going to beat Jeb Davis within an inch of his life. Jacob feels more than that."

"I believe Mr. Butler appreciates the things I've done with the children. He would be grateful," Olive said.

Beth chuckled. "Yes, I suppose he is grateful. Now let me get you changed."

Beth had Olive propped up and in her nightgown when she heard pounding outside. "What's going on?" Olive asked and held her aching head.

"I don't know," Beth said and leaned over the sink to see outside.

"Mr. Butler? What are you doing? Mr. Butler?" Olive called out.

A moment went by until Olive saw Jacob's large frame fill the doorway.

"Do you need something, Olive?" he asked.

"Mr. Butler, what are you doing? It sounds as though the house is coming down," Olive said.

"Framing the back stoop," he replied.

Olive waited for him to continue. "Why?"

"There's a floor already there," Jacob said.

Olive's lids closed slowly. Certainly this last month had taught her patience. "I know there's a floor there. Why are you framing it?"

"Adding a bedroom for you and the girls."

"That's not necessary," she began.

"You aren't staying in this house alone at night, anymore."

"But, Mr. Butler."

"No buts about it."

Jacob had the look about him that meant no amount of arguing would change his mind. Olive tried to take a deep breath and leaned back onto the pillows.

Beth listened to Jacob and Olive bicker and turned to Mary. "I brought dinner for tonight, Mary. But tomorrow, you'll have to see to the cooking. Your Aunt Olive will be in no shape to feed you."

Jacob stopped at the door and turned back to the women. "Nothing new there, Mary."

Olive rolled her eyes at his retreating figure. "He's right, of course. I don't know how to do many of the tasks that are required. But it certainly was ungentlemanly of him to point out my flaws so vividly." She watched Mary bite her lip and Beth smile.

"He's teasing you, Olive," Beth said with a giggle.

"No, he's right. Mary was teaching me how to do laundry when we had a visitor," Olive said. "I suppose, we'll have to begin again with that Mary."

"I got it all hung," the girl said.

"See, Beth. We wouldn't eat or have clean clothes if it wasn't for Mary," Olive said and smiled. "Come sit beside me, Mary. You've had a long day."

The girl sat down tentatively, and Olive touched her back. Mary looked at her, and Olive smiled and pulled the child to her shoulder. Olive held Mary tightly and kissed her dark hair. She had been so close today to losing this precious, brave child. She had been warned by the sheriff about Jeb Davis and paid scant mind to it. She had seen Mary's reaction to the mention of her mother's family and dismissed it. Olive's own stubbornness had put Mary and Peg in danger. The two of them lay together quietly entwined, and Olive felt her eyes close, even with the pounding and shouting of the men and children.

Olive awoke slowly, hearing the shouted whispers of the children and Jacob's attempts to shush them. She smiled as much as her mouth would allow and took a deep breath to ease the pain in her side. They were trying so hard to be quiet that Olive could not disappoint them and kept her eyes closed. One at a time, she felt a kiss from each of the children and heard Mark's cries slow as Jacob rocked him to sleep.

Olive lay still and listened to Jacob inch around the room. She felt the bed tilt and his hands gently pull her hair from under her back and arms. Olive kept her eyes closed and reveled in the feel of his hands as they sorted through her tangled hair. Is it a sin to let this man, not a husband, caress her like this? Would he know she didn't sleep? Would he do it anyway? Did she care? Olive felt the first tentative strokes of the brush and felt sure she had died a divine death and gone straight to her maker. Olive relaxed her neck and shoulders with Jacob's ministrations and succumbed willingly, deceitfully, to his strong hands.

* * *

Jacob sat in the rocker with Mark, pumping the floor and watched Olive and the children sleep. His anger, barely contained today, had drifted to fear, and he found himself looking from one sleepy face to another, as if to reassure himself all were under his roof. Jacob swallowed as he saw himself running to the house and all the horrible images that went through his head.

But the very real vision of Olive lying, battered and bruised on his porch, would not go away. Jacob lay Mark down in his crib and turned to Olive. Her lip was cut wide and swollen, and he didn't know if he wanted to be with Olive the first time she looked in the mirror. Not that she was vain, but still, Jacob imagined, no woman would want to see herself like this. Olive's hair was always pulled back tight and neat and her clothes clean.

Jacob looked at her hair, her crowning glory in her head, he supposed, and thought of how many years had it been that Olive had brushed the burnished mass faithfully before bed.

Jacob found her brush on the shelf and sat gingerly on the side of the bed. She was awake, he knew, but she had chosen not to face him. From the look on her face she was enjoying it. He brushed the long strands flat on the pillow above her head and had his own secret victory. To touch this hair on the sheets of a bed as if they had awakened together or having watched her fall asleep. He brushed through methodically; working knots out and lying combed handfuls aside.

Olive and his relationship to her was more a puzzle than he had ever known. He and Margaret had been simple, so suited, so meant to unite that he had never felt questions. They just were and would still be if she hadn't been taken from him. But what was Olive to him? He admired her, he knew. A woman from her background, charging forward to save a niece and nephew she had never met. And she was a smart one. Olive figured out what made these children tick in no time. She loved them all, and they loved her gifts of discipline and patience. But most of all, Jacob respected her courage in the face of her shattered dreams and in the threat of real danger. He finished brushing, reluctant to quit, and placed the ivory backed brush on her valise.

* * *

The May morning came bright and crisp and clear through the window as Olive watched the children begin to stir. She was sore from head to toe and was wondering how she would get out of bed that day. Jacob started coffee, and Jack arrived soon after the chickens were fed and the cow milked. The pounding began again, and the children seemed to have forgotten the previous day's horrible scene. Peg helped Olive wash her face and hands, and she felt truly the invalid. Everyone ran to do her bidding, and she sat amidst the chaos, propped up, only to watch. A wagon rolled in the yard, and Olive heard the sheriff call to Jacob and Jack.

"Good morning, Miss Wilkins," the sheriff said as he came in the house and doffed his hat.

"Good morning, Sheriff. What brings you this way so early?" Olive asked.

"Few things. First I heard you had an unwanted visitor yesterday."

"Yes, we did," Olive replied and noticed Jacob had ceased his pounding to lean against the doorway. "I should have heeded your warning, Sheriff."

"What happened?" the sheriff asked.

Olive retold the tale, and the room grew somber. The sheriff asked Mary a few question, and she replied quietly.

"I hate the idea of you and the children facing that man alone, Miss Wilkins. How are you feeling? I should've asked first, I suppose," the sheriff said and pulled a chair beside Olive's bed.

"I'll be fine, Sheriff..."

"They weren't alone," Jacob interrupted.

The sheriff sat back in his chair and tilted his hat back. "Well, I don't think Miss Wilkins would be sitting here with her mouth split open if she hadn't been alone."

"I was plowing. Mary shot the gun, and I came," Jacob said.

Olive watched curiously as the two men stared each other down. "I'm sure you have all the information you need, Sheriff. You said a few things. What else brings you out this morning?"

"A crate and a letter came for you on the train." He stood and went outside and motioned Jacob to follow. The two men carried the wooden box back in the house, and the sheriff handed her a letter. Theda had written, and Olive could hardly wait to read her dear friend's reaction. She held the envelope, fine paper, with Theda's distinctive script boldly etching her name. Olive looked up, smiling with the thought, and saw the sheriff, hat in hand, holding a bunch of flowers.

"These are for you, Miss Wilkins. I hope they brighten your day while you're bedridden," he said and swallowed.

Olive knew her face colored, and she could not stop a shy and silly smile from forming on her face. "Why, Sheriff, how thoughtful. And tulips, yet."

The sheriff grinned and turned his hat in his hand. "I grow them out back of the jail. I'm a bit of a gardener."

"How wonderful. I have a beautiful garden at home. I would have never suspected you would have been interested in flowers."

"Pretty flowers for a pretty lady."

"Really, Sheriff," Olive said. "Thank you so much."

"You take care, Miss Wilkins. I'll be back in a few days to check on you, if you don't mind," the sheriff said as he stood.

Olive opened her mouth, but Jacob spoke sooner.

"She'll be fine. I'll look after her."

"Please do stop back and visit, Sheriff," Olive said.

"I'll be going then. Miss Wilkins. Children. Jacob," the sheriff said.

Jacob didn't reply but stood instead at the door until Olive heard the wagon pull from the yard. The children were clamoring over the crate, and Jacob dragged it close to Olive's bed.

"Do you know what it is?" Mary asked.

"Yes," Olive replied with a laugh.

"What is it?' Luke shouted.

"My sewing machine."

"What?" Luke asked.

"A machine that sews. I bought it last year. It stitches in half the time I can by hand," Olive said.

The boys lost interest quickly, but Mary and Peg edged closer. "I ain't never heard of such a thing," Mary said. She saw Olive's eyebrows raise and began again. "I've never heard of such a thing."

Olive smiled her approval and looked up to Jacob. "Would you open it for us?"

Jacob opened the box and lifted the wood cabinet out. Olive instructed him how to attach the black metal machine, and Peg touched the gold paint on the Singer. Jacob fiddled and tightened screws and set the foot pedal up. He stood back as Olive began to show the girls how it worked.

"Lot of fuss for someone who's not staying," Jacob said.

Olive's smile dropped. She looked down at her hands and raised her head slowly. "I wrote Theda, nearly the first day I was here, to ship my machine. I was making the children clothing at the time and knew I could do it in half the time if I had my Singer. You're right, though, I'll have to ship it back soon."

* * *

Jacob's shrugged his shoulders, and he thought how forlorn Olive looked when he had gone and opened his big mouth about her leaving. Nothing like the crooked smile she gave the sheriff when he handed her those damn flowers. It was downright pitiful to see the sheriff acting like a lovesick pup and Olive fluttering her lashes at the fool. He could hardly imagine Olive falling for the sickening sweet nonsense the sheriff had spouted. Apparently he was wrong.

"What did I see you and the sheriff bringing in the house, Jacob," Jack Steele asked from the doorway.

"It's Aunt Olive's sewing machine," Peg said and grinned.

"A sewing machine! Wait till Beth hears. Show me how it works so I can tell her," Jack said.

Olive explained the workings to Jack and Peg and Mary. Jacob stood back and watched the four of them nod and grin. Olive was smiling again, this time at Jack. He heard Olive tell him to bring Beth by soon and she would show her how to use it.

"If you get me a chair and help me into it, Mary, I'll show you how quickly we can finish your dress," Olive said.

Jacob slunk out the door and began to hammer. *I'm building her a room,* he thought, *do you think she's happy about that? No. I'm building shelves in a corner cupboard, too, so she doesn't have to keep her things in that silly suitcase of hers. Is she smiling and grateful? No. Just complaining about the noise.* Jacob dropped the hammer to his side, pausing. He suddenly and desperately wished Olive were smiling at him. He was building a room, trying to please a woman who was leaving. Leaving the children. Leaving him. By God, those children will miss her. He would miss her as well.

"Jacob?"

He jumped around to find Jack Steele staring at him strangely. Jacob picked up the hammer and began to pound again with fervor.

"What's eating you?"

"Nothing."

"You ain't talking to just nobody. I've known you all my life. Why you swinging that hammer like you're about to kill somebody?" Jack asked.

Jacob shrugged his shoulders but didn't cease his pounding. "Just don't know why I'm bothering with this room. Me and the children will be fine the way we were when she leaves."

"When's she going?" Jack asked.

"Don't know. With Olive you never can tell."

"Them kids will miss her something terrible."

"Yup." Jacob measured wood and began to work his saw.

Jack Steele sat down on the stoop and leaned back on his

arms. "Why don't you ask her to stay?"

"I told her she can stay as long as she needs," Jacob said. He stood the timber up and pounded the bottom in tightly. "I'm figuring Mary and John will be ready to go with her soon."

Jack swatted a fly from his pant leg and stared out over Jacob's fields. "Hard life out here, alone, with three kids."

"Yup."

"Olive seems to like it here," Jack said and stole a look at Jacob.

Jacob's hammer swung loosely at his side. "Don't start with me, Jack. I know what you're doing."

"Well, for pity's sake, don't act like it never occurred to you. Me and Bill ribbed ya a bit when she first came, being a spinster and all, but Olive ain't bad. I like her, and so does Beth. She'd make a good wife and mother," Jack said quickly.

"I'm sure Olive would make a good wife, and she's already a good mother, even if she doesn't know it. But that doesn't have anything to do with me," Jacob said without missing a hammer stroke.

Jack leaned back against a post and grimaced. "Well, I suppose you're right. It'd be tough in that regard."

Jacob stood straight and looked at his boyhood friend. "What in the hell are you talking about?"

Jack Steele looked around, as if checking for listeners and continued quietly, "Bedding her. She's getting on in years, and I'll be betting she's as cold a fish as you'd find. Skinny and pulled tight. Yeah, you're probably right. Wait around for some good lookin' young one to marry and bed."

Jacob's teeth clenched, and his jaw worked side to side. "Are you helping me build this room or just going to sit around jabbering?"

Jack jumped from his seat and grabbed a hammer. "I'm helping you. I'm helping you. Just saying she'd be the kind you'd be thinking about somebody else while you're doing it." Jack laughed and elbowed Jacob. "Like anybody, even a knothole."

Jacob's eyes flashed furiously. "Don't be talking about Olive like that. She's a lady. And she has more courage in her little finger than you or I." Jack stepped back as Jacob's finger neared his face. "There's plenty of men who would be proud to have her as a wife and be happy to bed her." A vision of Olive and Sheriff Bentley in bed together came to Jacob, and the thought incensed him more.

"Alright, alright, don't get your suspenders in an uproar."

"She has nice hair and pretty blue eyes," Jacob added.

"I'm sure somebody thinks she's as perfect as a sunset," Jack said. He watched Jacob nod solemnly on his words and bent to retrieve the dropped hammer. "Sure seems like the sheriff does anyway."

Chapter Six

O LIVE WAITED UNTIL THE CHILDREN HAD FOUND something to occupy them to read Theda's letter. A cup of tea beside her, she pulled the ivory stationery from its matching envelope.

Dear Olive,

I can think of nothing appropriate to say to you concerning dear John and Mary. I can only give you my heartfelt sympathies. The poor, poor children and your poor brother James. To have married someone of ill repute, I cannot imagine his shame. But being the gentleman he was, I'm sure the worst circumstance he handled with aplomb. Certainly his wife's tarnished reputation led to his untimely death. I am quite sure, though, he went bravely, and his last thoughts were of his family. Are the children doing any better? Has John spoken? I pray every night that God graces those children with their father's gentle spirit.

But Olive, (forgive my lapse in grammar, for my thoughts are coming quicker than my pen can scratch) could I have possibly understood your letter correctly? You are living with a man? Driving a buggy alone for an hour is one thing, unlike you as it is, but certainly living with a man is so far removed from your sensibilities that I barely know where to begin. My mother, when she could, and your mother certainly warned us of the dangers associated with this type of behavior. I beg of you, do not allow your sympathies for James's children to override your good judgment. You are resourceful and intelligent. There must, there simply must be another solution to this problem. The only hopeful thought in this area is that this Jacob person is far too young to be interested in you. Although sometimes youthful men have vitalities that are hard to restrain. And what of his family? Have you met his parents? What sort of position does Mr. Butler hold in the community? Please write and apprise me of the particulars and your solution to this problem.

Life here on Church Street remains the same, although I sorely miss your company. Mother is the same and requires much attention. Mrs. Benson has been ill for nearly a week, and I was told, although I am unsure of the veracity of the comment, that she is not long for this world. Your friend, Miss Johnson from the library, stopped by to ask me if I heard the date of your return. Rest assured, I revealed nothing of your letter or the circumstances of James' death, the children's condition or your living arrangements. They are anxious to hear from you though and miss you desperately "in the columns."

I have been chosen to read a Bible passage at the Ladies Aid Society meeting and have been unable to make a choice. Something from Matthew would be nice, but I am always inclined to hear the poetry of Mark's writings. Do you have an opinion? The meeting is not until next month, so I am sure you will be able to write and advise.

Mr. Gunnerson has checked on your house faithfully, and he has told me Tiger is doing well. Oh, I nearly forgot. Mr. Henderson asked me to accompany him to Bible Studies on Wednesday evening. I am quite perplexed. Would it be in poor taste to arrive with a gentleman at the pastor's home? Mr. Henderson has been quite honorable in his approach to me, but I fear three short years with his wife dead is not nearly long enough to be proper. Well, I have given you much to consider in this letter. Write soon and be well.

Sincerely,
Theda

Olive lay back on her pillow to reread Theda's letter. As she read, she could hear her friend speaking but she could have never replied what she was thinking now. Theda loved James. All these years. Olive had been clear in her letter about James's duplicity as well as Sophie's. But Theda had read only what she wanted to read. James was innocent and his unnamed wife, guilty. Olive closed her eyes and imagined Theda's unspoken longing and her own blindness, so like Theda, where James was concerned. "Jacob is far too young to be interested in you," her friend had written, and Olive reread time and again. So reassuring in her old world, so discouraging in her new. *She's right of course*, Olive thought. *Where have my good manners and breeding gone? Certainly nowhere to be found when Jacob brushed my hair, slept beside me or kissed me.* Olive's hand came to her mouth, unbidden, as she recalled his kiss.

Olive chuckled to herself as she continued reading, "Life is the same on Church Street." She both longed for that familiarity and dreaded the sheer sameness of it. More new, more different things had happened to Olive in these short weeks than in her whole life before. And what of it, Olive said aloud. *The differences, the challenges have yet to kill me, but I fear the boredom of life on Church Street quickly would. Within a blink of an eye, I would be back to my old habits, and Theda and I would sit up to the unheard of hour of ten o'clock, deciding her Bible passage for the Ladies Aid Meeting. I would mull over the correct number of years that a widow should wait before asking a woman to the pastor's home. The demise of my newfound perspective will make the time frame no matter, and I will simply wait to cease breathing, may it be one year or fifty. I will die there.*

With that thought, Olive saw clearly that she would not return home. Could not. But what was she to do? She could not stay with Jacob. Now her injuries were truly frustrating, for they would keep her from setting a new path. Olive's thoughts ran fifty ways at once as she envisioned her life hence, unchartered.

The week went by slowly for Olive. And by Friday, she thought she would, indeed, lose her mind. The house was a witness to her lack of attention, and the children were suffering from lack of attention. When the sheriff visited, she entrusted him with a letter for the president of Spencer's one and only bank. Saturday, she dressed and did a few chores with the help of Mary in the morning and had a long afternoon of study time with the children. The rain had made playing outside impossible, and Olive felt after only a few hours on her feet that she would surely pass out, so she gathered the children around the table and spelled and read and read and spelled.

Monday morning came, and Olive dressed and looked in her hand mirror at her injuries. She hadn't known that bruises could look worse nearly a week after the injury than the morning of it. Shades of yellow, brown and an awful green graced Olive's jaw, but she snapped the mirror closed tied her bonnet and went on the hunt of Jacob.

"Mr. Butler?" she called near the barn.

"Olive, what are you doing out of the house?"

"I've been looking for you. I'd like to borrow the wagon if I may. I need to go in to town," Olive said.

Jacob tilted his head. "Are you sure you're up to it? If you need something, I'll go for you."

"No, thank you. I have an appointment." Olive did not elaborate, and she watched Jacob narrow his eyes in wonder.

"Your room will be ready tonight," he said.

Olive began to smile, but the healing skin on her mouth pinched and she grimaced. Jacob had been scarce company the whole week with weeding and hoeing during the day and completing the bedroom in the evening.

"I know you've been working very hard, this week, with me laid up and the children unattended. The bedroom could've waited. But now that I know it's nearly done, when can I see it?"

she asked.

"Whenever you want."

"Well, then, as soon as I come back from town," Olive said and looked up. Jacob didn't move and Olive waited. "May I use the wagon?"

"I'll hitch it. Do you want me to ride in with you?" Jacob said.

"No, thank you. I'll be fine," Olive replied.

"Not sure if I like this, you alone on the road, and Jeb Davis out and about," Jacob said.

"I won't be a prisoner, Mr. Butler," Olive said.

"Suit yourself."

* * *

Jacob hitched up the wagon, helped Olive get seated and asked again if she would like him to accompany her. She refused as he knew she would, and he watched her pull away from the house. He hated the idea of her on the road alone, and it irked him that she had not revealed why she needed to go into Spencer. Near noontime he went to the house and found Mary.

"What's your aunt need from town?" he asked.

"Don't know," she said.

Mary shrugged and continued feeding mush to Mark. When he was near the door, dismissing thoughts of Olive, Mary stopped him dead in his tracks.

"Maybe it had something to do with the letter she gave the sheriff when he came out to see her. I don't know."

"What letter?" Jacob said as he turned back to the girl.

"The one she handed the sheriff. It sure did stink."

Jacob shook his head. "What stunk?" The girl turned to him eyes wide and exasperated.

"The letter. The letter stunk of lilacs or somethin'."

Olive gave the sheriff a perfumed letter, and now she was going to see him. Jacob sucked wind through his teeth and headed to the barn. *Lots of work to do*, he said to himself, but his mind drifted again and again to Olive. As he fixed his plow, he scowled at her behavior. Chasing the sheriff around and sending him notes like she was some young girl. Well, let the sheriff worry about Jeb Davis then, he thought.

* * *

"It's a pleasure to meet you, Mr. Holmes," Olive said and was seated in a worn but comfortable leather chair.

"As it is to meet you," the pinched-face man said.

Olive could tell the banker was all business. Ink-stained hands and stacks of papers piled neatly littered his desk. Nearly bald, Olive observed, with just a few wisps of gray hair, flopping around his ears. His white collar was oversized around his thin throat, and the skin hanging in folds. The banker wiped his smudged glasses on a white hanky and proceeded to skim Olive's letter.

"Well, Miss Wilkins, I believe I have compiled all the information you requested," he said as he nodded his head and read.

"Thank you so much."

"Pertaining to your house on Church Street in Philadelphia, your banker there, a Mr. Cummings, believes the house would sell for approximately $2000.00. Now, that is just an estimate, of course. Wouldn't be right to hold Mr. Cummings or me to the figure," the banker said over his glasses.

Olive's eyes widened. "I had no idea that my family home was worth that much money."

"In normal circumstances it would not fetch that much. But Mr. Cummings has had recent inquiries in your neighborhood.

Apparently a merchant is interested in buying a few homes adjacent to each other in order to build a store, and your banker is confident that negotiations would yield in that area," Mr. Holmes said.

"A store?" Olive asked.

"Yes, a mercantile of some sorts," he replied.

Olive sat back against the cool leather and frowned. What would her neighbor hood become? What did her elderly neighbors think? Nothing would remain the same on Church Street once a busy retailer set up shop. Crowded streets and buggy traffic would keep them in their houses and off their porches all summer.

"Has this merchant already purchased any property?"

"Yes, I believe he has. Things are already underway," the banker said.

Then this is truly for the best, Olive thought. "Can you wire Mr. Cummings and tell him to begin negotiations immediately. I would like all my funds transferred here to your bank from the sale of the property and what I have in savings. I will write my friend to handle the shipping of my housewares and furniture once the sale is complete."

Mr. Holmes nodded. "I will tell him as much when I wire him. Now about your brother's farm. You seem to be under some misconceptions concerning the mortgage."

Olive's shoulders dropped. What had James done? She took a deep breath. "What misconceptions?"

The banker rifled through a stack of papers and looked up to her. "Your brother never really owned that farm. And upon his death and the death of your parents, you became sole owner."

"What?" Olive asked, eyes wide.

"I've checked everything carefully, Miss Wilkins. Seems your father bought the property back in '83, and he held and paid the mortgage. We need to send death certificates to Mr. Cummings, but that's just a formality. The farm is yours."

"Do I still owe anything on the property?"

"No mortgage. Your father paid it in full. But apparently last year's taxes are overdue. Let me see here. Yes, here it is: $82.63 will clear the taxes. I can take care of that for you when your property on Church Street is sold, if you'd like," the banker said.

James never paid the taxes on his own property. Father paid them until his death, and Mother and I had no idea we owed anything. Olive felt betrayed by a family secret but empowered all the same. She was a property owner, a landowner with money in the bank and more to come on the sale of her house. She was free. When all was said and done, she would have enough to last a lifetime.

"Mr. Cummings mentioned that your family had always been judicious savers and careful spenders." Mr. Holmes smiled and said, "I'd be happy to help you in any way I can."

Can't wait to get his fingers in my money, Olive thought and smiled primly. "Thank you, Mr. Holmes, for everything but I believe you've explained everything I need to know."

The lilt of Olive's step was near a skip, and she, in all honesty, wanted to run down the street to the postmaster. The letter to her employer, resigning, so painstakingly written flew from her hand to the man behind the counter. Olive had been careful to leave the option of returning to the library open, but now the thought could not have been farther from her mind. She smiled and called to passersbys, grinning and nodding, and she wanted to throw the black bonnet far in to the air.

"Miss Wilkins, good to see you," the sheriff said as he stepped from the jail. "Feeling better then?"

"Much better, Sheriff Bentley," Olive said.

"You look lovely today, Olive. May I call you Olive?

Smiling and gay," the sheriff said and leaned closer. "Looks like those bruises are healing fine."

"I'm doing quite well today. Thank you. But I am very busy, and I must be getting home," Olive said.

"Where's Jacob?" the sheriff asked.

"At the farm," she replied.

"He let you ride alone in town? What was he thinking?"

"Really, Sheriff, it's fine," Olive said and placed her hand on the agitated man's arm. "I came to town to conduct some business on my own. I don't need an escort."

"Any young woman as lovely as you needs an escort. Let me get my horse. I'll ride out with you," the sheriff said.

"Young? Oh really, Sheriff, you do know how to spin a tale," Olive said. "But truly, I'll be fine." Olive turned from the man while he flustered and fluttered, and she headed down the street with a light step to the wagon.

Olive tilted her head back to the sun and stretched her back as she rode home. With the information Mr. Holmes had given her she felt a thousand choices were at hand for the taking. She was no man's wife, no parent's child, and she was truly able to decide for herself what she wanted to do with the rest of her life. Her obligations to John and Mary were the only consideration she had. And now, she could send the children to school or college, and they could live wherever they wanted.

Before knowing she owned James's farm, she had hoped only to continue paying the mortgage payments and fix the house for her and the children. But the money and her uncontested ownership of the property changed everything. She had hoped to employ a sharecropper to work the land, therefore giving her the bank payments and slowly make the shack of James and Sophie's a home. But that would be unnecessary. With no mortgage payment to make every year, her options were wide open. They could travel or live in a large city. Or on a farm, Olive thought.

Olive smiled to herself again, even though her ribs ached when the thought of living on the farm entered her head. I don't need to find the children and me a new home. We have one. Whatever drawbacks a town such as Spencer had, Olive was sure she would find more wherever she decided to raise the children.

Olive chuckled, thinking about the pitfalls of Church Street. She hadn't known they existed until she left, and she was sure Spencer would present problems of its own. But this solution would relieve so many aches in her heart. Olive had found she dearly treasured the land and its sweet smell in the morning. She had found love in the faces of Luke and Peg and even Mark. She had made friends in Jack and Beth and Bill and Florence, and they returned the friendship faithfully. And she had found Jacob. His quiet, strong demeanor, his loyalty and love to his lost wife, his devotion for his children was so true, she knew she would never meet a better man.

"Hello, children," she called as she pulled the wagon in front of the house. "I have peppermint sticks for everyone."

Luke and Peg were screaming and shouting, and John was jumping up and down with excitement. Mary stood at the door and waved to her.

"What are those for?"

"Because Mary, it's a beautiful day, and you've all been wonderful to me while I was in bed. These are a treat everyone deserves," Olive said and pulled the candies from the small paper sack. Mary shrugged and popped the candy in her mouth.

Olive saw Jacob coming from the barn. She was standing in the wagon handing out the treats when she noticed the look on his face. "A peppermint stick will surely fix that frown, Mr. Butler."

The children giggled with her teasing but sobered at Jacob's scowl, deciding to return to their game.

* * *

Jacob stood and waited til the children were out of earshot.

"Where in the hell have you been?"

"Mr. Butler, really, such language," Olive said but smiled. "The day is too wonderful for that."

"Did you find the sheriff?"

"What are you talking about?" Olive asked.

Jacob shook his head and looked away. When he returned to Olive's face, he stared, unforgiving. "Aren't you concerned what folk will think of you? I would've thought for Mary and John's sakes anyway you'd be awful careful."

"Mr. Butler," Olive said and climbed, unaided from the wagon. "What are you talking about? I haven't done anything to bring shame on those two children, and you know it."

"In the first place, I, I mean me and the children have been worried about you out this long. Anything could have happened. Could have run into Jeb Davis, the horse could've gone lame, you could have been stuck somewhere and then where would you have been," Jacob asked nearly shouting.

"I suppose Mr. Butler, I would have been wherever I was. I could have walked home. It is still the middle of the day," Olive replied.

Jacob continued as if Olive had not spoken. "And in the second place," he leaned to her, "what do you think folks will think of you throwing yourself at the sheriff. Sending him perfumed letters. A woman your age."

Olive's eyes opened wide. "I don't have the foggiest notion what you are talking about."

"Saw the sheriff today didn't you?"

"Well, yes..." Olive began.

"I suppose that's the reason for your high mood. Handing out treats to appease your guilty conscience."

Jacob could not believe what he was saying. But all these thoughts had gone through his head as he worried about Olive's safety, the whole morning. He was no talker, a doer, he supposed, but this woman deserved a tongue-lashing and by damn he'd break his silence to tell her.

"Although, I owe you no explanation, I will tell you what I did in town today. I went to see Mr. Holmes at the bank. I ran into the sheriff on my way out of town, and he offered to escort me home. I declined."

"And what of the perfumed letter?" Jacob said.

"That's the only stationary I have with me. I keep a sprig of lilac from my yard back home in the box. I had questions for Mr. Holmes, and I sent the letter via the sheriff," Olive replied.

The two of them stood facing each other until Jacob turned on his heel and went to the barn. *I've kept my mouth shut for twenty-five years; I should have kept it shut today.* Jacob shook his head and thought of the fool he had made of himself. He swallowed and swore again and didn't relish the thought of facing Olive over the dinner table. *She'll wrangle an apology out of me, probably in front of the children*, he thought. But Jacob had no time to stew as he heard Olive shrilly shouting his name.

"Mr. Butler," she shouted at his back. "Don't you dare walk away from me. Whatever conclusions you drew were wrong. I don't appreciate the implications that I was engaging in some unseemly activities. I can hardly believe you would think that of me. How could you think I was throwing myself at the sheriff? He asked me to dance, at a function where other adults were dancing. I don't get many invitations, Mr. Butler. I decided, not long ago, to stop letting life pass me by. Who are you to judge? Not everyone has experienced the pain you have, but all of us, by God, have our own hurts."

And I have added to hers, Jacob thought. When he turned to face her, his shoulders sagged at the demoralized look on her face. No matter when she smiled it seemed he managed to make her frown and when he realized she fought tears he dropped his head in shame.

"I was wrong, Olive."

"Yes, you certainly were," she said and turned from the barn.

When Jacob entered the house, long after dark, Olive, Mary and Peg were already asleep behind the closed curtain of their new room. Mark made soft sounds in his sleep, and the boys were huddled together on the bed. Jacob pulled the cover over the two and sat down at the table. Few times in his life had Jacob wanted, really wanted, a drink but this was one of them. He moved the boys over a bit and lay down beside them, fully dressed.

* * *

The next morning after a somber breakfast, Olive asked to speak to Jacob alone. By the time she had reached the house the night before, tears were falling and Olive's fists were clenched so tight her knuckles were white. She was angry at Jacob's conclusions that she was a woman of no character, no morals. Her beautiful day and news had fallen by the way side, as she fully comprehended Jacob's thoughts. Her lip trembled, and she fought the tightening in her throat. Her hair was pulled back tautly, and dark circles lined her eyes. She stood stiffly, facing him.

"I learned yesterday at the bank that my brother's farm is mine and mine alone. I have decided not to return to Philadelphia but intend to set up house keeping on James's farm as soon as I am able to get someone to build a house for me. Would you be so kind as to tell me who would be able to do the work? I will want it done quickly. I do not intend to infringe on your hospitality a moment longer than necessary."

* * *

This was why she was so happy yesterday. When did she decide to stay? How did she get her brother's farm? How would she make the mortgage unless she farmed it? And he was glad. Glad for her, glad for him, she was staying. Not under his roof, but still here in Spencer. This must have been a huge decision for Olive. She would have answered his questions yesterday before he made a jackass of himself. She might have even asked his opinion, although Jacob doubted it.

"You're welcome to stay as long as you want," Jacob said. Olive looked away, and he continued. "Jack Steele does some building once his crops are in. I'm sure he'll be happy for the work."

"I'll have to make arrangements to see him," she said.

"He was talking about bringing Beth over to see your sewing machine. Why don't I ride over and ask them to come for dinner on Sunday?"

Olive gave him a small smile. "That would be fine. Let's hope Mary is able to cook for so many."

Jacob knew Olive's barb was intended for him. He nodded, and she turned away and called to the children to begin chores.

* * *

While the children gathered eggs, Olive sat down to write Theda a letter. Much needed to be explained, and Olive struggled to make clear how she had come to her decision without naming Theda's letter as the culprit. Olive asked her friend to take care of the details she listed about her furnishings. She advised Theda to keep a few pieces for herself, send some treasured furnishings of her parents on, and sell the rest in preparation for the sale of her home.

Olive knew Theda would attend to every detail with precision, and although seemingly a great burden, it always pleased Theda to be occupied. Her friend's life was so rigorously scheduled around her mother, that a diversion of this nature would be welcome. She continued her letter and advised any verse from Matthew rather than the disciple Mark and told Theda to accept Mr. Henderson's invitation to Bible studies immediately. Hopefully the Gunnersons would keep her cat, and the thought of not seeing Tiger again made her pen lift from the page. There were things she was forfeiting, very dear to her, like Tiger and Theda's companionship, but it did not change her mind. Her decision was made, and it was best for all concerned. And she could not deny her happiness with it. She liked the work on the farm, liked the challenge of the children, and was anticipating planning a home all her own.

Sunday arrived, and Olive dressed for church with the girls. She had wanted to thank Jacob for the cupboard with shelves in the room, but she had seen little of him, and if truth were known, she was glad. Olive had enough to occupy her thoughts, and when she did think of Jacob, she could not help getting angry and hurt all over again. Nothing in her limited experience with men had prepared Olive for the pain she felt when she realized how little he thought of her. Her morals, in Olive's opinion, were so firm and clear that to hear them questioned by a man she both trusted and liked was devastating. She was no beauty, not charming or stylish or able to be coy and shy, but all of her life she had firmly believed that her greatest attribute was principled convictions.

"I won't be going to church with you this morning," Jacob announced at the breakfast table. "I have work that won't wait, but I'll be home for supper with Jack and Beth."

Olive nodded and continued to eat. When Jacob rose and left the table, Olive told the children she had some news for them. "I have decided not to move back to Philadelphia." Four heads turned her way, all smiling but Mary.

Peg's eyes grew wide and she smiled. "She's staying. She's staying."

"In Spencer, yes, but not here on Mr. Butler's farm."

"Where you going?" Mary asked.

"Not where am I going. Where are we going, Mary. I am building a small house on your parent's land, and we will live there," Olive said and held her breath waiting for a reaction. Luke and Peg and John's face fell, but Mary eyed her.

"When?" the girl asked.

"As soon as we can get a house built, Mary," Olive replied.

"Why?" Mary countered.

"Well," she said, "I found out last week that your farm was actually my father's all along. With your parents and grandparents gone, the land becomes mine. We can build it up, and when you are older, you and John will have working property. A start for you both."

Luke, Peg and John did not follow Olive's explanation and just sat staring. But Olive could see Mary's mind working in her eyes, and she knew the girl would have questions.

"My ma and pa never owned nothin'?"

"That's right, Mary," Olive answered.

"They was squatters?"

"They were squatters?" Olive asked. "No, I wouldn't say that. I'm sure there was some arrangement worked out between my father and yours. I can't say more. There is no one left to ask."

Mary tossed around the information, Olive could see. The girl laid down her fork and looked at her brother.

"We ain't livin' in our old house?" she asked.

Olive watched John look at his sister, and he looked away blankly from the others. Olive hurried to reassure him. "No, no. We're going to ask Mr. Steele today if he would have time to begin on a small house closer to the lane. We will be only a short distance from Peg and Luke and Mark."

The children looked at each other and evaluated. Peg looked worried, and Luke stared at his sister then at John's turned head. The boy shrugged and asked, "Can we come see you? Can we finish the book?"

Olive laughed. "Of course. You can come anytime, and we will make time for Charles Dickens."

Luke reached for the bacon, and Peg said, "Is there anymore eggs?"

"Are there any more eggs, Peg, and, yes, there are. Would you like some?" the girl nodded, and Olive eyed the children as they had seemingly received the news, processed it, and hurried on to something else.

"I'm done. May I be excused?" Luke said. "Come on, John, let's see if Pa's got the wagon hitched." Peg followed after stuffing her mouth, and Olive and Mary were left alone at the table.

"What do you think, Mary?"

The girl shrugged. "Does it matter?"

"Yes, it matters. Very much. We're a family, and I want you to be happy," Olive replied.

"I guess it'll be alright." The girl stood and carried the dirty dishes to the sink. "How are just the three of us gonna' work a farm?"

"I'm not sure, but I believe the best thing to do is find some sharecroppers to work the land until we're able to hire someone to do it. And then when John is old enough, he may want to work the land. Or your husband," Olive said.

"I ain't ever getting married," Mary replied.

Mary's experience with men would have certainly led her to that conclusion, Olive thought. "Never say never, Mary. I would have never dreamed I'd be living here with Mr. Butler or be building a house in Spencer. Circumstances can change, people and their ideas can change, Mary. I know I have."

"You were daggone sure we was all moving back to Philadelphia when you first come, came here." Mary didn't face Olive but continued quietly, "Are ya sure you want us, I mean John and me? I don't want him getting settled somewheres and then you up and decide ya don't like us."

Olive stood and walked to Mary. She turned the girl by the shoulders and looked at her solemnly. "I will never not want you or John. We're a family. We're going to make our way together."

Mary bit her lip and looked away. "My ma used to say all her and Pa's troubles started when she had kids."

Olive swallowed at the bitter hurt in Mary's voice. "Then I, Mary, am exactly the opposite of your mother. My life didn't begin until you and John."

Mary looked up at Olive. "Goin' ta be hard work with just us."

"We'll figure something out, Mary. Between the two of us I know we'll come up with a solution."

"Shouldn't we ask Jacob? I mean he knows all about farming and such," Mary asked.

"No, Mary, Mr. Butler is busy with his own problems. We'll figure ours out on our own." The girl shrugged, and Olive tied her bonnet for church.

Jacob hitched the wagon, and Olive would not look at him. Church was raucous, trying to keep all five children quiet and in their seats. Luella Grimm stared openly at Olive, and Olive smiled and nodded to the woman in return. Luella turned quickly away, red-faced. Mark coughed and fussed, and Olive worried he was feverish, but he settled down as Olive rubbed his back and cooed in his ear. The child never looked directly at Olive, but he made a soft gurgling sound when she held him, and she imagined he was content in her arms. She touched his face gently, and he darted his eyes rhythmically, as if rocking himself to sleep. The brilliant blue eyes closed slowly, and Olive tried to concentrate on the last few minutes of the sermon.

The children were excited, with company coming and the sun shining brilliantly. Olive taught the children a song, and they sang and clapped the whole ride. The Steele children, Bess and Jack Junior were nine and seven years old respectively and had played with Jacob's children on many occasions. Mary and Olive had started beef stew before church, and Olive had bought fresh bread for the dinner.

When Jack and Beth and the children arrived, the noise level increased ten-fold. Olive and Beth decided to feed the children first and then let them run as they were clamoring to; then, hopefully, the adults could eat in peace. Olive taught Mary and Bess hopscotch, and the two girls seemed to get along fine. Mary didn't say much, Olive noticed, but Bess was a quiet child as well, and the two of them satisfied themselves, watching the young ones and getting to know one another. When Bess asked her mother if she and Mary could walk to the creek, Beth nodded, and Olive was glad. Maybe a friend her own age would help Mary, and Bess seemed suited to her. Jack and Jacob had Luke, John and Jack Junior in the barn doing what, the two women didn't know, but the house was quiet except for Mark's gurgling.

"Jacob said you're staying on in Spencer," Beth said.

Olive rocked Mark and looked from the infant to the woman across the table from her. "Yes, I am. I'm going to ask Jack to build me a small house on my brother's, well, my property."

"I'm glad you're staying, Olive. What a big change, though.

What brought it on?" Beth asked as she drank her coffee.

Olive tilted her head. "I think the idea had been creeping up on me actually. Then a letter came from my best friend Theda. I received it the day the sheriff brought my sewing machine, and I don't know if I can really explain it other than it made clear how sheltered and, well, dull my life had been."

"Dull?" Beth asked. "How could life in a big city be dull? Aren't there shops and theatres and things to do all the time? I know life on a farm gets pretty boring sometimes."

Olive lay Mark down in his crib and looked out the window. "Maybe dull isn't the right word." She turned back to Beth and said, "My friend Theda and I lived so rigidly conscious of what others thought that we never did anything out of the ordinary. We attended church functions, and I worked at the library, but other than that we just waited."

Beth tilted her head. "Waited?"

Olive smiled. "Yes, waited. Waited till an elderly neighbor died so we could send a meal. Waited till our parents aged so we could care for them. Waited for the next correct and dutiful thing to do, and we did it and waited again. We would have never dreamed anyone lived his or her life any other way. Especially spinsters."

"Were you and Theda waiting for husbands as well?" Beth asked softly.

Olive turned her head to the shadows cutting across the floor. "When we were young, yes, I suppose. But if anyone did come to call, we found a thousand reasons they were unsuitable." Olive lifted her head to Beth and continued, "Not the right family or work or called a minute too early or too late. Brought chocolates on the second outing rather than the third. We congratulated ourselves when they stopped calling and now, looking back, I think we were just scared."

"Scared of what?" Beth asked.

Olive laughed. "Of everything. What if we had to move to a new house or city? What if we had to make our lives with another person? All those what *ifs*."

The two women sat quietly together at the table.

"It must have been scary for you to come out here for John and Mary," Beth said finally.

"Theda and I talked for weeks about this trip of mine. And we thought I'd be rescuing little miniatures of myself and James and taking them home to Philadelphia and continuing to raise them as I assumed they had been raised so far."

"Your brother's, well, life, must have come as quite a shock," Beth said.

"A shock? I still can barely comprehend it. And I'm angry. Angry at James and Sophie. Angry with my father. But most of all angry with myself. I won't make the same mistakes again. I'll decide the children's future and mine from now on."

Beth tilted her head. "Why are you angry with your father?"

Olive told Beth what Mr. Holmes had told her about James's property. "I think my father knew all along that James was wild. That's why he bought the property in the first place rather than lending James the money to get started."

"So the land is yours?" Beth asked.

"Yes," Olive said triumphantly. "Mine to make into a home, in a new town."

"Aren't you scared?"

"Petrified," Olive said and chuckled. "But I won't be waiting for something to happen to someone else. I'll be making things happen on my own, for me and John and Mary."

"Jacob seemed very happy, well as happy as Jacob gets these days, that you were staying in Spencer."

"Humph," Olive said. "He implied I had made unseemly advances on the sheriff. I'm sure he'll be glad to see me go."

"What?" Beth said. "I don't believe it."

Olive told Beth of Jacob's accusations and their conversation the day Olive went to see Mr. Holmes at the bank. She sat back on her chair, eyes downward. "I was terribly hurt that day. I had begun to admire and like Mr. Butler, but I knew then I should hold my regard."

Beth smiled. "Olive, don't you see? Jacob's jealous."

"Really, Beth. Mr. Butler has no interest in me. I'm ten years his senior. I'm nothing like his first wife, not attractive." Beth giggled and covered her mouth. "I don't cook or bake or can or do any of the things that would interest a man in a woman out here on a farm."

"I don't usually talk about these things. Unless, of course, I'm with Florence, but I know something Jacob may be interested in you for. The same thing men are interested in women for everywhere, city or farm."

Olive looked at the woman across the table and asked, "What, what about me could possibly interest a man or make them jealous?" Olive could not believe what was coming out of her mouth, but the subject of Jacob vexed her so greatly, she threw propriety to the wind.

"Well, he may want to, you know, he might be itchy," Beth said, eyes wide, lips tight.

Rarely did Olive misspeak, speak out of turn, or say something she meant to keep private. But on Beth's last word, her inner thoughts rolled off of her tongue before she could stop them. "I know that's not true. He flew away from me as if I had two heads."

Beth sat back in her chair as Olive's eyes rounded, and her face colored. Just then the door opened and Jacob and Jack stepped in.

"What have you two been gabbing about all day?" Jack asked.

"Nothing," Olive said quickly.

"Where are the children?" Beth asked the men but did not take her eye from Olive's face.

"Playing in the haystacks. Can we eat?" Jack asked.

"Jack, really, you shouldn't ask. It's not polite," Beth said.

"No, no that's fine," Olive said and nearly knocked her chair over, trying to get away from the table.

Beth came to the stove beside her and whispered. "If Jacob is jealous and is sorry he upset you, then I'll bet any amount of money he treats you real special and sweet for awhile."

Olive stole a look over her shoulder to find the men looking at her sewing machine. "Why do you say that?" she asked.

Beth sliced bread and whispered under her breath. "'Cause they're too stupid to know their own feelings, and they get mad instead of glad. You watch, Olive."

Olive nodded and gave Beth a half-smile. *The poor girl has no sense of reasoning or deduction,* Olive thought. She turned when Jacob walked over to the stove and picked up the Dutch oven.

"Here, let me get that, Olive," he said and placed the stew in the center of the table.

Olive stared at him. "Thank you," she said.

Jacob nodded and said the blessing.

"Did you show Beth the sewing machine, Olive?" Jack asked.

"Why, no, we were so busy getting dinner ready, we didn't have time," Olive replied.

"It certainly smells delicious," Jacob said.

"It sure does at that, Jacob," Jack said and lifted his plate for Olive to serve.

"I want to show you how the machine works, Beth. You would be welcome to use it then," Olive said as she passed plates.

Jacob accepted his dish and looked up to Olive. "I've been wanting to see myself how it works. Maybe you can show Beth and me after dinner."

Olive's head cocked, and the ladle of stew stopped midway to Beth's plate. She looked at Beth, and the woman looked up to Olive's slack-jawed face. Olive finished serving and seated herself. Jacob certainly was being solicitous. But Beth was surely wrong. Could he be jealous? Olive dismissed the thought and proceeded to eat.

"Jack, I am interested in having a small house built on James's property. Mr. Butler said you occasionally do that kind of work. Would you have the time, and would you be interested?" Olive asked.

"Absolutely," Jack replied. "My planting will be done in a week, and I can always use the work. What did you have in mind?"

Olive's hands came together at her chin as she smiled and described to Jack Steele the home she envisioned.

"Three bedrooms, a sitting room and a kitchen. With a big porch. I can do that. Going to be a bit costly, though, with the price of lumber the way it is," Jack said.

"Can you give me an estimate?" Olive asked.

"Surely," Jack said. "Let me do a drawing and show you. Then I'll get some prices from the mill. I'll be able to be pretty close that way."

Olive felt as if doors were opening to her. She had property, someone to build her a house, and she would be seeing a drawing to change or add to her dream. She smiled fully at Jack. "Thank you so much."

* * *

Jacob watched the exchange between Olive and Jack. Jacob had never met a woman who made these kinds of decisions on her own. His Margaret didn't, and Beth certainly didn't. "I'll look over the plans for you when Jack is done with them," he said.

"That's very kind of you, Mr. Butler. I'm sure, though, I'll be able to decide if the drawing I see is the house I would like," Olive said.

"I'm sure you don't know anything about building houses. You may need some advice."

"I may need some advice, you are correct. But if I do, I'll either research my questions or hire an architect."

"Now, that's just plain dumb. Where would you do research, and what architect would you hire?"

"You have been kind enough to allow me to stay here, but that does not entitle you to make my decisions."

Jacob shook his head. "I'm not trying to make your decisions. I just thought I'd offer help if you need it. Women don't know much about building is all I'm trying to say."

Jack and Beth's heads swung to and fro from one end of the table to the other as Jacob and Olive argued.

"Well, Mr. Butler," Olive said with a thin smile, "if my mind and constitution is too fragile for the construction of my own home, then may hap I'll ask the sheriff for advice. I'm sure he'd would be happy to help."

Jack and Beth sat straight in their seats as Jacob gritted his teeth and slapped his hands on the table. "I never said you weren't smart enough, Olive, and you know it. And leave the sheriff out of this. I know I was wrong, and I admitted it."

* * *

Olive was having an honest-to-goodness argument and it felt wonderful. She didn't mind her words, just parried back with the only man she ever felt the comfort to do so. Her voice rose to match his.

"Very wrong, Mr. Butler. To think after all this time that

you thought so little of me. I was hurt at first, but I'm just angry now. My father deceived me, my brother was a liar and a cheat, and you… you think I'm a loose woman. No wonder Mary doesn't ever want to get married. Men are… are jackasses."

"A jackass, you say. I've never heard anything stronger than fiddle-dee-dee from you," Jacob said and stood. He placed his hands on the table and leaned forward, red-faced, "I wasn't a jackass when we were kissing on the front porch, now was I."

Olive's eyes widened wider than the frame of her glasses, but they would not leave Jacob's face, as he slowly glanced from Jack to Beth. She stood abruptly and turned to Jack.

"More stew, Mr. Steele?" she asked calmly.

"Well…" Jack said and leaned back in his chair.

"Take me out for a walk, Jack," Beth said as she wiped her mouth and stood.

Jack looked up to Jacob and grinned. "Pretty as a sunset," he said.

"Didn't your wife ask you to take her outside?" Jacob said.

"Come on, Jack," Beth said.

Jack slowly slid out his chair and joined his wife. He turned back to Jacob and smiled. "Don't worry Jacob, everybody fights. But the making up is usually good." Jack howled at his own joke, and Beth grabbed his arm, dragging him through the open door.

Jacob dropped into a chair and ran his hand through his hair as Olive cleared dishes from the table.

"Well, Mr. Butler, you've done it now," she said finally.

"What have I done?" Jacob asked.

"Now, Jack and Beth think I meet the sheriff for disreputable purposes and then run home and kiss you on the porch. This is going to be my hometown. I would hope to keep my reputation untarnished."

"Oh, Olive, for God's sakes, they don't think you met the sheriff for some two-stepping."

"Two-stepping? Another colorful phrase for me to add to "itchy."" Olive filled the bucket in the sink with wash water. She tilted her head and said, "You're probably right. Who would ever dream of the Spinster Wilkins' 'two-stepping' with anyone?"

Jacob jumped from his seat and turned her from the sink. "Me, goddamn it. Me. I've been thinking of two-stepping with you for quite a while."

The water trickled slowly over Olive's hands as Jacob held her arms. His words replayed in her head as their eyes met and would not part. Olive swallowed and looked away.

"I don't two-step, Mr. Butler." She returned to his gaze. "I never have and doubt if I ever will."

Jacob released her arms. "I bet you'd dance pretty good if you'd let yourself."

"Dancing, Mr. Butler is for married women. Young married women. It happens to be how the human race produces children, if I'm following your metaphors."

* * *

Jacob sat down at the table. Twice in so many days he'd spoken without thinking. His blood was racing, he was mad at Olive, had a hell of a good fight with her, and now, damn Jack anyway, he wanted to kiss her til her legs wobbled like a new-born calf. And he told her that he was thinking of doing more. *What is wrong with me? Maybe nothing,* Jacob admitted. Because these last few weeks, he had felt more alive than he had in a long while. Fighting with Olive would probably be a highlight if they ever married. He smiled to himself. Screaming, yelling, getting everything off your chest, kind of arguments followed by loving in the middle of the night that makes a man realize how lucky he is to not be alone in this world. He would miss her influence on the children and a clean house, no doubt, but more than that, he would miss her smile and her sass when they disagreed.

"We started this argument over the house if you remember. I didn't mean to insult you, Olive. I think you're the smartest person I ever met. Don't ever think different."

Olive dried her hands and sat down at the table. "I don't really think you're a jackass. But I have a different view of the world and my life now, Jacob. I am all those two children and myself have to rely on. I'm not the meek mouse, accepting what men tell me, anymore."

Jacob laughed. "A meek mouse, Olive? You haven't been meek for two seconds together since I've known you."

Olive told Jacob about her meeting at the bank with Mr. Holmes

She finished her tale and looked up at Jacob. "So do you blame me for getting angry? I find out in one day my father deceived my mother and me. I own property and have money. I make huge decisions for the children and myself. I'm thrilled with what I've decided, frightened as well, and then you accuse me of well, you know."

Jacob picked her hand up in his and stroked her palm. He watched his fingers as they moved slowly over her white skin. His inner battle raged, and he finally decided to fess up. *What the hell*, he thought, *he already told her he wanted to two-step with her.* She was moving to her own house, the temptation would be gone but he was lured in an odd way to be totally honest with Olive. Whether because of her self-doubt that he wanted to assuage or because she made him think and feel without grief for the first time in a year, and he was in her debt. But either way, she deserved to know she was not the spindly, dried-up old maid she saw herself as. He looked in to her eyes, and she returned his look, seemingly frightened and compelled by the touch of his hand.

"I was jealous, Olive. I thought you and the sheriff had

something going on, and it bothered me."

* * *

The words registered in Olive's head and heart, but her reply made Jacob's eyes widen. "That's what Beth said."

"What?"

"Beth said you were jealous, and she said you'd be especially nice to me if she were right. Then you carried the Dutch oven for me and asked to see how my sewing machine worked. She was right."

Jacob looked away and scowled. "Yeah, well, Beth Steele's a know-it-all."

"You were right all along as well, Jacob."

"About what?" he asked.

Olive swallowed nervously. "I don't know anything about what goes on between men and women."

Their eyes met, and Olive felt the world and her problems melt away. She could have been standing in a ballroom in Vienna or on the streets of New York, and Olive would have still seen and felt nothing but Jacob's gaze. At that moment he was her world, so completely, so fully, tears welled in her eyes.

Jacob stood slowly. Olive followed and they stood, inches apart, fathoms too far, and yet completely joined.

"A kiss wouldn't hurt anything, would it, Olive?"

She shook her head, and a fat tear rolled down her face. Jacob wiped it away with his thumb and inched closer to her face. Their doubts, their fears, their own devils, fled from their minds as the distance separating their lips disappeared.

Olive's hands crept slowly up thick forearms to broad shoulders, physically imposing, yet so tender in their embrace. The touch of his lips to hers made her shiver and wonder how a man so handsome could be kissing her. It was as though she was the frog in the fairy tale and with this prince's kiss came alive.

And, certainly, Olive had never felt before this overwhelming instinct to lie with a man. She cringed at the thought in her mind, but yet that was clearly it. The urge, from deep within the same place in her psyche that compels humans to eat and sleep and protect their young. And mate. His body covering hers, in a union, shrouded in mystery, with a history that dated to the very conception of man. As she stared into his eyes, she knew he felt the same.

* * *

How could I have found her undesirable, Jacob thought, as he deepened the kiss and wrapped her thin frame in his arms? Every spot of flesh that touched sparked, as he turned his head to cover her mouth completely. When their lips broke, they stared at each other inches apart, panting and wanting. And he knew, fleetingly admitted, that he wanted this woman in his bed, under him, kissing him, as their bodies joined.

Jacob watched recognition dawn on Olive's face. She wanted him, and she knew it. He laid his forehead on hers and closed his eyes.

"Olive," he whispered.

"This may have been unwise, Jacob."

He murmured his answer. They stood quietly in their embrace, reluctant to face the parting, yet frightened to stay. Jacob's hands moved slowly up and down Olive's arms, and he breathed softly into her hair. They listened as Beth called to children, and the replies the children shouted.

"We have guests, Jacob," Olive said finally, pulling from his arms.

Jacob looked into her eyes and nodded. He ran a hand through his hair and turned to head out the door.

* * *

Olive was cleaning the table when Beth came into the house.

"Everything all right?" Beth asked.

Olive nodded, reluctant to reveal anything of Jacob's and her conversation. He had patiently listened to her about Mr. Holmes and how she had come to the decision to stay in Spencer. Her father's deception, her brother's irresponsibility, and her triumph at being free to decide her future. And then he had kissed her. And that kiss unearthed long buried desires Olive never thought she'd be tempted by. But as long as she didn't voice the feelings Jacob's kiss evoked, maybe she could forget them, avoid them, deny them.

When at last the house was quiet and the sleep sounds were rhythmic, Olive closed her eyes, gave in to temptation and let her mind wander to Jacob. She could not resist imagining the feel of his arms around her or the sheer, raw, masculine beauty of his face. Skin, tanned from the sun, and rough from whiskers, stretched taut over angled cheekbones. A long straight nose between green eyes and above full, heart-shaped lips. Jacob's hair, too long she had thought at first, curled en masse over his collar and shone blue-black in the sunlight. Its texture, she blushed to admit, was that of her silk stockings.

Chapter Seven

JACOB LAY AWAKE IN THE BED BESIDE THE CRIB and thought of Olive. He had not been able to vanquish the vision of Olive in his arms, even as Jack had droned on and on about her house as he helped his friend hitch his wagon. Jacob closed his eyes, willing himself to sleep, when a picture of Olive, slowly revealed itself. He squirmed, as the image formed, wondering if she had the long thin legs, he envisioned. Her skin would be the milky color, maybe even paler, of her face, and he knew it would be as soft. She had full breasts, he could tell, as he held her against him, and he swallowed, thinking those breasts, high and soft, rose-tipped, he imagined, were just feet away, covered in thin cotton. Jacob ached as he lay still, and the throbbing beat a drumroll to his head.

He stood slowly, to not wake the children and padded softly to the kitchen. He knelt in his long-john bottoms and reached under the sink to a bottle of whiskey he hadn't touched since Margaret's death. As he knelt and held the bottle, his thumb moved slowly over the faded yellow paper of the label. Jacob had nearly finished the bottle in the days following Mark's birth. It had numbed the hurt briefly, but the pain blew back with a vengeance when he sobered. His shoulders shook with a laugh when he thought of Margaret's scolding when he occasionally drank. He smiled, ruefully, hearing her threats, and he realized this was the first time he had remembered Margaret and not felt tears in the back of his eyes. Their time together had been good, wonderful in fact, but she was gone, and he faced a life without her. The question that remained was whether would he live a full happy life or would her death ever overshadow anything good. He took a swig, still squatting, and knew his sweet wife would not want him to miss a moment of joy for his grief.

"Oh, Margaret," he murmured to the bottle and the night air.

* * *

Olive stood in her nightgown, under the drape of the curtain and watched Jacob drink and heard him call his wife's name. She turned quietly, hoping not to intrude, but the swish of the curtain dropping brought Jacob's head around.

"Olive?"

She peeked around the curtain and saw Jacob stand, bare-chested. He was tall, wide and cut through with muscles and sinew. A smattering of blue-black hair, held her eyes and the milk she had sought to ease her to sleep was forgotten.

"I didn't mean to intrude. I couldn't sleep."

"Me neither. You want a nip?" Jacob asked and held up the bottle.

She inched into the room. "I don't drink alcohol."

* * *

The light from the window in Olive's room answered Jacob's question. Long, lean, shapely legs revealed themselves, shrouded in a mist of white, coming together at her hips. He stared, unable to move his gaze from the spot where those legs joined. He cleared his throat and reached for two glasses on the shelf.

"Then it's time you tried it."

"I don't know, Jacob," she said as she stood at the table.

Her hair was a mass of curls and hung over her shoulders. Olive's glasses reflected the moonlight, and he watched her pull her hair to one side. "Sit down. If we can't sleep, then maybe a little snort will help us both."

She seated herself and pulled her arms, tight under her breasts. Olive sipped tentatively, eyes watering. "Oh, dear."

"Don't drink it too fast," he said.

* * *

When Jacob turned to the table, she stared straight at his naked mid-section. He poured the whiskey and re-plugged the bottle, and her eyes wandered from a flat hard stomach to the top of Jacob's long johns and below. Something hung and swung loose and bulged through the soft red cotton of his under-drawers. Yee Gads, she thought and sipped at the small glass of whiskey.

They sat together silently, and Olive warmed to the heat of the whiskey as it burnt a path to her stomach. "Were you thinking about your wife? Before, I mean." Olive's lips felt oddly numb and the words played slower to her ear than the movement of her lips.

Jacob nodded. "I nearly drank that whole bottle one night after Margaret died."

Olive watched Jacob, and she knew he was remembering. "Did it help?"

"No."

"You said to me once that nothing does, except time. Is that true?"

"I still miss her," Jacob said and tilted his glass to drink.

"But time lessens the hurt. I have children and a farm, and I couldn't let my grief mean more to me than they did. Margaret wouldn't have wanted that."

Olive was quiet and swirled the amber liquid in her glass. "You loved her very much." Jacob looked up to Olive, and his anguished smile pulled at her heart.

"More than life itself. I will love her until the day I die."

"You are lucky then," Olive said, as tears threatened.

"Lucky?" Jacob asked.

"Yes, lucky. Some of us don't ever love like that. I imagine most of us don't. Even though she's gone, you'll always know you were blessed with that kind of love."

"I guess you're right." Jacob looked down at the table but then back to Olive quizzically. "What about you? Was there a man back in Philadelphia for you?"

Olive smiled and tilted her head. "No, there was never a man back home that evoked those kind of feelings for me."

"Never?" Jacob asked softly.

Olive's lip trembled. And she knew that she could not answer him honestly. The pull of her heart and her body to Jacob was so strong and so sure that she realized then she was lucky as well. Because she loved him truly. Loved a man who would mourn his dead wife until the day he died. Loved a man strong enough to put his grief aside and care for his children. Loved a man compassionate enough to rescue John and Mary from the nightmare they lived in. Like Theda, loved a man, younger than she, and unattainable as well.

"Never," she whispered.

Jacob nodded, tight-lipped. He reached for her hand then and held it softly.

Olive stood abruptly, and Jacob followed. He touched her chin, and she shook her head, making the halo of her hair glisten and dance. Jacob pulled her hard in to his arms and kissed her.

Olive's head swam from the whiskey and the feel of Jacob's bare arms around her. Once admitted, love propelled her to accept his touch, his lips, his body. Where their hips clenched, she felt the unmistakable rise of his passion, hard and thick, pulsing into the soft flesh of her stomach. She pushed herself from his hold and held him at bay with her hands and the anguished look on her face.

"No," she said.

Jacob shook his head. "I'm sorry, Olive. I would never force you to do something you didn't want to. I didn't mean to scare you."

"I'm not scared of you Jacob," she whispered. "You are the kindest, gentlest man I've ever known."

His head tilted, and he questioned her without speaking.

Olive backed up slowly, arms chilled where Jacob had held her, lips bereft of his kiss. She touched her mouth and said, "It's me I'm afraid of, Jacob. Not you. Never you."

* * *

The morning came through the window, and Olive lay still and smiled at the rough wooden ceiling. With the abject pain of sure rejection came the sweet inner peace that love brought. And that peace wrinkled a smile to her lips even as she heard, in her head Jacob's voice declaring his undying love for his wife. How tragic, she thought. He loves a woman unable to return his love, as she loves a man unable to return hers. Will I spend my remaining days watching Jacob from afar? She had grown comfortable living with a man and the children as a family. Will I sacrifice that comfort to remain true in my heart? Or will I marry, someone like Sheriff Bentley, and make the best of what the rest of my life presents me?

The thought of marrying anyone was shocking to Olive,

but as many of life's sureties fell by the wayside, so did the idea that she was never meant to marry and raise a family and find comfort and intimacy and strength in another human being. Was she not as deserving as the next woman? But her smile faded again as she pictured a dinner with Mary and John and a husband. The man seated at the gingham-checked table was not the sheriff. Nor a stranger she had yet to meet. The man in her dream was Jacob.

Olive baked biscuits for breakfast and heated ham on the stove. "After everyone's chores are finished, I would like to begin on today's studies."

"Why so early, Aunt Olive?" Luke asked.

"Because I would like to do some sewing today. I need some skirts for myself to work in, rather than the heavy dresses I brought."

"What are you going to do with James's land?" Jacob asked.

"Well, Mr. Butler, I've actually been thinking a lot about that question. And I was hoping you would be interested in farming it for me. It is good land?"

Jacob shoveled ham into his mouth and nodded. "Oh, yeah, prime land. You'll need a barn, though."

"I was wondering about that. I'll have to have something for a horse and chickens and a cow. Are you interested in farming my property?"

* * *

The income from additional crops would surely make a difference for Jacob and his money woes. And he would see the children and Olive often. He wondered which would mean more to him. "I think we could come to some agreement."

Olive smiled. "Good. That's good. If I am to be partners with someone, then I'm happy it will be you. I want John to learn farming the right way, and I know I can trust you."

"Usually a sharecropper is an employee, not a partner, Olive."

"Well, then, I'm just going to be unusual. I will need help, and I'll have to rely on you to get us the best prices for our crop and all the other things that will have to be decided. If you agree to work my farm, then we'll be partners until you choose not to or when John is old enough to work the farm himself. Or...or if I were to marry."

Jacob looked up to Olive with questions, and she brought her shoulders up with a breath and looked down at the table.

"Do you have any plans in the works to marry?" he asked.

The children listened intently and waited for Olive's response.

"Well, no. Of course not. But I, well, you never know. Life seems to hold great mysteries for me. And I've decided I'm not too old to find someone to care about. Who would care about me."

"Well, hell's fires, you're not too old. You're the only one that thinks that," Jacob replied.

"You said she was too old to dance with the sheriff, Daddy," Luke reminded him.

Jacob sucked air through his teeth. "That's not what I meant."

"Oh, yes it is, Daddy. You said she wasn't acting her age," Peg said.

"How old do ya have to be to dance?" Luke asked. "Mary danced with you. Ain't she old enough?"

Jacob laid his hands on the table and looked everywhere but Olive's face. When he did he only saw her lips soft and ready for more kisses, felt the hollow of her back where she arched in his arms and smelled the lilacs and summer in her hair.

"Daddy?" Luke said.

"What?" Jacob shouted.

Luke's eyes grew wide. "I was just wondering if it weren't about time for grandma to come see us. The last field is almost planted and you said last year, I remember, that grandma is as regular as pig shit."

"Luke!" Olive cried.

"Well, he said it," Luke replied. "I'm just repeating it."

Jacob realized his son was right. Ma will be pulling up in her wagon any day now and won't she have a time of it if Olive's still here. "When did Jack say he could start on your house?"

Olive's head tilted. "Anytime soon. Is your mother coming for a visit?"

Jacob turned in his chair, crossed his legs and drank his coffee. Shit, he thought. "Yeah, she'll be here any day."

"Will your father be coming as well?"

"I doubt it. Those two look forward to the week she's here and they're out of each other's hair."

* * *

Olive contemplated meeting Jacob's mother. She was curious about his parents and his upbringing and why his mother's visit would elicit such a response.

"If there's anything you'd like me to do to get ready, I'd be happy to," she offered.

"Not much to be done, but count the days til she's gone."

Olive's eyes widened, and she let her fear get the best of her. "Why do you say that?"

Peg pulled on Olive's sleeve and giggled. "Grandma's real bossy. Ma even used to say so. She said it took her a month of Sundays to put her house back the way it was before Grandma's visit."

"Oh," Olive said. "We used to look forward to overnight

company. My mother would make special desserts, and we would have tea in the afternoon and a house party for them with all the neighbors." Olive looked away dreamily.

Jacob leaned across the table. "I'll guarantee you my ma won't drink afternoon tea."

"She'll sew with you, though, Aunt Olive. She brings her shears and cloth and always helped Ma make us new clothes," Luke said.

"Well, that sounds wonderful, then," Olive said.

Jacob harrumphed and stood to leave. "When the boys are done with their studies, I could use them in the fields. Send them out."

"It's awfully hot for the boys in the sun this time of year, don't you think?" Olive asked.

"Trust me, we won't be hurrying."

"Why not, Daddy? Didn't you say you wanted to get the planting done?" Luke asked.

"Yeah, well, that was before you reminded me that Grandma's coming. If the plantings done, we won't be able to get out of the house."

"Goin' to leave us with her, huh, Jacob?" Mary asked.

"I'm going out to plow. Send the boys when they're finished with their studies," Jacob said.

* * *

The next day Jacob took the boys to the fields, and Olive stood in the kitchen in her chemise as Mary pinned a skirt around her waist. Olive held her arms up, and Mary struggled to follow her aunt's instructions. The facing to a waistband to a seam and Mary stabbed Olive in the side for the tenth time.

"Ouch," Olive said. "Yes, that's where to pin it, Mary. Make sure you catch the facing."

Mary and Peg and Olive's heads turned as they heard a rumbling in the yard. "See who it is, Peg. Get ready to close the door and latch it if it's not someone we know," Olive said.

Peg peeked out the door and shouted, "Grandma!"

"Oh, dear," Olive said. "Mary can you hurry and get that pinned. I'm not dressed."

"Hang on, Aunt Olive, I'm almost done."

Peg was jumping and shouting on the porch as sweat began to run down the underside of Olive's arm. "Quickly, Mary." When Olive looked up to the doorway, she saw a woman, a large woman holding Peg.

"What in the Sam Hill's going on here?"

Mary jumped and dropped the pins and the fabric from Olive's waist. Olive stood still, took a deep breath, and as she did the unfinished garment made a slow descent to the floor. She refused to be cowed, though and graced the woman with a pleasant smile even as her face reddened.

"You must be Mrs. Butler. I've heard so much about you. Won't you come in?"

"I reckon I will. Seeing how this is my boy's house," the woman said and narrowed her eyes.

Olive excused herself and hurried behind the curtain of her bedroom. She quickly dressed and combed her hair. Olive listened through the curtain as Peg tried to explain who Mary and Olive were.

"Her mommy and daddy got killed, and Daddy went to get them, and this is Aunt Olive. She lives here."

This massive woman, stood hands on her hips, nodding and looked up to Olive as she came around the curtain.

"Don't rightly get all that. Who are you?"

Olive held her hands folded at her waist and explained to Jacob's mother who she was and how she came to live with her son. "And so you see, I am building a home of my own and my niece Mary and my nephew John and I will be moving soon. I hope we won't interfere with your visit."

"You always stand around the house half-naked?" Mrs. Butler asked.

"Well, no, Mrs. Butler, I was making myself a new skirt, and Mary is learning to sew. It just took us a little longer than usual."

Up until that time, Mrs. Butler had fired so many questions Olive's way that she had not noticed a young woman stood behind the massive female replica of Jacob. "Please come in. I've made some cold tea since it's so warm. Would you like some? Or would you?" Olive asked Jacob's mother and the other woman.

"This here's my neighbor's sister's girl. Audrey. I brung her for Jacob."

"Brought," Mary said. "Brought her, not brung her."

Olive's eyes widened, and she glared at Mary. Her niece returned the look with a sly smile. And then the woman's words sunk into Olive's brain. The rosy-faced girl, no more than seventeen, tilted her head and smiled.

"Pardon me?" Olive said.

"I brung her for Jacob," the woman said and stared at Mary, lifting a brow. "Been more than a year since Margaret died. Time he was getting a new wife."

"Oh," Olive said. "Has Mr. Butler met Audrey before?"

"Nope."

Olive looked at the girl. She was a darling thing but appeared far too young for Jacob or marriage or anything but dolls. And she seriously doubted Jacob would appreciate his mother's interference.

"Audrey, it's a pleasure to meet you. Welcome to Jacob's home," Olive said.

The girl began to reply, but Jacob's mother spoke first. "Look around, girl. This'll be your house, and this Peg here your youngin' till Jacob gets you carryin' one of yer own."

Olive's eyes widened at Jacob's mother's comment and watched the girl blush furiously. "Please sit down or look around if you'd like," Olive said.

"You been helpin' look after Jacob's youngins'?" Olive nodded, and the woman continued. "Well, then I guess I'm in yer debt. Lookin' after my grandchildren. I'm Martha Butler."

"Pleased to meet you, Mrs. Butler," Olive said.

"No need for the *Mrs.* I spect. Don't spose we're but a couple a years apart. I'm in my forty-second season. How 'bout you?"

"I'll be thirty-six this June." Martha Butler graced Olive with a huge smile.

"I'm real good at guessing a body's age. Pa said it's a gift."

"Is Grandpa coming?" Peg asked.

"No, darling. He waved goodbye and plopped down to take a week's nap while I'm gone. I don't go in for laziness, and Zeke Butler can be a son of a gun if someone's not watching him."

Peg inched close to Audrey. "Want to see some kittens in the barn?"

The girl smiled widely and held her hand out to Peg. Mary harrumphed and followed them. She leaned close to Olive and whispered, "I can take her if you want me to, Aunt Olive. She wouldn't look nearly so good with a black eye."

Olive shook her head at Mary and spoke to Jacob's mother. "Let me help you bring your things in, Martha.",

"Me and the girl's just got one poke a piece. Let's set a spell."

Olive sat down and watched Martha Butler as she lowered herself into a seat. The chair groaned in time with the woman and Olive noticed work-worn hands, clean but callused, lay flat on the table. The woman's calico dress was high necked, worn and serviceable. Martha Butler's thick black hair was streaked with gray and was wound tight into a neat bun. Although Olive knew it was none of her business, she could not resist asking.

"Does Jacob know you were bringing Audrey for him to court?"

"Court? Who said somethin' about courting. I'm planning to have 'em married 'fore I leave. That boy's waited too long to get hitched. This girl'll give me some more grandchildren, right quick," Martha said and winked.

Olive's mouth opened in a half-smile. "What if they're not suited? I mean, what if Audrey doesn't like Jacob, or Jacob doesn't care for her?"

"She'll do fine. Built to breed, that one," Martha Butler said and winked again but then sat back in her chair and scowled as she stared at Olive. "You have your eye on my boy?"

"Why, no," Olive said, quickly.

"Good. Not that there's anything the matter with ya. Ya seem like right good people, coming for your niece and nephew and helping out Jacob." Martha smiled at Olive and continued, "I can tell about folk. But, hell, get to our age, a woman don't want some young buck chasing us around, now do we?" Martha Butler chuckled and sat back in her seat.

"I didn't know Jacob was interested in having more children."

"Oh, he'll be interested alright," Martha said and grinned. Olive smiled wanly, and Jacob's mother continued. "Now, don't get me wrong. I know he may not like the idea at first, but he needs a wife. A farmer needs a wife to care for the youngins' he has, to clean his house and cook his meals. It's a hard life, and my heart aches that he's been struggling alone. That's why I'm right thankful you were here. To help my boy."

Olive could not deny the woman's reasoning. She had seen first-hand the work involved with a farm, and she often wondered how Jacob managed it all. And she could tell Jacob's mother spoke from the heart. She loved her son and worried over him. Apparently Martha Butler had come up with a solution for his problems.

"Jacob has been very kind to me as well. Allowing me to stay here with the children."

"What happened to your brother?" Martha asked bluntly.

Olive told the unvarnished truth and looked up to find Martha regarding her.

"Them kids watched their ma get killed?" she asked.

Olive nodded.

The woman whistled and shook her head. "Don't seem right sometimes what happens to some youngins'. Luke and Peg and Mark with no mama and your brother's kids seeing the ugly in this world so young. No, it don't seem right." The woman looked away but turned back to Olive. "But who are we to question the Maker? If the Lord intended them children to go through what they did, then he must a had a good reason."

Olive nodded on the woman's wisdom. "I've asked myself the same question time and again. All I can try to do now is make a home for them and love them."

"You're a wise woman, Olive Wilkins. Too bad yer past yer prime. You'd be a good one for my Jacob."

Olive cringed, but Martha smiled genuinely at her, and she knew the woman meant no insult. Her reasoning was obviously built on the experience that a hard life had brought.

"You don't think Audrey is a bit young for this life? For marriage?" Olive asked.

"Naw, I was half a year younger than her and had a baby and fifty acres of rock for a farm. She'll do fine. Her family's hard workers."

Olive realized Jacob might feel exactly the same way. Why wouldn't he want a young, strong, and buxom girl to cook and clean and sleep in his bed? Loving him and being the right mate for him were two different things, Olive supposed. Martha

Butler's no-nonsense reasoning were why families survived here. Hopefully, Audrey could make him happy and coax a smile from his lips once in a while. And Jacob would be kind to her, Olive knew. He would help her get adjusted to life here on the farm and to the children, just as he had done for Olive. He would try to ease Audrey's worries as he had done for Olive so many times. He would kiss her tenderly and stroke her arms and pull her tightly to him, Olive imagined. But she could go no further in her mental musings without bringing tears to her eyes. She was awakened roughly by shouting from Luke.

"Grandma!"

"Here, boy, come give me a kiss. You look so much like yer Daddy when he was yer age, it brings tears to my eyes." Martha gathered the child to her chest and looked over to John. "I hear yer name's John. Good Bible name. Come here, boy. Don't be shy. I'm Luke's granny, and I got enough room on my lap for the two of you."

John stood still and stared at the woman. He inched over to her, and Martha ruffled his hair. He shyly stepped closer and allowed her to lift him on to her other knee. Martha smiled up at Olive, and Olive returned the smile.

Olive noticed Jacob stood in the doorway.

"Ma."

"Jacob. That's no way to say hello to yer ma. Get on over here and give me a kiss," Martha said and then turned to the two boys on her lap. "He thinks he's too big for that but yer never too old to kiss yer ma. I'll take him over my knee when he stops."

The boys giggled, wide eyed and Jacob leaned down to kiss his mother's cheek. "I'm sorry I wasn't here when you got here, Ma. I was planting the last of the fields."

"No, you ain't sorry, boy. Don't lie to yer mother," Martha said and chuckled. "I didn't expect find a naked woman in yer kitchen, though. But Olive and I did fine. Had a nice chat."

"Mary was fitting a skirt for me when your mother arrived," Olive explained.

Mark's cries stirred the adults, and Olive reached into the crib for the child. He drooled, and his head tilted into Olive's shoulder. She cooed in his ear and laid him back down to change his diaper. When Olive stood with the child, clean and dry, Martha reached her hands out to hold him. The boys scooted from her lap, and Olive watched tears form in Martha's clear green eyes. Jacob's mother held the child fast and closed her eyes.

"God gives us burdens. Yes, he does."

"Mark is no burden, Ma," Jacob said and reached for his son.

Martha glared up at him. "Leave his grandma hold him for a minute, Jacob. And even though you won't admit the boy has problems, the rest of us know."

"He's my son," Jacob bit out quietly.

"Don't ya think I know that. I know he's yer son, and ya love him and I do, too, even if his birthing took his mother. But that don't mean I won't admit the child has problems." Martha looked up to Olive. "You got sense about ya, and you've been livin' here. You know the boy's got troubles nobody can fix."

Olive sensed this was an argument that had been aired before. The room was silent, and Olive was careful of her words. "Yes, Martha, I know Mark has problems." Martha nodded and turned to Jacob as Olive continued, "But I don't think talking or dwelling on them will fix them. Mark was a gift from God, just like Luke and Peg."

Jacob looked up to Olive and met her stare. He appreciated her defense of him, and she knew he did, without a word passing between them.

Martha Butler watched the two of them and stood up,

handing Mark to Olive. "Luke, run out to the barn and fetch your sister. There's a woman with her I want your father to meet."

Martha Butler turned from her son and asked Olive what was started for supper. Olive admitted that she hadn't begun the meal, and Martha sent Jacob to her wagon for her bags and a box of canned goods she had brought. Jacob set the box on the table and turned as Peg and Mary came through the front door with a young blond girl.

"Jacob, this is Audrey Hooper. Mary Hooper's younger sister. Say howdy," Martha said and smiled.

The girl stood at the door and stared wide-eyed at Jacob. Her eyes fluttered, and she said, "Hello, Mr. Butler."

"No need to call him Mr. Butler, girl. Jacob will do. Didn't I tell you he was a good-looking one? Handsome, my boy is," Martha said.

"Hello, Audrey," Jacob said and turned back to his mother. "What's this about, Ma?"

"Just needed company on this trip. Ya know I'm not as young as I used to be, Jacob. Just wanted some company."

Jacob's eyes narrowed in disbelief. "That's all it better be, Ma."

"Did ya see the kittens, girl?" Martha asked.

Audrey's eyes lit up. "They're so cute. Can we... I mean will you be...I mean I hope you keep them all."

"Take one with you when you go home, Audrey," Jacob said.

Martha turned to the stove. "Audrey, take the youngin's outside for a spell, while I talk to my boy."

The children inched their way to the door, hanging on every word, and Olive shooed them along. "Come along children. Mr. Butler and his mother need some time to talk. Let's show Audrey the swing your father built."

"Don't go, Olive," Jacob said.

"I don't want to intrude," Olive said from the doorway.

"Let Olive go with the children, Jacob. This is between you and me," Martha said.

"Olive stays, or we don't talk," Jacob said, never turning from his mother's regard.

Martha Butler stared back and then shrugged her shoulders. "Suit yourself."

"Why did you bring that girl, ma?" Jacob asked.

Martha glanced at Olive's back where she stood at the sink. "'Cause it's time, Jacob. Time for you to get a wife."

"I'll decide when it's time for me to get a wife."

"No, I don't think so. You're still grieving over Margaret, and she's dead and gone a year. A nice young girl will make you forget," Martha said.

Jacob's head snapped up. "I'll never forget Margaret. Don't ask me to."

"Well, for pity's sake, Jacob, I ain't askin' you to forget, but this farm life is hard. I know. You need a helper and someone to warm your bed," Martha said.

"Ma!" Jacob shouted.

"What?"

"Olive is a lady. Don't be talking about that kind of thing in front of her," Jacob said, red-faced.

"And yer own ma ain't a lady? Listen here, Jacob, just cause we're ladies don't mean we're not women with blood running through our veins," Martha said.

"Ma, Olive's a sp... has never married," Jacob said quietly.

Martha Butler turned her large body in the chair. "Just cause yer acting like ya ain't listening, don't mean you ain't. You got sense, Olive, turn around here and tell Jacob he needs a wife."

Olive turned slowly and looked at Martha Butler. "I don't think your or my opinion really matters in this affair. Jacob must decide on his own when and if to remarry."

"I know that, Olive. But I'm saying, just saying, it's time Jacob thinks about it. Don't you think it's time?"

"I don't know, Martha," Olive replied.

"Isn't a year and more, time enough?" Martha asked.

"I think everyone's different. I think Jacob loved Margaret dearly, and who's to say he'll ever stop loving or grieving for her."

Martha Butler sat silently and shook her head. "You think that a body only gits one chance in this life to love or be happy? I don't. You seem like a smart one, Olive. Do you think we only git one chance?"

"I believe in a merciful God. I can't imagine One who would deny someone love to see him grieve."

"See there, Jacob. Olive agrees with me, and she said it awful pretty, too."

"Do you think it's time for me take another wife, Olive?"

Martha's questions tore at the very heart of Olive's grief. She raised her head to Jacob's question and the feel of his eyes on her. She stood silently, opened her mouth to speak and closed it quickly. From six feet away, she felt Jacob's presence around her, as though they stood entwined and alone.

Olive's lips were pale and her speech halting when she finally replied. "I don't think convenience or the want of a helpmate are good reasons to marry. I think... I think the only reason to marry is for love."

The air was silent and thick as Jacob stared at Olive.

"What if you're not sure you could ever love again?" Jacob asked.

Olive tilted her head and smiled. "I think if you were in love you would know, and that question would not need answered."

"How do you know, Olive. For sure, I mean. Didn't you tell me you were never in love?"

Olive could tell Jacob waited for her answer, and she felt as if her whole life and happiness depended on how she replied. She could not lie again, nor could she tell Jacob how she really felt. How her love for him was the greatest gift she had ever received and how she counted on that love to warm her when she lived apart from him. How she begged her God to give her the courage at this moment to reveal that love with no expectations. To tell Jacob that she loved him and would love him until she drew her last breath. Her eyes misted, and she begged him silently to not press her for an answer. When he turned away from her indecision or cowardice, Olive lifted her skirts and ran through the door.

* * *

Jacob leaned on the dry sink and heaved a breath. When he heard the rumblings of a kitchen chair, he remembered he was not alone.

"Do ya love her, son?"

Jacob's head dropped and shook. "Why would you ask me that?"

"Well, one thing's fer sure. She loves you somethin' fierce," his mother said.

"I don't know, Ma. Olive's different from any other woman I ever met."

Martha Butler smiled kindly and with the wisdom age and life brought. "She loves ya alright. It's as clear as a summer morning. And," Martha said as she stood and her bones creaked, "I think you love her, too, maybe. But yer fighting it. Think you'll tarnish what you and Margaret had by lovin' another woman."

"You don't know how I feel, Ma," Jacob said on a sigh.

"Then tell me, Jacob. How do you feel about Olive?" Martha said and laid her hand on her son's back.

Jacob looked out the window above the stove. No matter how old a man gets, he thought, his mother has a way of wheedling out feelings and making him take a hard look at things he may have chosen to avoid. "When she first came here, I thought she was a dried-up old prune of a spinster."

"Well, hell, Jacob, she's nearly as old as me. Could be a grandma ten times over by now. Some women, though, weren't meant for marriage and loving."

Jacob turned quickly. "Olive is meant for all those things and more. She's brave and strong and didn't flinch when two crazy kids were dumped in her lap. She didn't have the foggiest notion of how to get by on a farm, but she's learning and working herself to the bone doing it. Olive never had a chance to love, other than her mother and father, but by God she loves John and Mary and my kids, too, as if she had them herself. Making clothes for them and teaching them their letters and reading to them," Jacob trailed off.

"Yer the one who said she was old, Jacob," Martha said and stared hard at him. "A dried-up old prune of a spinster."

Jacob stood straight and stared out the window. Audrey sat on the swing laughing and shouting as Luke pushed her. "I know I did, Ma. Maybe I was wrong. Maybe age doesn't mean so much."

Martha turned to see what held Jacob's attention. And there swinging was Audrey. She glanced to her son's face and found him not looking at the young blond frolicking but looking past her to Olive as the older woman walked towards the trees.

"Well, then if that's the case, Audrey there ain't too young for you. Might be suited to you if ya gave the girl half a chance."

"I'm not interested in Audrey," Jacob said.

"Huh, what young buck like you wouldn't be interested in Audrey? Blond curly hair, clear skin, good teeth."

"She isn't a horse, Ma," Jacob said.

Martha studied her son and watched him crane his neck as Olive disappeared into the trees. "She ain't Olive either, is she, boy?"

Jacob left his mother's question unanswered and walked through the open door.

Chapter Eight

THE WEEK THAT FOLLOWED REVEALED MUCH for Olive. Martha Butler was an endless source of information. Olive wrote recipes and struggled to explain in her writing what a "handful" consisted of. How the feel of dough, wet or dry, predicted how the bread would rise and how to stretch a pitiful collection of ingredients into a meal. Olive did as she was told, and Martha passed on a lifetime of cooking and caring for a family with each day. What plants yielded medicines for burns. How to make soap and candles, and her butter, sweet-smelling and rich. Olive understood how a young wife like Margaret might have resented this woman, but Olive listened carefully and squeezed the years a young farm girl watched her mother and learned into seven days.

Martha Butler was fascinated by the sewing machine, and Olive stood tall, knowing she had one skill Jacob's mother did not.

"Ya sew a fine seam, Olive," Martha Butler said as she squinted at a dress for Mary.

"The machine makes it easier and faster," Olive replied.

"Ya put too many gee-gaws on these dresses for me, but I'll say they sure are nice."

"Thank you, Martha," Olive said.

Jack Steele had come by and shown her plans for her house the day before. Olive made a few changes, asked Jacob his opinion, and told Jack to begin immediately. She and the children and Martha had ridden to the spot Olive had chosen for her home on the day the lumber arrived. Martha insisted that Jack build the house facing south so the morning and afternoon sun would not heat it, and the breeze blowing east to west would cool it. Olive had chosen a plot with an oak tree, and she envisioned a swing for Mary and John that she could see from her window.

By the time the end of Martha Butler's visit came, the markings where the timber for her home where linked with string, and Olive knew she genuinely liked Jacob's mother. Bossy was an understatement as she watched Martha argue with Jack Steele, but the woman was full of wisdom and wit and willing to share what life had taught her. Olive honestly felt as though she were prepared for living alone on a farm, and the credit went to Jacob's mother.

They stood on the porch and Jacob loaded his mother's and Audrey's bags in the wagon. Olive turned to the older woman. "Martha, I want to thank you so much. You have been generous and helpful to me about things I didn't even know I was supposed to be doing. I have enjoyed your visit and hope you will stop and see me next year in my new house."

Martha watched as her grandchildren helped their father and shook her head. "I miss these youngins' somethin' terrible after I visit. Somethin' about children that brings us hope and a reason to get out of bed in the morning." She turned, faced Olive and continued. "I've had a real pleasant time, too. Seeing yer sewing machine and listening to the story you read the youngins' at night. Yer gonna do just fine, Olive Wilkins."

Martha stepped down from the porch and stopped. She

turned back to Olive. "Thank you for helping with Jacob's youngins', teaching them and all. And thank you for being here for Jacob. He needs you. He don't know it yet, but he does."

Olive breathed deeply and let Martha's words settle. "He's been kind to me as well, Martha. Good upbringing, I imagine," she said.

Martha harrumphed and smiled. "You take care of my boy, ya hear?"

Olive heard Martha's voice crack, nodded and watched the woman heave herself up into the seat. Jacob handed Audrey a kitten, and a dazzling smile lit the girl's face. The children gathered around Olive, and they watched until the wagon was small on the horizon and disappeared over the hill.

"Children, you are so lucky to have such a wonderful grandmother. We're going to begin writing her letters. I truly think she'll enjoy reading about all of you," Olive said and smiled.

Mary called to the children, and Olive was alone with Jacob.

"Margaret hated when she came," he said.

Olive laughed. "I can understand why. Especially if Margaret was as good a wife and mother as you say she was. But I never learned all the little tricks of life on a farm. Martha was a fountain of information."

"Ma seemed to take to you, too," Jacob said.

Olive nodded and smiled. She tilted her head and asked, "You avoided her, Jacob. Why?"

"Because my ma can be a meddling pain in the ass."

Olive looked down and then out over the fields. "You mean about Audrey and you remarrying?"

Jacob nodded.

"She means well. She knows first-hand how hard this life is. Especially alone. Martha's just worried."

"Yeah, I guess," Jacob agreed. He turned, began walking

away, stopped and turned back to Olive. "She convince you this week that I should marry?"

"The subject was never brought up. Not since the day of her arrival."

"A year's not very long," Jacob said haltingly.

Olive smiled softly. "A moment in time to some," she said and turned away from Jacob's regard. *A lifetime to others*, she thought.

* * *

Olive's house went up faster than she expected, and she found herself hurrying curtains as she watched windows fill with glass and walls divide her house into rooms. In her mind, she foresaw her mother's settee near the stone fireplace and worried when her stove would arrive. Some of her things began to come by train, and the sheriff took it upon himself to accompany every delivery.

When the July day arrived for Olive to move, she felt energy and joy and a melancholy as well. Theda had shipped her clothes and china, trinkets, and pots and pans alike. Olive's bedroom furniture had already been installed in Mary's bedroom, and Olive had purchased a bed and dresser for John. Her mother's fine bone china and everyday plates had come through the transportation unscathed, but her father's mantle clock had been broken. Olive was hoping to have it repaired and now waited only for her parent's mahogany bedroom suite, which she would use as her own. A trunk arrived with bed linens, and Mary's eyes widened at the handmade wedding ring quilt that Olive now spread flat across the girl's bed.

"Your ma and pa must have been rich," Mary said and fingered the fine stitches.

Olive laughed. "Not really. Some of these things were

passed down from my mother's mother. My father did have a good-paying job, though and my mother an eye for quality. We didn't buy often, but when we did, it was built to last and remain beautiful."

"And you say you sold some of your stuff as well?" Mary asked.

"Some, yes. I told Theda to keep some things for herself and sell the rest. My old house had more rooms than this new one. The money will keep us in good shape until Jacob can farm this land." Olive paused and looked contentedly around her new home. "I confess, I worried this house may be too small, but now that I'm here, I have to say it is perfect, just perfect. Cozy and homey. Do you like it, Mary?"

The girl shrugged. "I never had stuff this fine. But it sure is pretty."

Olive smiled and hugged her waist. "I can't wait till the sheriff brings my bedroom furniture today."

"He sure is being nice," Mary said and eyed her aunt.

"Well, him being in town and receiving all my goods from the train certainly has been convenient. I would have had to ride in nearly everyday and hire men to load my things."

"Like I said, he sure is being nice."

Olive turned from Mary's knowing look. She looked out the window of Mary's bedroom to the oak tree that shaded the front of the house. The morning was clear and warm, and birds chattered in the tree. When she left Jacob's house that morning, knowing she would not live there with him and the children again, her heart lodged in her throat. Peg wouldn't cuddle with her at night, Luke wouldn't pester her with a thousand questions, and Mark would not reach for the sound of her voice. Bittersweet, as well was the look on Jacob's face when he left for the fields that morning. Their eyes had connected, and she held her breath, fearing the release of a sob. He was smiling at her, but when his head tilted and he nodded, she knew he was thinking the same as she. Two souls had drifted together for comfort and help. And now they would drift apart.

The rumble of a wagon at the top of the hill snapped Olive from her melancholy, and she watched the sheriff slowly guide the team and the wagon towards her home. Large blankets made massive blocks of color in the bed of the wagon. Who was that riding beside the sheriff, she asked herself. Olive squinted and strained and felt John at her sleeve tugging.

"Yes, I know, John. My furniture is arriving. But who is with the sheriff?" she said as much to herself as the boy.

Olive opened her front door and stood on the porch with John and Mary. The woman in the wagon began to wave frantically, and Olive stepped down into the yard to get a closer look. When recognition came, tears followed quickly.

"Theda," Olive shouted.

She ran, holding her skirts and waving back. Theda's hand covered her mouth and Olive knew she was crying as well. In an instant, sweet memories ripped through Olive's mind, and the heartache of separation from all she had known, all of her life, filled her throat to closing. When the wagon finally stopped, the two women stared at each other and smiled through their tears.

"I had resigned myself to never seeing you again," Olive said.

"It wouldn't have been proper to not make a housewarming call, now would it?" Theda said.

Olive laughed. "All the way from Philadelphia?"

Theda turned to the sheriff. "Sir, can you not see that I need help from this wagon?"

The sheriff's brows rose, and he pulled on the brake. He climbed down, and as he passed Olive, he nodded and smiled. "Olive, you look lovely today. I have your furniture and not a scratch on it."

"Thank you, Sheriff."

"Really, sir, I need help," Theda clamored.

The sheriff offered Theda his hand and she climbed down from the wagon. When Theda turned to her, Olive stepped close and hugged her. "My God, it's good to see you," she said.

Theda leaned back and nodded. "And you as well."

Olive's eyes opened wide. "Theda! Has something happened to your mother?"

"No, no. Mrs. Gunderson is staying with her while I visit."

Olive's shoulders dropped. "Thank God. I just thought of her, and, well, I've never known you to be away for more than a day."

Theda smiled. "I do have a surprise for you from back home, though." She reached into the wagon and lifted a small box covered with a blanket. "Here. Open it."

Olive reached for the box and the weight inside shifted and made her nearly drop the package. Then she heard a sleepy meow and looked up to Theda. "Tiger!" Olive's eyes misted yet again, and she put her arm around her friend of many years, leading her to the house, carrying her orange tabby close to her. "There are some young ones I'd like you to meet, Theda."

Theda shaded her hand for a view of the children on the porch but shouted over her shoulder. "Sheriff, do hurry with my bags, won't you?"

"John, Mary, this is my dearest friend in the whole world, here from Philadelphia. Miss Patterson," Olive said as she neared the porch.

"Hello," Mary said while John clung to her side.

Theda smiled at the girl and then turned to John. Her face sobered, and Olive feared she would faint.

"He... he is the very image of James at that age," she whispered.

"He is a handsome boy," Olive said.

Theda crept slowly up the steps and touched Mary's face softly. The girl's eyes darted to Olive, but she stood still as a post. Theda reached tentatively for John, and he ran into the house. Theda turned to Olive with questions.

Olive shook her head. "He's terrified of strangers. It takes him awhile to warm up. But he will."

Theda clasped her hands at her waist clutching a beaded handbag and looked again at Mary. "You, child, are very fortunate." Mary stared up from under her brows. "And I am as well. For in you, I see my closest childhood friend at ten years of age."

Theda turned to Olive, and the two women stared and remembered and felt the weight of the passing years descend as if only a second had eclipsed.

"Come into the house, Theda. You must be exhausted. I made tea this morning. We'll have some."

"Olive?" the sheriff said.

"Oh, Sheriff, would you like some tea?" Olive said and turned.

"Maybe when I get back. I'm going to ride over to Jacob's and see if he'll help me unload your furniture. I'm going to take your hitch if you don't mind. Don't want to be chancing a scratch on your things. Mary, John, want to ride along?"

"Sure," Mary said and grabbed John by the hand.

"Come on in, Theda," Olive said and opened her screen door. Tiger jumped from her arms and went off, exploring his new home.

Theda sunk into a chair and untied her bonnet. "It feels wonderful to be seated in something that isn't moving."

Olive laughed. "How was your trip?"

"Fine," Theda said and sipped on her tea. "I will admit I was a bit unnerved at riding out alone here with the sheriff. In the middle of nowhere."

Olive smiled and recalled her exact thoughts those few months ago and how silly they seemed now.

"But Olive, I must say, you look quite different. A skirt and blouse and your hair down. And it almost looks as if your face is tanned from the sun. You haven't been going without a bonnet, have you?"

Olive seated herself, straightening the skirt she recently made. "It's different here, Theda. Less rules and expectations and, really, I may go days without seeing another soul other than the children."

"That's never been a reason to let out skin exposed to the sun. The wrinkles, Olive. But I must admit you have a certain healthy glow about you," Theda said.

"I still can not believe you traveled all the way out here, Theda. If you were anything like me, you were terrified," Olive said.

Theda's head tilted. "I must admit, I have never been fond of traveling alone, but truly, I wanted to see you so much, I did it anyway."

Olive laid her hand on her friend's. "I can't begin to tell you how glad I am you came."

Theda gazed thoughtfully at Olive. "If truth be known, I had to see first-hand these children and this Jacob fellow who seems to have you in a dither."

Olive's head dropped. "I'm hardly in a dither, Theda."

"Well, you certainly weren't yourself in your writing."

Olive looked up at her life long friend. *No,* she thought, *I was you.* With her black hair pulled back tightly and navy blue traveling dress, buttoned to the top, Theda looked to Olive just as she had probably looked to everyone in Spencer. A prim, proper spinster whose lips pursed at the slightest infraction of propriety. Uncomfortable with any mention of the very real, sometimes painful, occasionally embarrassing facts of life. A brother's shortcomings, a father's secrets, children's suffering but most clearly that mystical joining of men and women in the marriage bed that haunted Olive's dreams.

"I will admit, Theda, my stay in Spencer has changed the way I look at things."

"It certainly must have. When I read that you had decided to stay here and build a home, I was shocked. I must have read the letter three times, and yet still I could not believe it."

Olive looked down at her folded hands and back to Theda's unwavering regard. She knew her closest friend was waiting for a reason or an explanation and chose her words carefully.

"When I first came here and saw how James had lived and what a terrible condition John and Mary were in, I admit, I wanted nothing more than to run back to Church Street and hide. But I knew I could not abandon them, either. And at first when Jacob offered to let me stay at his house, I was shocked and offended. But what was I to do? Mary barely spoke a civil word, and John didn't speak at all. They looked like street urchins and smelled like them, too. Jacob was the only constant and steady influence in their lives. And I decided to put aside my own fears and sometimes silly notions of right and wrong and do what was best for those children."

"Being married before living with a man is not a silly notion."

Olive laughed. "I know that, Theda. We hardly lived together as man and wife. He stayed in the barn with the boys until Sophie's father paid us a visit."

Theda questioned her, and Olive retold the story of the beating she had received at the hands of her brother's father-in-law. Theda's eyes opened wide, and her hand covered her mouth.

"My, God, Olive, what kind of people are they? Monsters?"

"Horrible people, Theda. And that's who John and Mary would have legally belonged to if I hadn't claimed them," Olive said.

"Dear, merciful God. And that's why you decided to stay. The children wouldn't come, and you could not leave them."

"There are other reasons as well." Olive could not stop a smile. "I found I liked it here. It's beautiful and clean. I've made friends. I came to adore Jacob's children, and things happened that have never happened to me before."

"Such as?" Theda prodded.

"The sheriff asked me to dance at a social apparently because he wanted to," Olive said.

"Did you?"

"I most certainly did. Life is slipping away from us as we speak, and I refuse to let another second of my life go by without some pleasure for myself," Olive replied. Theda's look of shock and confusion was nearly comical.

"But, Olive, we're spinsters. We always will be spinsters. Pleasure is not a pursuit meant for women like us."

"What are women like us meant for?" Olive asked quickly.

"Well, well..."

"We sit and worry and wait and God forbid we enjoy something, anything, in the meantime. Well, I for one refuse to live like that again. Mother, Father, James, all dead, and we will be as well, Theda, faster than we realize." Olive halted and stared hard at Theda. "Jacob kissed me, and I would do it again. And even more, maybe."

Theda's mouth dropped, and her eyes widened. "I knew it. He compromised you. I just knew it. Well, don't you worry, Olive, I'm here, and I'll set him straight. Of all the arrogant..."

Olive heard the wagon pull into the yard. "No, no, Theda. It wasn't like that."

But the women would not be stopped. "And you in a vulnerable state with the children and James's death. Some men just cannot control themselves, Olive. Your mother and mine as well warned us of this behavior."

The sheriff, Jacob and all five children came through the front door on Theda's last words. She stood, straight and stiff, eyes hard and lips tight as she focused in on Jacob's face.

"You... you cad!" Theda shouted.

Olive's hand flew to her mouth as Theda screeched at Jacob. Jacob's eyes widened, and his mouth opened to speak, but not before Theda began again. "To take advantage of a woman in her state, well, it's just too much to bear."

"What are you talking about, woman?" Jacob said.

"I'm not your woman and neither is Olive," Theda snapped and stepped close to Jacob.

The sheriff stepped between Jacob and Theda. "You took liberties with Miss Wilkins, Jacob?"

"No, I mean, it was nothing... "

"Not nothing where I come from. Let's step outside and settle this like men," the sheriff growled.

Olive could not squeeze in a single syllable above the shouting, and she glanced at Mary as the adults argued. The girl watched wide-eyed, and a sly smirk formed on her face.

"There's nothing to settle here, Sheriff. Nothing much happened and anyway it's between us if it did," Jacob shouted.

Mary yanked at Theda's sleeve, and the woman turned. "He sure was kissing her and holding her tight on the porch when I saw them."

"And in front of the children. Have you no shame?" Theda shouted shrilly.

Olive gave Mary a look that shut the girl's mouth and stood trying to get everyone's attention. "Enough," she yelled.

All heads turned Olive's way with her shout. She was red-faced and angry, but when Olive looked from one seething face to the other, she could not deny the humor in the drama before her. Never had the word *irony* had a truer meaning. *Theda's convinced I've been compromised, the sheriff wants to settle it with fists, and poor Jacob's caught in the middle. All over her,* she thought. Olive the spinster. Her belly laugh began as a giggle and the sheriff and Theda stared wide-eyed at her. "I'm sorry," she managed to say. "I know... I know I shouldn't laugh, but..."

"She's hysterical, Sheriff," Theda said. "I wonder if there are smelling salts in the house."

"I'm not... I'm not hysterical," Olive said after she took a deep breath. "Not that it's anyone's business, but Jacob and I exchanged a few kisses. That's all. Certainly nothing as dramatic as all this."

The sheriff narrowed his eye and said, "You're sure?"

"Yes, certainly I'm sure. Theda misunderstood something I said and got the wrong idea. It's not like we were two-stepping or anything," Olive said.

"Two-stepping?" Theda asked.

The sheriff, Olive and Theda exchanged glances, and when recognition occurred, Theda's face grew scarlet, and she hemmed and hawed, looking at everything but another face. Olive's head turned when Jacob laughed out loud. And kept laughing.

He tried to draw breath but could only mumble something about the look on Theda's face. Olive found his laughter contagious and was soon giggling as well. The sheriff walked out of the house and slammed the door. That only brought more peals of laughter from Olive and Jacob.

Theda looked at her hands and primly asked, "I would like to freshen up if you don't mind."

Olive opened the door to her bedroom. Theda sashayed through, head high, skirts swinging. Her exit did nothing to quiet Jacob.

Jacob and Olive's eyes met, and they began to laugh again. Olive held her mouth pursed trying to calm herself. "I think Theda was shocked," she said finally.

"That's an understatement. I thought her eyes were going to bulge right out of her head when she realized what two-stepping was," Jacob said and smiled.

Olive's eyes flew to the ceiling, and her face colored as she thought about what Theda had been thinking and how the same thought rarely left her head. But her smile for Jacob, remained.

"What's two-stepping, Daddy?" Peg asked.

Olive and Jacob turned around and saw four sets of eyes regarding them. "Well..." Jacob began.

"That's what the sheriff and Aunt Olive were doing at the dance," Luke replied.

Olive swallowed. "It is a dance step of sorts, children." She felt Jacob's eyes on her, and when she looked at him he was grinning at her.

"Come on, boys. Let's get Olive's furniture unloaded," Jacob said and stopped at the door. "Unless the sheriff dumped it out of the back without us." Jacob winked at Olive and stepped on to the porch.

Olive could not understand why her heart missed a beat at Jacob's acknowledgement of their secret with a sly wink. But it did, and she sighed aloud. She turned and saw Mary holding Mark and regarding her. Olive forced herself to appear serious as she reached to take the infant from the girl's arms. Olive cooed to Mark, and he turned into her as she watched the men unload her furniture.

Olive could see Jacob's temper grow short, though as she had the men move her furniture time and again in the small room.

"There's only so many ways all this junk's going to fit," Jacob said.

"It's not junk," Olive said as she moved the dresser another quarter of an inch. "There," she said finally and surveyed the room. "Perfect."

"This is how you had it in the beginning. An hour ago when we started."

"I just needed to see all my options," Olive said and placed embroidered dresser scarves atop the polished wood.

"I'm getting something cold to drink," Jacob said.

"It looks beautiful, Olive," Theda said.

Olive smiled and watched Peg fiddle with the matching brass knobs on the wardrobe.

"You take your time placing your things where you want them," the sheriff said, red-faced from the exertion. "I'll come back and move them for you again if you like."

She looked up from the sheriff and realized his casual words where a challenge of sorts. "Would you like some tea, Sheriff?"

"Don't mind if I do," he said and pulled his hat from his head to wipe his sweating forehead.

Theda served the tea and explained to Mary the correct service as she went. "Yes, dear, hold the glass at the bottom."

Mary rolled her eyes and did as she was told. The kitchen was silent until Jacob spoke. "You put your sewing machine in the kitchen, Olive?"

Olive nodded. "Since I use it so much, I wanted to have it in here. Where all the activity is. I can watch the children from the window and see to supper on the stove as I work."

"Olive?" the sheriff said. She turned to him and smiled. "There's another dance this Saturday. I would be happy to come out and escort you and Miss Patterson, if you'd like."

"I'm close by here, Sheriff. I'll drive them if they want to go," Jacob said.

"Well, I'm asking Miss Wilkins if she'd like me to come out and escort her," the sheriff fumed.

"I'm sure Olive," Jacob paused, "would be as happy as pie if I drove her in."

The two men eyed her, waiting for an answer. "I didn't even

know there was a dance on Saturday," Olive said.

"Always is before the crops come in," the sheriff replied and glared over his glass at Jacob. "I don't ever remember you coming to often to the dances."

Jacob smirked and leaned forward. "I think I'll be coming to this one."

The sheriff's face colored.

Olive watched and listened to the undercurrent between the two men. She could not stop the foolish notion of herself as the damsel as two knights battled for her hand. This was a new feeling for Olive, and she conceded it felt wonderful.

"We'll have to see at the end of the week. Theda and I may want to stay home."

"You just let me know, Olive," the sheriff said. "I sure hope you decide to come, and I'd like you to save me a dance if you do."

Olive smiled at the sheriff and turned to find Jacob watching her.

"She may not have too many dances to spare, Sheriff. A single woman as pretty as her," he said.

Olive's shoulders dropped, and her stomach flopped on Jacob's words. Her eyelashes fluttered, and she could have only described her own words as tittering. "That's sweet of you to say."

"Don't you have to be getting back to town, Sheriff?" Jacob asked.

The sheriff eyed Jacob and slowly stood from his chair. "Yeah, I guess you're right. Can't be lollygagging around, like some."

Jacob sat still in his chair as the sheriff nodded at Theda and tipped his hat to Olive. He went to the door and turned. "Just let me know about Saturday, Olive."

She smiled and thanked him for his help with the furniture.

Jacob nodded stiffly to Theda, and Olive followed him onto the porch. "Thank you, Jacob."

A slow smile crept to his lips as he asked, "Will you tell me what your friend has to say about two-stepping?"

Olive grinned. "Ladies never, and certainly not Theda and I, acknowledge publicly any understanding of two-stepping."

Jacob's eyes heated and bored into Olive. "I told you, I'd be happy to show you. If you're ever curious."

Their conversation, to Olive's surprise, had turned quickly from casual bantering to a smoldering exchange of understanding. She blushed and looked away. "Really, Jacob. That's not something you say to someone other than a wife."

"You're right, Olive. I'll tell you, though, I haven't belly-laughed like I did today with anyone other than Margaret. Maybe that makes us, well, I don't know, more than just friends. What do you think?"

"I consider you a friend."

"Good. 'Cause I sure would be wondering why the notion of you dancing with the sheriff puts me in a foul mood, if we weren't at least friends." Jacob gathered Mark in his arms and called to Luke and Peg.

Olive watched the children smile and wave as Jacob drove them away. She entered her house in a fine mood and found Theda staring at her strangely.

"You remind me of Hester Hawkins," Theda whispered.

Olive's eyes rounded as she thought of the woman back home. Hester, in Theda and Olive's opinions, threw herself at every unmarried man within a hundred miles. Olive wondered now if her judgments were too harsh. "Hardly, Theda," she said and carried glasses to the sink.

"Really, Olive, I thought there for a moment you were going to swoon or drop a hanky to see who would pick it up," Theda said quietly, looking at Mary.

"I have to say I enjoyed the attention," Olive said.

"Is that why you were making eyes at Jacob on the porch just now?" Mary asked.

"Mary, were you spying on us?"

Mary smirked. "I just went to the door to see what Miss Patterson was looking at."

"I was trying to see where the other children were, that's all," Theda answered casually.

"So you both were eavesdropping," Olive gasped.

"Couldn't hear much," Mary added and looked from one woman to the other.

"Mary, why don't you go check on John," Olive said. The girl stood slowly and inched her way out of the room. Olive watched her tarry and waited patiently until the screen door slammed. "Theda, I can hardly believe you would listen to my conversation."

Theda's eyes narrowed. "Blame me if you will, but as your closest friend I felt it was my obligation to see exactly how far this relationship has gone. Remember Alfred Smith?"

"Alfred Smith?" Olive said. "What does Alfred Smith have to do with this?"

"He was fast," Theda whispered. "You knew that as well as I did, and yet you still went to the ice cream parlor with him."

"We were fourteen-years-old," Olive shouted.

Theda's eyes rose, and she primly looked at Olive. "You needed my advice then and you may need it now."

"I'm an adult. What I do with Jacob Butler can hardly be compared to a sallow-faced boy I knew twenty years ago."

"So tell me, Olive, what do you do with Jacob Butler?" Theda asked.

Olive's face colored, and her head tilted. "Nothing really."

Theda leaned in close and checked right and left for listeners. "Has he touched you in any place you consider private."

Olive knew what Theda meant. It was how their mother's warned them of boys a million lifetimes ago. "He kissed me. I nearly fainted the first time."

"The first time, uh huh, there have been other occasions," Theda said and sat back in her chair, drumming her fingers on the kitchen table.

Olive felt her face redden, and she was mentally transported back to her bedroom as her mother questioned her about Alfred Smith. "The first time he kissed me was while he was apologizing for rubbing on my backside while I was sleeping."

Theda's eyes widened. "He had his hand on your...backside?"

Olive's mouth pulled to one side. "Well, not his hand exactly."

Theda's mouth dropped. She cleared her throat and stumbled, "What exactly was rubbing on your backside?"

Olive could not answer and sat and stared at her friend.

"I see," Theda said, wide-eyed.

Olive knew for a fact that Theda did not see. "There was a storm after the last dance. By the time we got home, we were all soaked, and I had left the window open above the girl's and my bed. The roof came off the barn over his and the boy's bed, and it was wet as well. The children were frightened by the storm, and we all slept in front of the fireplace. When I woke up, Jacob's arm was around my waist, and he was asleep with his stomach up against my back."

"And?" Theda persisted.

Olive's eyes flew to the ceiling as she recalled the most intimate moment of her life. "Well, when I woke up, he was rubbing his hips against my backside."

"Oh," Theda said and sat quietly for a moment. "Were you in your bedclothes?"

"Yes. We were sleeping," Olive said impatiently.

"Oh."

The two women sat silently, and Olive continued. "The next day, I tried to excuse his behavior and continue on since I was living there with him, and he ended up kissing me."

"Oh." Theda said. "Was it, the kiss I mean, was it pleasurable?"

She is as curious as I, Olive thought. "Like nothing that ever happened to me before." She leaned forward to Theda and whispered, "He put his tongue in my mouth."

Theda's eyes widened and a look of revulsion crossed her face. "His tongue?"

Olive fiddled with her hands and looked up to her friend. "Yes. And I thought I'd faint dead away."

"Really?" Theda said in wonder.

Olive nodded. "Then I had some whiskey with him one night when I couldn't sleep, and he kissed me again."

"You were drinking whiskey?" Theda said as her hand came to her throat.

"Just a sip," Olive conceded.

"Well, well, well," Theda said and nodded and stared.

Chapter Nine

ALTHOUGH SHE WOULD NOT ADMIT IT, OLIVE believed Mary went to bed early that evening just to be in her own room. The girl had folded her belongings, neatly in the dresser, changed into her new white nightgown and sat cross-legged on the bed.

Olive peaked her head in the door and asked, "May I come in?"

Mary nodded and sat still looking around the room.

"We'll have to get some pictures or do some cross-stitch for in here. The walls seem awfully bare," Olive said and began to sit down on the edge of the bed.

"Careful," Mary said. "You were cooking in them, those clothes. I don't want anything getting my spread dirty. You did say it was mine, right?"

"It's yours all right. I'll be more careful next time," Olive said with a grin.

"Do you think if I gathered wild flowers and dried them they'd look good on the walls?"

"I think that would be perfect. I think whatever you want will be just fine, Mary. What do you think of my friend, Miss Patterson?" Olive asked.

Mary shrugged. "Seems pulled tighter than a noose, I'd say."

"Mary. That's no way to talk."

"She's alright, I guess. She reminds me of you when you first came here," Mary said and looked up at Olive from under her brows.

Olive's eyes closed, and she harrumphed. "I was thinking the very same thing. A few short months has certainly brought some changes for me."

Mary's eyes rolled in her head. "That's for sure."

"I suspect bigger changes than I'd thought. Some big changes for you as well. We've both changed, Mary," Olive said.

"Yeah, I guess you're right," Mary conceded with a shrug.

Olive leaned down and kissed the girl's hair. "Goodnight."

Mary scooted back and ducked under the blankets. "I might just lie here for awhile. Not go to sleep right away," she said and rolled to her side.

Olive smiled and replied, "That's fine." As Olive reached for the door, she heard Mary turn over and looked back at the girl.

"I like it here, Aunt Olive."

"I'm glad," Olive said and felt tears brim at the back of her eyes. She closed the door softly and felt oddly as if this was her first real night as a mother. Settling a daughter to bed, talking about the day, and looking forward to the future.

Theda had spread a sheet on the davenport and was sitting at the end by the kerosene lamp, embroidering. Olive sat down in the rocker, and the two women sat quietly, Mary in her room, and John asleep in his bed.

"Are you sure you don't mind sleeping out here?" Olive asked.

"Not at all. I wouldn't dream of moving one of you out of your bed on your first night in your new house," Theda replied.

John's door opened then, and the sleepy boy stood in the

doorway looking at Olive. "What's the matter, John?" Olive asked. He turned his head, looking away and Olive said, "Why don't you come sit on my lap for awhile?"

John crept over to Olive, and she pulled him into her arms. She reached for a quilt thrown over the back of the rocker and spread it over John and her legs. The boy snuggled tight, and Olive rocked and kissed his head.

"It's been a big day, John," Theda said and smiled. "Lots of new things to get used to."

He stared and held tight to Olive's arms. The groan from the wooden rocker, as Olive's foot pushed the floor in rhythm, was the only sound in the room. Soon his eyes fluttered shut, and Olive felt him relax against her. She looked up to Theda and smiled contently.

"It seems as though mothering comes naturally to you, Olive," Theda said softly.

Olive smiled. "I don't know about that. But I will say I can't remember when I've ever felt as useful or needed."

"Do you miss Jacob's children?"

"I was just thinking that," Olive said and kissed John's hair again. "You don't know quite when or how children find a way into your heart, but they do."

Olive stood slowly, holding John against her and turned to Theda. "Good night," she said.

Olive lay John down in her bed and pulled the covers back from under him. She crawled in beside him, relaxed and breathed deeply. Fresh wood, the scent of lemon furniture polish, and little boy filled her nose. Olive could not remember a time when she felt this happy and at peace. As if all of her life she had been waiting, filing away memories and knowledge, preparing for this purpose. Waiting for the day, through tragedy and boredom, to begin her own life in a new home, with her own family. She said her prayers silently, eyes closed, as she had done since she was a little girl, thanking God for the long crooked path that brought her to this bed, under this roof.

* * *

Morning came brightly and swiftly to Olive, and she awoke as John began to stir, and Tiger stretched lazily in the sunlight. She heard someone in the kitchen and rose, pulling on her much-missed green flannel robe. Olive was so glad to have all her things from back home. It made her new home feel right. Like a bride wearing something old and something new, her treasured family belongings brought sentiment and history to a new beginning.

"Good morning," Theda said. "I've put water on for tea."

"Good morning. You're up and dressed early," Olive said and yawned.

"I didn't want to bother anyone," Theda said as she measured tea leaves into the pot.

Olive sat contentedly while Theda heated biscuits from the last night's meal and poured tea into Olive's mother's china teapot. Olive lifted the gold-rimmed cup and admired the delicate painted roses. "We didn't always realize how lucky we were, did we, Theda?"

Theda sipped her tea. "We were lucky, weren't we?"

"Always enough to eat, never worried about anything more important than what dress we would wear to church," Olive said and pulled her robe tightly around her.

"We took for granted that everyone went to school and had clothes and people to care for them," Theda said wistfully.

"Mary didn't want me to sit on the wedding ring quilt, for fear I would dirty it," Olive said and chuckled.

"From the sounds of it, that's the finest thing that girl ever owned," Theda said and frowned.

"James did a poor job of providing for his family, among other things. Mary told me she didn't go to school because it was too far to walk home. I guess James wouldn't leave his card game at the end of the school day," Olive said and felt a surge of anger.

"I just cannot believe James," Theda said and stared hard at Olive. "Do you think that wife of his was responsible for his poor behavior?"

Olive stared back and didn't blink. "No, Theda. I don't think anyone made James lose sight of right and wrong. I think he did that all on his own."

Theda's head tilted, and she looked down at her hands. "Something must have happened."

"Yes. Something happened all right. Mother and Father spoiled him and gave him everything he ever wanted without working for anything." Olive looked away then and said quietly, "I suppose I was guilty as well. Me being older didn't help. I did all his chores so those beautiful blue eyes of his wouldn't tear up."

"He was the most handsome boy I ever laid eyes on," Theda admitted quietly.

"And we worried about whether men were honorable in their intentions to us and all along, my baby brother, the least honorable of them all."

Theda opened her mouth but didn't reply. The two women sat quietly in their thoughts as they had done hundreds of times before.

"Good morning, Mary. How did you sleep?" Olive asked as the girl walked into the kitchen.

"Good," the girl replied. "I'm goin to keep my door closed. I don't want that old cat of yours pulling its claws on my spread."

Olive and Theda exchanged glances while Mary's back was to them.

"I nearly forgot," Theda said and jumped from the table. "I brought gifts for you and John."

Mary looked at Olive from under her brow while Theda dug through her valise in the sitting room. "Probably some book on how to serve tea," Mary whispered.

"Whatever it is, be gracious and thank her," Olive said quietly.

Theda stood up triumphantly and returned to the kitchen. "Here, Mary, this is for you," she said and handed the girl a velvet-covered box.

Mary's eyes widened, and she fingered the soft fabric. "What is it?"

"Open it and see," Theda said and grinned at Olive.

Mary laid the box reverently on the table and lifted the lid. Her mouth fell open and then closed. "I shouldn't take something so fine."

"Yes, you should, Mary. Your Aunt Olive and I got our own brush and comb set when we were about your age. Go ahead, lift them out," Theda said.

Mary held up the ivory backed, horse hairbrush and turned it over and over in her hand. She tucked it back in its spot and pulled out the matching comb. "They got an 'M' on them."

"Your initial, Mary," Theda said.

"Oh, Theda, they're beautiful," Olive said and smiled up at her friend.

"I'll be afraid to use them," Mary whispered.

Olive laughed. "The one I use on my dresser is the one my father bought me when I was eleven years old. I use it every day."

Mary replaced the comb and closed the lid formally. "I'm going to sit them on my dresser, right now. Ah... ah thank you, Miss Patterson. I never had a gift like this before. Sometimes on my birthday, Pa would bring me some new ribbons or something, but never, ever anything like this."

"You're welcome, Mary," Theda replied.

The girl went to her bedroom, and Olive smiled at Theda. "What a thoughtful gift, Theda. Mary loves it."

"Well, after reading your letter, I wanted to get Mary something to treasure. It sounded like she didn't have many things of her own," Theda said.

"She had nothing of her own. I'd be embarrassed for you to even see the house they were living in."

"Good morning, John," Theda said. "I have a gift for you. Well, actually, they belonged to your father. Come see."

Olive turned and smiled to John as he came into the kitchen and wiped the sleep from his eyes. She looked up to Theda and asked, "From his father?"

"Olive," Theda said excitedly, "I found them when I was supervising the move at your house. Here, John."

Olive watched the boy accept the worn leather bag with the strings knotted and her breath caught in her throat. "James's marbles. Where ever did you find them?"

"Wedged behind the dresser in James's room. Do you remember when he lost them?"

"How could I forget, Theda? Our house was in an uproar for days," Olive said and sat back, drifting to memories long forgotten. She watched John slowly untie the bag and pull a marble out. He turned it carefully in his hand, and when the morning light caught the center, he sank slowly to the floor, examining each one.

Olive and Theda watched the boy finger the smooth glass, and Olive saw Theda's lip tremble.

"My God, Olive," she said softly. "If I didn't know better, I would think we were girls again watching James do the same thing."

"I know," Olive said.

"Have you ever played marbles, John?" Theda asked. The boy stared at her blankly. "Will you come outside with me? I'll show you what to do." Theda offered her hand, and John considered. He carefully placed the marbles in the string bag and stood up, placing his hand, tentatively, in Theda's.

Theda's face beamed over her shoulder as she looked at Olive, and Mary came into the kitchen.

"Where they going?" the girl asked.

"Theda brought your father's marbles for John, and she's going to teach him how to play," Olive said smiling.

"She knows how to play marbles?" Mary asked.

Olive laughed. "We entertained your father when he was a boy more times than I can count. I was never very good, but Theda was the acknowledged neighborhood champion."

"Just can't imagine her playing marbles," Mary said. "Aunt Olive? Will you come in my room?"

Mary stood beside her dresser. "See, I put them right there in the middle."

Olive looked at the girl's dresser, bare but for an embroidered scarf and the precious velvet box. "They look perfect. Why don't you open the box, then you'll see your comb and brush?"

Mary hemmed and hawed, opened the lid and closed it again. "I don't know. I like it open, but I sure don't want nobody coming along and swiping them."

Olive laughed and hugged Mary. "I don't think anybody's going to come along and swipe them. Let's go see how Theda and John are doing."

Olive could do nothing but smile when she looked out the screen door with Mary. There was Theda, kneeling on the ground, over a circle drawn in the dirt. "Now this one is a cat's eye, and this one is your aggie. You try to knock my marbles out of the circle. Like this."

* * *

Jacob arose, with kinks in his neck and sand in his eyes from too few hours of sleep. Luke and Peg had slept with him, and even though there were four of them in the house, it had taken on a tomb-like quality. He missed the steady hum of Olive's sewing machine and her voice reading to the children in the evening. Jacob envisioned Olive in her own kitchen now, sewing and smiling, keeping a close eye on John and Mary. Cooking the things his mother had taught her. A vision of domestic tranquility.

Luke and Peg had sat quietly, staring into the fire after dinner. Jacob had tried unsuccessfully to coax them into conversation. They only nodded and looked away. When Peg stood and announced she was going to bed, Jacob was shocked. The girl fought constantly to stay up, fearing she would miss something, Jacob supposed and now she voluntarily climbed into her bed. Luke followed soon after, quiet as well.

Jacob sat a spell in the still of the house trying to convince himself how wonderful it was to have his house back to normal. He stripped to his underwear and stretched out in the rocker. Jacob reached for his tobacco and rolled a cigarette, thinking how grand it was to sit, in his shorts and have a smoke unbothered by a woman and children. But soon his eyes were drawn to the sink filled with dirty dishes from supper. He leaned back in his chair and planned his day following and watched Mark stir in his crib. On the shelf above Mark's bed sat a neatly folded stack of clean white diapers and wondered how long they would last and if he had better add laundry to his list of chores. His eyes were drawn to the red gingham check cloth that now covered his rough table. Something else to wash, he thought.

But as he looked at the table and the crock of daisies in the center he was reminded of Olive as she stitched the ends of the cloth and spread it across the table before dinner. A last vestige of her influence in his house, now a bit more civilized, he conceded. Homier with the new matching curtains at the window and covers pulled down before bed for the children.

Jacob stood and stretched, shaking off the niggling feeling that his home and his children were bereft without Olive and worse off for it. "Shit," he said and stood, looking around at his home. It was fine before she came, and they would do fine again. His eyes, though, stopped and held as he noticed a spool of dark thread on the mantle. A threaded needle stuck out of its side. And he gave into the loneliness he fought as it swept a cool chill across his bare back. Jacob climbed into bed beside Luke, but soon Peg cried for him, and he tucked her under the covers with him. He lay stoically, as small feet dug into his ribs and bony legs kneed him, unable to sleep.

Near dawn, just as Jacob closed his eyes, Peg whimpered in her sleep. He awoke, pulled her tightly to him and kissed her head. "What's the matter, Peg? Did you have a bad dream?"

The little girl's long lashes fluttered with sleep and tears and she shook her head. "I'm just sad," she said.

Jacob pulled her tighter and saw Luke staring and awake. "I'm sad, too. We miss Aunt Olive."

Jacob swallowed and admitted to the children that which he had been unable to admit to himself. "I miss her, too."

* * *

Theda's visit went by quickly. The two women talked and sewed and tried with little success to turn ground over for a garden.

"Well, Theda, everyone out here has a kitchen garden. Much more than our little beds of flowers and spices back home," Olive said and straightened. "Flo and Beth feed their families all winter on what they can in the fall,"

"You can do the same with canned goods from the mercantile, Olive," Theda said and wiped the sweat from her forehead.

The two women turned as they heard the roll of a wagon at the crest of the hill.

"Jacob and the children," Olive said and smiled. She shaded her eyes and waved back, walking out to greet them.

"Aunt Olive," Peg cried. Olive stretched her arms out and as Jacob pulled the wagon to a stop, Peg jumped down and raced to Olive. "I miss you."

"I miss you too, Peg," Olive said and squeezed the girl. "Hello, Luke. Where's your brother?"

Luke ran to her. "I caught a toad yesterday, Aunt Olive."

The children were smiling and yanking on Olive's skirt as she laughed and pulled them close for a hug "Did you? How wonderful. My, my, Luke I think you've grown since I last saw you, and it's been less than a week."

Jacob climbed down from the wagon, Mark in his arms. "Olive," he said.

"Jacob," she said and turned to him with a soft smile.

Olive's hair was tied back loosely with a scarf, and dirt streaked her nose and cheeks. Her white blouse as well was marked with dirt, and her hands fumbled in her skirt. She continued smiling at Jacob, and he grinned back at her. Sweat glistened on her forehead in the noon sun, and he shuffled his feet.

"You two look like you've been wrestling a pig," Jacob said.

Olive's hands flew to her face and hair. "Oh, my. What a sight I must be. Theda and I were turning some ground over for a garden."

Jacob looked over her shoulder as Luke and Peg ran off with Mary and John. "I'd have never guessed."

"The ground's much harder than I'd thought it would be."

Jacob walked to the spot Olive had marked off with twine and sticks. He picked up the shovel and quickly black earth gave contrast to the prairie grass.

"Why didn't you tell me you wanted a garden? I would have turned it for you."

"I just decided. Is it too late?" Olive asked.

"For some things, yeah, but peas and beans and beets will do alright."

Jacob worked methodically as Olive watched, and he spoke to her without turning. "I'll be here at five tomorrow to take you to the dance, Olive."

She smiled at his broad back as he continued working. "We'll be ready."

* * *

Olive hurried a cream-colored scoop neck blouse on her Singer Saturday morning. She had sewn tiny tucks down the front of the shirt and fitted it with pleats in the back. Olive had taken apart an out of style, burgundy taffeta dress from her trunk and made a full skirt to match. She taught Mary the basics of the sewing machine with a scrap of the material and now had a matching tie for her hair. Olive removed the dark red buttons from the bodice of the scrap dress and sewed them to her new blouse as Mary stitched on the machine. When the house was straightened and John and Mary dressed, Olive tried on her new outfit.

She stood and twirled in front of the mahogany framed oval mirror in her room and listened to the crinkle of the fabric as she moved. When the door opened, she said, "Come in, Theda. What do you think?"

"Are you wearing your hair down and loose like that? The tie will never hold all the curls," Theda said as she came to stand beside Olive in the front of the mirror.

"Yes," Olive replied and preened in the mirror. "I think it softens my features, and you don't notice my glasses so much."

Theda stood stiffly beside Olive, turned sideways and pulled her hand tightly down the front of her dress. "I've always felt I looked my best in black, don't you?"

Olive looked at the reflection of herself and Theda in the mirror. Her friend's stiff posture and tightly-pulled lips certainly did complement the austere look of her outfit. Theda's hair, black but for a few gray wisps, was pulled back into a small bun. Theda had beautiful skin, Olive knew, but not an inch other than her face and hands was revealed. Olive's head tilted at the picture she beheld in the mirror and could not believe the differences she saw. Granted, Olive had looked the same as her friend three months ago, but now, she could pass for Theda's daughter. My friend looks old, Olive thought and well... pulled tighter than a noose.

Olive heard the rumble of a wagon and Mary's shouts and hurried out of her room, straightening her hair and new dress, one last time. She stood in the doorway as Peg climbed out of the wagon in the pink flowered dress Olive had sewn. Luke wore his denim pants, and Olive noticed they were getting a bit short in the leg. Jacob climbed down carrying Mark, and Olive hurried down the steps to take the child.

* * *

Jacob watched Olive come to him and noticed the new outfit she wore. His heart raced when he saw her. Her waist was cinched in tight, and as he looked down at her as she talked softly to Mark, his eyes found the edge of her blouse and the cleavage peeking above it. He wanted to tell her she looked like a young girl, all fussed up and pretty. But Olive was no young girl, and she knew it.

"You look beautiful, Olive," he said.

"Thank you," she said and smiled broadly up at him. "I have something for you in the house, Jacob. Come in."

Jacob nodded to Theda, but the woman seemed intent on continuing their unspoken conflict. Her lips pulled together as she nodded back and held her head stiffly.

"Here, Jacob. I made this for you, and I've been meaning to give it to you," Olive said and handed him a newly-made shirt. "I... well... I've made everyone else something new to wear, and I realized I hadn't made you anything."

Jacob accepted the gift and watched Olive as she held her hands behind her back and waited for a reaction. He shook out the shirt, gray and black plaid soft flannel and held it up. "Thank you, Olive." He looked closely at the double-stitched cuffs and patch pocket and knew she had spent some time making it.

"I mean... well... you helped move me here and turned over my garden and all, and I wanted to repay you," Olive said, flushed.

"No thanks necessary, but I appreciate the gift anyway," Jacob said and smiled.

"Well, then, children, I guess we're ready to go," Olive said.

"Wait a second, here," Jacob said and began to unbutton his homespun shirt. "Everyone else is wearing new duds. I think I'll wear mine."

* * *

Olive could not tear her eyes from him as he slowly pulled his shirt from his pants. She knew her face colored as she watched the material slide from Jacob's thick arms, revealing a solid, muscled chest, more intimidating, more enticing than her dreams of him. Olive swallowed and felt hot and unable to catch her breath. She felt as if every eye in the room was watching her. But the children were busy looking at John's marbles, but Theda's eyes were as big as half dollars. Olive watched her friend stare at the only male chest she had ever seen. Olive cleared her throat. Theda's head snapped around, and her face colored.

"Come along children. Let's get in the wagon," Theda said. She primly swept past Jacob and said, "There are rooms with doors Mr. Butler. Changing clothes is usually done behind them."

Jacob rolled his eyes as he looked over at Olive. He held his arm out stiffly, and her shoulders dropped with a sigh as she curled her hand around his forearm.

* * *

The dance was held in the same barn as the last, and when they finally arrived, Olive hailed Flo and Beth and introduced Theda.

"Pleased to meet you, Theda," Beth said.

Flo stared unashamedly at Theda and Olive. "My God, Olive, you've changed. You looked just like Theda here when you first came."

Beth and Olive exchanged embarrassed glances.

"I understand what you mean, Mrs. Williams," Theda said and nodded. "I told Olive she had best start wearing her bonnet again, and this loose fashion she's taken to wearing her hair just won't do. Pieces come loose from the ribbon, and her hair, well, looks slovenly." Theda turned to Olive and nodded.

"Oh, yes, well," Flo stuttered.

"Your outfit is beautiful," Beth gushed to Olive. "I bought fabric last week, and I was hoping I could come to your house and use your new sewing machine."

Olive smiled and looked down at herself. "Anytime, Beth. I'd love to help you. What are you making?"

"Some new shirts for Jack and a dress for myself. I'll see

when I'm done, what's left over to use for the children."

"I doubt Mrs. Steele will want a neckline as low as the one on this new blouse of yours, Olive. Maybe we can piece a pattern from one of my dresses before I leave," Theda said.

"Oh, Theda, the neckline on this blouse is hardly revealing," Olive said.

Theda's cheeks receded as she slowly gave the front of Olive's dress a look. "What do you think, Mrs. Williams?" Theda leaned in conspiratorially and whispered, "One can almost see the tops of her bosom."

The corner's of Flo William's mouth turned down as she peaked over the top of Olive's blouse. "I don't think so Miss Patterson. And, anyway, if a man that looked like Jacob Butler was hot on my trail, I might have done away with another inch or two of that blouse."

Theda's eyes widened, and Olive turned to her. "Flo is teasing you, Theda. Come on. Let's get something to drink."

The children were playing games with other youngsters, and Olive's eyes were drawn to Jacob as he stood talking to other men and holding Mark. He winked at her, and her eyes did not leave his face as she followed Theda to the table for refreshments. Until she ran square into the sheriff.

"Oh, Sheriff, pardon me," Olive said.

"The fault is mine," the sheriff replied. His eyes slowly perused Olive's form and as he met her eyes, his jowls trembled, and he held his hat over his heart. "Miss Wilkins, Olive, you are as pretty as a picture. Not a woman here holds a candle to you."

Olive smiled softly but beheld in the sheriff's eyes what she had felt in her own heart many times before. His hound-dog face pleaded for a word of encouragement or interest. "That's very kind of you, Sheriff. Theda, you remember the sheriff, don't you?"

The sheriff's face snapped from his prolonged revelry of

Olive when Theda spoke. "Well, of course, Olive. He was kind enough to drive me to your house. Sheriff."

Theda nodded and stretched her lips into what resembled a smile. Olive knew this was Theda's stab at coquetry, but the attempt only managed to make her lips disappear and her nose wrinkle unattractively.

"We're on our way for some punch, Sheriff. Would you care to join us?" Olive asked.

"Certainly, ladies," the sheriff said and held an arm up to each woman.

Olive smiled and hooked her arm in the sheriff's and nodded to folks as they passed. She glanced over her punch, around Theda's back and over her glasses for Jacob and still managed to continue a reasonably intelligent conversation with the sheriff and Theda, nodding where necessary and grimacing when she thought appropriate.

When the fiddler started in a fast clip, Olive watched the dancers begin to take the floor, and she smiled at being part of the gaiety.

"What lively music," Theda said and smiled at the sheriff.

Olive watched his eyes dart as he toyed with Theda's comment. He glanced from one woman to the other, nervously, when Theda spoke up again.

"I haven't heard "Turkey in the Straw" for years."

Chivalry won out as he turned to Theda resignedly. "Miss Patterson, would you care to dance?"

Theda's eyes widened, and she gave Olive a short nod and smile. "How lovely, of course, Sheriff. I would be honored."

Theda's thin neck seemed to be pulling out of her collar as she held her head high and walked out into the crowd of dancers, on the arm of the sheriff. Olive watched the dancers and tapped her toe in rhythm to the music. She had lost sight of Jacob and searched in the crowd of dancers for him. Olive found him in the midst of a bevy of young tittering women, and her shoulders dropped as he met her eye. He leaned close to a particularly attractive redhead and whispered in her ear. The young girl beamed a smile up to him and accepted Mark into her arms.

Olive watched as Jacob turned her way and slowly made his way through the crowded barn. Their eyes parted only when Jacob was out of her view, and her breath came in shallow gasps. Olive stood still, warming from her stomach to her ears as she felt the seduction of the closing gap between them. Pulled, yet patient, fearful and fascinated, clinging to the lure of Jacob approaching her. He stopped once, drawn into a conversation, but his eyes never left Olive's face. This dance they stepped to was powerful, and she waited, as a maiden would have, watching a man come to claim her. By the time he stood close to her, Olive feared she would faint, she had held her breath so long. The fiddler began a new song, slower than the last, and Olive swallowed as Jacob's eyes bored into her.

"Dance with me, Olive."

A shrill sigh escaped her lips as he put his hand at the small of her back and directed her into the dancers.

When she was in his arms, moving through the steps, she watched other dancers to avoid meeting Jacob's stare. *One look, she thought, and I will pitch over from the sheer intensity that Jacob's gaze held.*

"What's the matter, Olive? Did you have your heart set on two-stepping with the sheriff?" he asked.

She grinned and tilted her head shyly. "No, Jacob."

"Then what is it?"

"Nothing," she said and nodded to Flo as she passed.

"Look at me, Olive," he said.

Olive's head turned slowly, and the carnal look in Jacob's eyes made her breasts heavy and her knees come undone. But once latched, their locked eyes held. Her lips were dry, and her heart pounded in her ears as she leaned, soft-boned into Jacob's arms and chest. His thumb moved slowly over her palm in an erotic rhythm that mimicked a touch she sought but did not understand.

This feeling, this want, has brought kings to their knees and shattered nations, Olive thought. *Men have walked away from fortunes and power through the years for this heady feeling. For what could be more powerful or irresistible than this magnet, this undeniable force between a man and a woman.* She shook her head softly in fear at what she would do or become to have Jacob's hands on her. Always.

* * *

This woman, his woman he thought increasingly, made his heart pound and stirred to life the bothersome want in his groin. "I smell lilacs," he whispered.

"My talc," Olive whispered.

Jacob's gaze dropped, and he pictured Olive as she dusted the powder over the already white flesh of her breasts. His eyes shot back to her face, and one side of his lip lifted in a feral growl. He knew townsfolk and friends stared and smirked at their slow grind, and he met staring eyes with a cautionary glare. When he saw the sheriff, watching them, Jacob regarded him with a proprietary look and pulled Olive closer still. The dance ended, and Jacob pulled Olive close and kissed her forehead softly. Her eyes closed as his lips touched her. His hand did not release hers until they came to the young, redheaded girl holding Mark.

Jacob watched Olive take Mark with a smile and the little boy calm in her arms. He wondered if Olive were too old to have children. He hoped not. He would solve this ache he felt when they slept on the same sheets. When he watched Olive move under him and saw her stomach grow from their mating. That mark on a woman that proclaims to anyone near that she was in her man's bed and took his force and that she was, unequivocally, his.

And Jacob relaxed with the wisdom of his decision. He would marry Olive. She would raise his children, and he would take care of her. This would solve the children's misery without her and the growing ache in his groin. Best for everyone, he thought and nodded with surety.

* * *

Olive's face was flushed, and she watched Jacob as he tilted his head in confusion, turning to her moments later with a broad smile.

Jacob stayed close to Olive for the rest of the dance. His hand would touch her elbow when someone approached, and Olive reeled from the intake of breath the connection brought. The sheriff eyed them, and Olive glanced up at Jacob as a sly, slow smirk formed on his lips. His head tilted at the man in challenge and Olive looked nervously away. Jacob was different. Suddenly different and... settled. As if he had worked through some long-standing argument with himself and come to a conclusion. Olive shrugged off the thought and enjoyed his attentions. She talked with Flo and Beth and heard Theda's shrill laughter for the sheriff.

When the dance ended, Olive and Jacob gathered the children and said their good nights. Theda nearly moaned when Olive told her they must get the children home. The ride home was a perfect cool foil to the heat of the day, and Olive admitted to herself, she had never been as happy. The children laughed and sang songs Theda taught them. Theda gushed endlessly about the pleasant town Olive had chosen and the wonderful people who lived here. Olive watched Theda breathe heavily and sigh and look out over the darkened landscape. She knew Theda was overwhelmed as she had been with the attentions of a man and the diversions life away from Church Street brought. If she were like Olive, she was, at this minute reliving every moment of her dance with the sheriff. Because Olive could not stop herself from drifting to Jacob and the feel of his hands on her as they danced.

Jacob winked at Olive as Theda repeated for the fourth time what a gentleman the sheriff was. She shook her head at him but it did not stop Jacob from asking, "So did you like two-stepping with the sheriff, Miss Patterson?"

To Olive's shock, Theda giggled into the night air.

"Really, Mr. Butler, what a thing to ask," Theda said.

The children's excitement and shouting, slowly wound down until Olive heard the chirp of the crickets in the distance. Jacob called softly to the horses, and Theda stared dreamily to some unknown spot. Olive breathed deeply of the night smells in farm country and thanked God for all that had happened. John and Mary liked the house she had built, and Olive hoped they felt the roots of the land twine to their hearts as she did. Her dearest friend Theda had ventured here, and Olive knew what a sacrifice it was.

Jacob, to Olive, seemed to be at peace as well. Whatever grief hung from his heart he seemed to be making peace with. He smiled more, and he looked her way often, and she hoped she could be as good a friend to him as he was to her.

Her house came into view vaguely in the twilight, and Olive's spirits lifted further still. Her home. How all of the tragedies thrown her way had brought confidence to Olive, she did not understand. But she knew she could do this. This life of farming and working and raising children and making her own decisions. She smiled to herself. She, Olive Wilkins, could do this. Up until now, this joy would only come to Olive when she read a book and lived through the author's words, another's life. She did not need to live through Charles Dickens and Jane Austen any more, though. She had her own life, of her own design and whatever was thrown in her path, she knew, she would work around or over or under. On her own. For herself and John and Mary.

When Jacob whoaed the horses, Olive stood up in the wagon.

"Wait, Olive," he said. "Let me help you." He took Mark from her arms and reached his hand up to take hers.

"Thank you, Jacob. I had a wonderful evening," she said.

"Me, too. Here, hold Mark. I'll carry John into bed."

Theda held Mary's hand, and Olive kissed Peg and Luke as they slept in the back of the wagon.

Jacob pulled the door closed to John's room and nodded to Theda. "Good night, Miss Patterson. Olive, do you want me to drive the two of you to the train station tomorrow?"

Olive's shoulders dropped as she realized Theda's visit was coming to an end. "No, Jacob. Would you mind if I brought the children to your house while I take Theda?"

"Not at all." He gave Theda a nod and turned back to Olive. As naturally as Olive imagined he drew breath, he leaned down and kissed her cheek. "I'll see you tomorrow then."

Chapter Ten

OLIVE BOILED WATER FOR TEA ONCE THE children were in bed and turned when Theda came into the kitchen in her nightclothes.

"You love him, don't you?" Theda asked.

Olive's head tilted, and she dropped her eyes.

"Don't be embarrassed, Olive," Theda said. "You feel about Jacob what we have only dreamt about all these years."

"I do love him, Theda."

Theda pulled the chair out and poured a cup of tea. She sighed and sipped and looked at Olive. "He's a good man."

Olive smiled and nodded, holding back a whimper. She knew she didn't need Theda's approval but once spoken, realized how important Theda's opinion was to her.

"He is a good man. Unfortunately," Olive said and closed her eyes, "he still loves his wife. A charming attribute, Theda. One we value. Loyalty."

"But he cares for you. It is clear." Theda turned her head. "And more importantly, he sees past your age and looks to the wonderful person you are. Who you are. He admires in you all those things we've cherished and clung to all these years. There could be no greater compliment."

They sat silently until Olive looked at Theda with a wise smile. "I know now what it feels like to love. And to live. Beyond the reaches of parents and the boundaries of spinsterhood. I won't go back, Theda."

Theda nodded. "And you shouldn't. You've lived more in three months than we did combined for sixty-some years. You must promise to write and tell me every detail. Soar, Olive, and I will watch."

* * *

A steady drizzle set the mood for Theda's departure. Theda kissed Mary's cheek and John's head before they jumped from the wagon at Jacob's. The two women rode silently, much left unsaid, mostly unnecessary. They sat together on a bench awaiting the train's arrival, and Olive could not look at Theda for fear of crying foolishly. Olive wanted to beg Theda to stay, start her own life, but she knew it would not be so.

"I... I envy you," Theda said, and Olive watched a tear run slowly down her friend's cheek. Their eyes met, and Olive nodded.

"You'll give your mother a kiss from me and tell all the neighbors hello," Olive said and picked up Theda's hand, suddenly now desperate for more time as she heard the blow of the train coming in the distance.

"Yes, of course. And you'll bring John and Mary to visit soon," Theda said as fat tears rolled down her face.

Olive nodded and cried, and they stood together as the train rumbled to a halt. The conductor stepped down and placed a wooden step on the platform. Theda bent down to pick up her bag.

"We will see each other soon." Theda said as she took a step to the train and then stopped, dropped her bags and turned to hug Olive. "I will be long past my prime when I am free, Olive. But you, you can live out all of our dreams," she whispered in Olive's hair.

"I can't imagine you past your prime, Theda Patterson. And there is someone out there for you. Don't doubt it," Olive said and held back yet another sob.

Theda dried her eyes and stepped up into the train. Olive walked down the platform as Theda found a seat, and the woman lifted her hand in a wave. Olive waved back and pressed into memory, like flowers held between the pages of a book, the face of her lifelong friend. They both knew they might never see each other again. This could be a final goodbye, and tears streamed down Olive's face as Theda stared at her, as well, and remembered.

* * *

Olive's ride to Jacob's was wet and depressing. When she stepped into Jacob's house, he looked at her and stood. He came around the table and held her arms.

"Theda made the train?" he asked.

"Oh, Jacob," she cried and buried her face in his chest. He patted her back and rubbed her arms, and Olive cried until she had no more tears.

"You'll see her again," he said softly.

"Perhaps," Olive said. "Perhaps not."

The children watched from the table as Jacob held Olive.

"Why are you sad, Aunt Olive?" Peg asked.

Olive dried her face and sat down beside Peg. "My friend, Miss Patterson, left on the train today. I will miss her."

"Oh," Peg said and leaned close to Olive. "Like I miss you."

Olive nodded and smiled.

"I know what will make you feel better. Start the new book.

The one about the boy on the Mississippi. Please," Luke begged.

Olive laughed as she looked from one face to another. *They can lift my heart as nothing else in this world,* Olive thought. Until she felt Jacob's hand on her shoulder.

"Maybe Olive doesn't feel like reading, children," Jacob said.

She looked up to him and smiled. "No, Jacob, I think they're right. Where is the new book?"

* * *

"Why are you wearing your go-to-church clothes, Daddy?" Luke asked. "I thought we were going to work in the barn today."

"Come on, children," Jacob said.

Luke and Peg watched their father race frantically around the house. He stopped to look at his reflection in the cracked mirror where he shaved. Jacob touched his cheek where he had cut himself and ran his hand through his wet dark hair. He pulled his neck up and out of the stiff, tight collar of his best white shirt and pulled straight the cuff over his wrists. "Mrs. Steele is going to watch you for awhile today. Are you ready?"

"Where are you going?" Peg asked.

Jacob hemmed and hawed. "To see Olive."

Both faces lit up, and the children raced for their shoes.

"Why didn't you tell us we were going to see Aunt Olive?" Luke asked.

"You two are going to the Steele's house today. Not Olive's."

Both shoulders dropped in disappointment and Peg asked, "Why?"

Jacob was afraid of this. He decided to ask Olive to marry him on this Wednesday in July, he wasn't sure why, but he had decided on that day and had asked Beth to watch the children.

He knew Olive would want to tell all the children together of their plans and so was at a loss as what to say to Luke and Peg.

"Olive and I have business in town," he told the children.

"Where are Mary and John going? Are they going with you?" Luke said.

"Why can't we go, too?" Peg cried.

"No. John and Mary are not going with us to town. You haven't seen Bess and Jack for a while. You'll have fun there."

"Are John and Mary going to see Bess and Jack, too?" Peg asked and twisted her hand in her skirt.

"Listen, children," Jacob said and knelt down. "Olive and I have grown-up business to talk about." He held his hand up to Peg's mouth before her protest could begin. "I don't leave you behind very often. But I must today."

"Is that why you're all dressed up and pretty?" Peg smiled and touched the collar of his shirt.

Jacob looked down at himself, hoping he didn't look pretty, but agreed, regardless. "Yes, Peg. That's why I'm dressed up."

Jack Steele's wagon rumbled into the yard, and Jacob stepped on the porch to greet him. Mary and John were in the wagon.

"Beth told me to pick up Olive's kids first," Jack said and grinned. "Give you some time alone."

Jacob nodded and his stomach rolled. His decision, although right, was causing his palms to sweat. Luke and Peg jumped up into the wagon, and Mary reached down for Mark. Mary stared at Jacob and he felt uncomfortable with the piercing look she gave him. "Have a good time, children. I'll be out in a bit to fetch you."

Jack Steele slapped the horse's rump with the reins and called over his shoulder. "Take your time, Jacob."

The rumbling of the wagon trailed off in the distance, and Jacob found himself alone and still standing in front of his house. He nodded to himself and swallowed and headed to the barn. The day was as beautiful as he had hoped, thinking he and Olive would sit on the porch when he asked her. Ask her to marry him. Once riding, he sighed and spoke aloud to the crisp blue of the sky and the bubbles of white clouds above him.

"Margaret, it's time."

He knew his Margaret would be smiling, and he gave himself one long last thought of her face. Jacob wouldn't let a new marriage be overshadowed by the haunt of a dead wife and vowed to himself to focus on Olive and their new life. Margaret's sweet smiling face came to view and closed his throat.

"It's not that I would ever forget you, Margaret, but I owe it to Olive to think of her now." Jacob knew his heart was at peace with this decision, but he felt oddly obligated to say the words aloud and hoped Margaret could hear the wisdom of his decision.

Olive's house came into view, and all other thoughts left Jacob as he imagined himself asking for her hand. He cleared his throat and practiced. "Olive, I think it would be best if we married." No, no. "Olive, we care for each other and get along and I think we should marry." Better. "Olive, I can't wait to see you naked." His eyes opened wide, and he watched Olive step out onto her porch and shade her eyes.

"Jacob, what a surprise. Jack Steele just stopped by and took the children with him. Said Beth had plans for them all day. Where are Luke and Peg and Mark?"

"With the Steeles," Jacob said as his voice hit a high note.

"Well, isn't that nice. The children will love it." Olive's head tilted. "Are you going to town?"

"No."

"Oh," Olive said and cocked her head. "You're all dressed up."

Jacob nodded.

"Would you like some tea?"

Jacob followed Olive into the house and watched as she poured two glasses. "Sit down, Jacob."

"If it's alright with you, let's sit on the porch a spell," Jacob said.

Olive smiled and led the way. She seated herself on the wicker settee. Jacob squeezed himself in beside her and she moved her skirts and looked at him quizzically.

"Jacob, is something wrong?" Olive asked.

"No." He sat his tea on the porch, suddenly feeling like an oversized bull, dressed for church. He laid his hands flat on his knees and looked out into the yard. "How's the garden?"

"Fine," Olive replied. "I may actually have something to can. Probably just beets, but it's a start."

"That's good," Jacob said. "My crops look like they'll do better than last year."

Olive's smiled. "That's nice."

"Prices are going up for corn, too."

Olive smiled vaguely.

"That means I'll get more money for my crop," Jacob said and stole a glance at Olive.

"I'm glad for you, Jacob," Olive replied and laid her hand on his. "I know how you worry. And farming my land next year will make it even better."

Jacob hemmed and hawed and turned to Olive, sat back in his seat and sighed, thinking what a fool he was making of himself. "Maybe we ought to think about working the two farms as one," he said and turned to her.

Olive's brows lifted and the corners of her mouth dropped. "I don't see any harm in thinking of the two farms that way. If it would be easier for you."

Jacob turned in his seat and regarded her intensely. "I don't mean thinking about the farms as one. I mean the farms being one."

Olive shook her head softly. "I'm not sure I understand, Jacob. As long as I own my property and you own yours, they're not one."

Jacob looked down at her hands lying in her lap. He picked one up slowly and kissed her fingertips. When he lifted his head, he met Olive's bewildered stare. "They'd be one if we married."

Olive's eyes opened wide. She shook her head as if to clear a strange dream and looked up at Jacob. "What did you say?"

Jacob stood from the settee and awkwardly knelt down on one knee in front of Olive. "I've been thinking a lot about this Olive. I think we should marry." He watched Olive's face cloud with confusion and a sweet joy come to her face. Encouraged, he continued. "We'll have a large farm together and be able to make a life for ourselves with the profits. The children miss you, and so do I. It will be the best for everyone."

Olive's lip twitched. "It sounds like you'd rather have influenza than small pox. The better of two bad choices."

Jacob's head shook and he hurried to correct a rather uninspiring proposal, consisting of crop prices and disease. "No, no. It's not like that at all, Olive. I want to marry you. I want to take care of you and help you, and I want you to raise my children."

"And?"

Jacob swallowed; knowing he was out of his depths and had no clue as to what Olive wanted him to say. "My ma was right, Olive. It's time I remarried. And I can't think of another woman I'd want to live with and raise my children. Or bed."

Olive's eyes widened. "So, you get a farm, a mother for your children and a warm body in your bed. What do I get?"

Jacob stood and ran his hand though his hair. "Now wait a second, Olive. You're twisting my words. Tell me what you want me to say, and I will. I want to marry you."

* * *

Olive's lip trembled and every fear she had known, she swallowed and looked up to Jacob, her heart on her face. She sat silently staring, finally voicing in a whisper what she wanted to hear. "Love, Jacob. I want to hear that you love me. Because... because I love you more than life itself." She watched his eyes widen, and she plunged ahead. "I won't settle for less from you, Jacob. Not anymore."

Jacob put his hands on his hips and turned to survey the horizon. "I don't think I can say that, Olive. Not right now. Maybe someday."

Tears poured from Olive's eyes. Would she risk a life alone, without Jacob, or accept what he offered? But how could she accept less than what she had only recently come to understand. Six months ago she would have turned down Jacob's proposal in fear of the new. Would she turn him down now, for fear of not having all she had hoped for? She swallowed, knowing there was no turning back. Her life had gone from a blank and unturned page to a richly-written world and she was convinced that a story of love was not written by one heart, but two.

"I love you, Jacob. I love your children. But... but that doesn't mean I will give up a life I've just begun, unless you love me as well."

Jacob turned back to her. "We're suited, Olive. Isn't that enough? I like having you in my home, and I think you like being with me. I wouldn't have asked you to marry me if I didn't care for you. Respect you. The children miss each other, and Mary and John could certainly use a father in their lives. People marry all the time for less reasons than that."

Olive stood and went to Jacob and held his hand. "People marry for many foolish reasons. I don't believe I can. You are the handsomest, kindest, gentlest man I've ever met." Her head dropped. "I don't think there is another man on the face of this earth I would want to spend my life with, but I won't be cheated. I've come too far."

"So you would rather be alone?" Jacob asked.

"No," Olive cried but stiffened her back. "Jacob, don't you see. What I was before, scared and blind, I'm not anymore. I have a new home in a new town and a chance to make a good life with John and Mary. I want what my parents had. They loved each other so dearly. And I deserve it. And you deserve to marry a woman you love."

The air was silent and thick as Jacob and Olive understood each other's denials, and their disappointment surrounded them like the humid July air. Olive sat and stared at the landscape unmoving, her chin and heart in her hand. Jacob took a step, stopped and brought his hands to his hips and shook his head.

"I thought this would make you happy, Olive. I thought, well, I thought," Jacob turned quickly and tilted his head. "Does this have anything to do with the sheriff?"

She turned her regard slowly. "Not a thing."

He nodded and turned his hat in his hand. "I guess I better be going then."

Olive's lip trembled. Her hope of a loving pronouncement dashed. "Fine, Jacob." As Jacob climbed into the wagon, Olive hurried into the house, unable to watch his retreating figure as he pulled out of her yard and away from her heart. She awoke, hours later in the descending light of the evening, face down on her bed. Eyes swollen and dry from the hour of crying before sleep rescued her from reality. But the consequences of her decision trickled back through her mind as she rolled onto her back and stared at the ceiling. Jacob had come to her, nervous, asking for her hand in marriage. Shaven and shorn and dressed with care for the task of admitting he needed a wife and that she was the candidate.

She should be flattered. She was. She should be grateful that a man as wonderful as he had deemed her worthy of raising his children. She was. *He wants to sleep with me,* she thought, *he admitted it.* He wants to care for the children and for me. Then why was her heart torn in two and of her own making? Because I refuse, Olive said aloud and sat up, refuse to be or have anything less than what I deserve. Olive headed to the kitchen, calming herself with her own declarations. More confident in her decision and herself than ever. But as she passed the screen door and the breeze rattled through it, her eyes were drawn to the wicker settee and the vision of Jacob kneeling before her brought fresh tears and regrets.

* * *

Jacob's ride home let Olive's refusal sink deeply. His head reeled. He had counted on a shy, happy yes. Not once had he considered she might refuse him. When she had first asked him to declare love, Jacob had not realized that she would not accept less. She had told his mother that she wouldn't marry for less than love. Why did he think a few months would have changed her mind?

Even as he stepped from her porch, he was sure she would come to him. Accept him for what he was and what he had to give. But the slam of the screen door reverberated through his head and made Olive's refusal clear.

Fine, then, he thought, *if she needs some fairy tale let her read one from a book.* I'm no knight in shining armor, no stupid sap with dog eyes and love words. I'm a man and she's a woman, and we care about each other. That should be enough. It is enough, damn her. So what if I can't mouth some silly words, they'd be a lie. Would Olive want me to lie? "Hell no," he shouted aloud as he let his anger consume him. Jacob had himself riled and aching for a fight, better suited for that emotion than the sting his pride took and the hurt his heart felt. He managed to convince himself that her refusal was for the best if she was going to be some lame, swooning girl waiting to hear the words. But his lip trembled, and he blinked as he heard in his head her words. Her declaration. For him. 'I love you, Jacob.'

He jumped down from the wagon when he reached Beth and Jack's house and the children begged to stay a few more minutes. Jacob stepped into the kitchen.

Beth turned from the sink with a brilliant smile and asked, "Jacob, where's Olive? What did she say? Did she cry? Did you kneel down?"

Jacob took off his hat and saw Jack eyeing him. "What happened, Jacob? You sure don't look like a man who just asked a woman to marry him."

Beth's face dropped, and Jacob flopped down at one of the kitchen chairs. He tilted his head and tried to maintain a casual tone. "She said no. That's it. Probably for the best."

"She said no?" Beth repeated.

"Yeah, she said no. Anything cold to drink around here?" Jacob asked.

Beth narrowed her eyes. "I've got to check on the children. There's water in the pitcher."

Jack sat down at the table across from him and stared. Jacob poured his water and sat back down. "How's your mare doing now, Jack?" he asked.

"My mare's fine," Jack replied.

"Good," Jacob said and turned the water glass in his hand. "How's your corn coming in?"

Jack smirked a laugh. "Now I know why Beth and Olive think men are jackasses."

Jacob lifted his brow in response.

"What happened, Jacob?"

"She said no. As simple as that. She said no," Jacob said and stared out the window.

"No why, no reason, just no?" Jack said.

Jacob nodded. "Yup."

"Well, what did you say?" Jack asked.

Jacob shrugged. "I told her that I thought it would be best if we married. She didn't agree."

"Nothing else happened. You walked into her house, said I think it would be best if we married, she said no and you left," Jack quizzed.

"Pretty much," Jacob replied, nodding.

The two men sat silently and listened to Beth call to the children. "Something's missing. Something you're not telling me," Jack said finally.

Jacob stood and ran his hand through his hair. "You're like an old woman. Prying and wanting to hear every detail."

"Yeah, and you're acting like a stubborn fool. Something else happened, something you're either embarrassed or mad about. Don't try and fool me. I've known you too long." Jack waited patiently, hands folded on the table. "Get on out of here. I'll get John and Mary home," Jack said as he walked to the door.

Jacob waited until he heard the turn of the knob in Jack's hand. "She wanted me to tell her I love her."

Jack turned slowly and said to Jacob's back, "So?"

"Well, I didn't want to lie. I didn't say it, so she refused."

Jack shook his head as he came back around the table and waited until Jacob faced him. "You didn't tell her you loved her?"

Jacob tilted his head and looked away. "I told her maybe someday I could say it. But not now."

Jack sat down slowly and whistled. "You are a jackass. You don't think you love her?"

"Hell, I don't know. How the hell are you supposed to

know?" Jacob said.

Jack's mouth dropped and he held his hands up in the air and shouted, "What a damn fool thing to say. I mean do your palms sweat when you're around her and does your heart race? Do ya feel like you're going to melt into the ground when she smiles at you? For God's sake, Jacob, how did it feel with Margaret? You were in love with her."

Jacob's head snapped to Jack's face. His lip twitched and he snarled at his friend. "And she's gone. Margaret's gone." Jacob stood and walked to the sink. He blew breath in a heavy sigh and continued, "I don't think I could take it again."

"Take what, Jacob? What are you talking about?"

Jacob turned and shouted, knowing Beth and the children would hear his every word, but unable to stop the pain. "I couldn't take it, Jack. If I love Olive and she dies, I couldn't do it again." His eyes glittered and Jack sat back in his chair as Jacob beat his fist on his chest. "I can't lose someone else. I didn't think I'd survive after Margaret died. I just worked and lived and tried not to feel. I can't do it again."

The air was silent, and Jack looked around the room. Everywhere but Jacob's face. He swallowed and digested the pain in his friend that he had yet to feel. The raw open wound of Jacob's loss was festering, and he was at a loss as to how to help.

Jacob turned to the door, placed his hat on his head, and nodded at Jack.

Jack reached out to touch Jacob's arm. "Just because you're afraid to love her, doesn't mean you don't."

Jacob's eyes revealed the pain he had kept hidden, buried from everyone. He nodded and went past Jack, resentful of the pity he saw on his friend's face.

The children sat quietly with Jacob on the ride home, and he was glad. Luke held Mark and Peg stole glances at her father. Jacob brushed the horse and stepped into his quiet household.

"Where's Peg?" he asked.

"Playing with her dolls in her room," Luke replied.

Jacob sat wearily down at the kitchen table and held his head in his hand. He had not wanted to reveal his private fears to Jack, but they bubbled out of his mouth before he had had a chance to think. He could not love Olive. The merciful God she often spoke of would snatch her away from him if he did. His head snapped up when Luke spoke.

"How's Aunt Olive?" his son asked.

"Fine, Luke. Just fine."

Luke inched towards him, head down and slowly pulled out a chair. "Did you get the big people's business decided?"

"What, son?"

"The big people's business. That's why you went over there, isn't it? Why Peg and I couldn't go?" Luke said.

Jacob sat back in his seat and grimaced. "Yeah, it's decided."

"Was it about farming Aunt Olive's land?"

"Something like that," Jacob replied.

Luke nodded, eyes downward. "Are you mad at us, Daddy?"

"No, Luke, I'm not mad at anyone."

The boy fiddled with his fingers and looked up slowly. "Are you sad then?"

Jacob closed his eyes, wishing for a few moments of silence and knowing he would not have it until he made some explanation. He leaned forward and folded his hands together, wishing Olive were here to explain a delicate adult subject to an eight-year-old.

"I asked Olive to marry me today." Jacob paused and faced Luke. "She said no."

"Why?" Luke asked.

"Well, it's hard to explain. When you're older, you'll

understand," Jacob said.

Luke sat quietly, and his eyes darted from his father's face to the table. "Doesn't she like us?"

Jacob shook his head quickly and covered his son's hand with his own. "No, no. Olive likes you and Peg and Mark, too. That's not it."

"Doesn't she like you?" Luke asked.

Jacob sat back in his chair, heaved a breath and spoke to no one in particular. "She told me today she loved me and you children."

"Then why won't she marry you?" Luke whispered.

Jacob knew then he was backed into a verbal corner. "That's the big peoples' part that you won't understand."

Luke watched his father for a few minutes then rose from the table. He pulled his shoes on and opened the door.

"Where you heading, Luke? I'm going to heat up some ham in a minute," Jacob said.

"I'm going to ask Aunt Olive why she won't marry us," Luke said.

Jacob jumped from his seat and whirled around. "No, Luke. That's not a good idea."

"Aunt Olive tells me big people stuff sometimes. Like why Momma died and why Mark is... Mark. She'll tell me so I can understand."

Jacob stared at Luke. "What did Olive tell you about Momma and Mark?"

Luke twisted his shirt nervously. "That, that, Mark was in Momma's belly too long and wouldn't come out. That Momma tried with all her might to get him out, but something went wrong. That it was nobody's fault. It just happened."

A lump lodged in Jacob's throat. "Why didn't you ask me, son? I would have told you."

Luke looked away. "I don't know. It makes you sad,

though."

"So you didn't ask because it makes me sad?"

Luke shrugged a reply. "It's alright, Daddy. I talk to Aunt Olive about Momma, or sometimes I talk to Momma when I hold my special pillow."

"Your special pillow?" Jacob repeated.

Luke smiled a lopsided grin. "Aunt Olive found a dress of Momma's and made pillow covers for Peg and me. I remember the dress. And when I hold the pillow and shut my eyes real tight, I can see Momma at the sink in that dress."

Jacob's lip trembled. His own children dealt with their grief better than he. He turned slowly back to his chair and sat, feeling old. A small hand touched his arm.

"It's alright, Daddy. I miss her, too. And see, Aunt Olive helped me with that so I figure she'll be able to tell me why she doesn't want to marry us," Luke said.

"Sit down, son." Jacob's grimaced as he tried to think of how he could explain to Luke the morning's disappointment. He turned to his son and said, "I loved your mother very much. I never had anything hurt as much as when she died. I don't think I'll ever love anyone like I loved your mother. And Olive feels that we should love each other if we were to marry."

Luke listened with rapt attention. He concentrated and pulled his lips to one side. "Well, since Aunt Olive said she loves you, it must be you that doesn't love her. And that's why she won't marry you?"

Jacob began to nod and heard a sniff from the bedroom curtain. Peg was peeking around the fabric and fat tears rolled down her cheeks. "Then tell her, Daddy. Tell her you love her. I want Aunt Olive to be my momma." Peg stepped through the curtain, clutching a pillow covered in fabric Jacob recognized. He held out his arms and Peg launched herself onto him and buried her face in his shirt. "Tell her," she whispered.

* * *

Mary looked suspiciously at Olive when she saw her Aunt's red and puffy eyes. "What did Jacob want this morning?"

Olive turned hurriedly from the child's knowing look. "Nothing."

"He sure was duded up for nothing then." Mary waited a while and watched Olive scrub dishes furiously at the sink. "What did he want?"

Olive flew past the child to the cupboard never meeting her eye. "I don't think what Jacob and I discussed is appropriate subject matter for you, that's all."

"I thought we were a family now. Talked about everything. I guess not."

Olive looked at Mary with stricken eyes. "We are a family, Mary. You and John and I."

Mary stared hard at Olive until she turned away. Olive busied herself at the sink, hoping Mary would concede and leave the room. But she never felt or heard the girl exit. Olive's hands clutched the edge of the sink, and she stared out the window as her shoulders dropped. "Jacob asked me to marry him today. I declined."

Mary whistled softly. "Why?"

Olive's head tilted. "He doesn't love me."

"So?"

"Mary," Olive said and turned from the sink. "I can't marry a man who doesn't love me. I couldn't live with myself. We all need our pride."

"What do you mean pride?" Mary asked.

Olive seated herself across the table from her niece. "Respect for ourselves, Mary. I am worthy of having a man, a husband, love me. I deserve it."

"Do you love him?" the girl asked.

Olive nodded. "Yes, I do."

Mary sat back in her chair with questions. "So you love him, but you won't marry him because he doesn't love you."

Olive looked out the window, chin in her hand and sat quietly with Mary. The girl rose, went to the door and turned back. "Don't worry Aunt Olive. You're better off without him. You'll see."

* * *

The weeks rolled by as August turned to September. The air was heavy, the ground dry, and the nights warm. Olive sewed, read to Mary and John, and missed Jacob and his family. Having rejected him, she lost his children as well and many days she found herself preoccupied with what they were doing while their father brought in the crops. Beth stopped by one afternoon with Bess and Jack Junior and Olive was thrilled for the company and curious about Jacob.

"How are you, Olive?" Beth asked when the children had ventured outside.

"I'm fine. The children keep me busy. It is different than life back on Church Street. There were always neighbors on their porch, and I talked to people at the library. It can be very quiet here."

"You mean lonely?" Beth asked.

Olive smiled. "Sometimes." She hemmed and hawed, but finally asked Beth what she was aching to know. "Have you seen Jacob and the children?"

"A little. This is a busy time of the year."

Olive swallowed. "How is he? How are the children?"

Beth shook her head. "Miserable. And as far as I'm concerned he deserves it."

Olive looked down at her hands. "I never wanted to hurt

him."

"Do you know what he told Jack?" Beth fumed.

"No," Olive said and shook her head.

"He couldn't love you because if you died he couldn't take it." Beth sat back in her chair and continued, "As if he doesn't love you. Just because he won't say it doesn't mean it isn't so."

"He thinks I'm going to die?" Olive asked.

"He's afraid something will happen to you. Like Margaret. You and I both know Olive, there are no guarantees in this world."

Olive sighed deeply. She had been afraid of this. It wasn't as though Jacob may grow to love her in time as she had hoped. He was afraid to love. They chatted awhile longer, but Olive was preoccupied with what Beth had told her and only half-listened.

"Come by early Saturday, then. Flo will be there. Bring anything you can from the garden, and we'll teach you to can," Beth said as she settled herself in the wagon seat.

"Alright, Beth. I'll be there," Olive replied.

Chapter Eleven

MARY AND JOHN WERE EXCITED TO SEE OTHER children and escape the boredom of the house. They piled their small collection of produce in the wagon and set off early before the heat of the day was oppressive. Olive peeled more vegetables than she thought was humanly possible, and by noontime she and Flo and Beth were dripping in the sweltering kitchen. Over the stove, boiling jars and lids and beets and tomatoes, the three women labored. But the time passed quickly with company and female chatter. The children played in the creek, and Olive envied them.

"Come on, Ma. Come see the toad that Mary caught," Jack Junior shouted through the door.

The woman decided a walk out of the hot kitchen was deserved and wound through the trees in the cooler air until they came to the stream. The children were huddled around Mary in the middle of the low water.

"Come see," Flo's daughter Sue said.

Flo plopped down on the moss and undid her shoes. As she rolled her thick stockings down over her legs, she looked up to Beth and Olive. "Nobody's around. I'm cooling off."

Beth and Olive exchanged glances and promptly stripped

their shoes and stockings as well. Olive held her skirt up and stood in the moving water. "This is heaven," she called to the other women.

"Well, this is a sight to behold," a masculine voice from the bank called. The three women's head snapped around to see Jack, Bill, and Jacob, holding Mark at the edge of the water.

Jacob and Olive's eyes met for the first time since the day of the proposal. Olive's breath caught on a hitch, and although Jacob's masculine presence compelled her, she knew she wanted his heart. He looked away, and Olive heard Peg and Luke call to her. The children, barefoot already, raced to her through the water.

"Aunt Olive," Peg cried and clung to her skirts.

Luke attached himself to her other side, and she knew then how sorely she missed these children. Peg showed her a skinned knee, and Luke told her he hadn't been sleeping so well. She kissed their heads and pulled the children to the edge of the water. "Let me hold Mark, Jacob."

Their hands touched with the passing child, and their eyes met yet again. Olive looked away first to coo and cuddle the infant. He turned into her and sighed. Luke and Peg were soon playing with the other children in the creek, and Olive reached down for her shoes.

"I'll get them, Olive," Jacob said.

"Thank you," she said and looked up to him. The other adults drifted away to the house, and they stood staring at each other. "I know things are awkward between us, Jacob. But please bring the children by. I miss them desperately."

Jacob nodded. "They miss you. I do, too."

Olive's lashes dropped. "I miss you as well, Jacob." As they walked slowly through the trees, Olive felt at peace and whole with Jacob near. She donned a brave face knowing that completeness would be gone with their parting.

Peg and Luke sat on her lap or hung on her skirts through the casual, stand-up supper, Beth had prepared. Jacob stayed to the other end of the kitchen, showing John how to whittle. Olive caught herself staring at the only man she knew she would ever love. When their eyes met, Jacob turned quickly away, obviously uncomfortable with their proximity. Olive swallowed the pain of the insult and wondered if she would regret telling Jacob she loved him.

Luke whispered in her ear as the men went to ready the wagons. "Daddy told me that you love us, but you won't marry us 'cause he doesn't love you."

Olive's eyes widened. She pulled Luke into her lap and leaned close to his ear. "Your daddy's right. I love you all very much."

"I showed Daddy my special pillow. It made him sad. I think he misses Momma too much."

"I think you're right," Olive said and gripped the boy tighter as he relaxed against her.

"Aunt Olive?" Luke said as he played with the buttons on Olive's blouse.

"Yes, Luke?" she said and smiled and turned her head to face him.

"I love you."

"Oh, Luke, I love you and your sister and brother very much."

"Daddy, too?"

Olive's eyes closed. "Yes, Luke. I love your father, too."

* * *

Jacob watched Olive whisper to Luke as he stood at the door. She looked as beautiful today as Jacob had ever seen her. Even soaked with sweat and red-faced, Olive appealed to him on every level. Her hair had clung to her face in the heat of the kitchen and now curled in ringlets around her face. When Jack had told a silly story about Reverend McGrath, Olive's eyes lit up, and her smile was dazzling. *If only she was smiling at me*, he thought. The children had hung at her side and to her every word, all day. Now, Luke was on her lap as Olive held Mark in the other arm, and Peg sat by her feet. His thoughts were interrupted as Mary approached.

"Aunt Olive told me you asked her to marry you."

Jacob nodded.

Mary smirked. "She turned you down."

He nodded again.

"I told her she was better off without a man," Mary said.

"Is that right?" Jacob said.

"Don't ya have nothing to say for yourself?" Mary asked and narrowed her eyes. "Still in love with your dead wife?"

Jacob held his temper as Mary baited him. "Feeling bad, grief about my Margaret, hasn't been easy."

"Loved your wife, huh? Had a great life with her, like in one of Aunt Olive's books?" Mary leaned close and snarled. "You were good to John and me, taking us in like you did, but I think you're stupid. I'm only ten, but I'm smart enough to know that my ma wasn't a very good ma. But I still didn't want to watch her get her throat slit. I'm getting over it, and even if I never told her, I know I loved my ma and my Aunt Olive, too."

Jacob watched the tears form in Mary's eyes and felt small and selfish beside the young girl. She had a bad, a horrible life but still managed to get past it, and he knew that was the message she was sending. He looked away, and Mary snorted and left him in his thoughts.

* * *

Over the next month's back-breaking work of getting the crops in, stored and sold, Jacob's house grew somber. Luke was called on to help in the fields, and Peg was often left alone with Mark. Jacob worried, knowing the situation was grim but was at a loss as to how else to solve it. Worse yet, Peg rarely smiled, and Luke became increasingly sullen. Clean clothes and baths and hot meals went by the wayside as Jacob struggled to drag himself back home every nightfall and deal with his family. The only high point in his dismal day was that corn prices, were holding and his land had yielded a bountiful product.

Luke walked to Olive's early in the morning one day to ask if John could help in the fields. "Daddy wouldn't want me to ask, but we need the help."

Olive looked at Luke standing on her porch in the early morning gray light and was shocked at the appearance of the boy. "We'll get him up. Luke, you look so thin and tired. Are you feeling alright?"

The boy's head hung. "Just a lot of work this time of year."

"Can't Mr. Williams or Mr. Steele help your father?" Olive asked.

"They have some, but they have their own fields to do," Luke said.

"Who's watching Mark?"

"Peg," the boy replied.

Olive's shoulders dropped. She called to Mary and John to get up and dressed and heated oatmeal for Luke for breakfast. She stacked canned goods and a ham on the table while the boy ate and John and Mary got dressed.

"Where we going in such an all-fired hurry this early?" Mary asked.

"Jacob is trying to get his crops in, and Peg and Mark are home alone. I have a feeling they haven't been eating very well either," Olive whispered to Mary.

"So what are we going to do?" Mary asked and scowled.

"Help, Mary. It's what neighbors do."

The girl rolled her eyes and muttered under her breath. Olive ignored her and loaded the wagon while Luke and John hitched the horse. "Come on, children," she shouted as Mary shuffled along.

When she arrived and saw the state of Jacob's home, she was shocked. Peg burst into tears and clung to her dress when she saw Olive. The girl had burnt her finger on the stove attempting to heat mush for Mark. Olive kissed her and the thumb and helped Peg into clean clothes. To Olive's surprise, Mary dug into the dirty dishes and piled muddy clothes windowsill high. Mark's rash was back with a vengeance and the infant howled and fussed. Olive bathed him and made a cornstarch paste. He greedily ate the mush Olive fed him and nearly fell asleep in his chair. Near noon, Olive started a fire for laundry, and Mary carried the earth and sweat-laden pants and shirts outside.

"I'm going to take Jacob and the boys some lunch. Mark's asleep, and Peg is playing with her dolls," Olive called to Mary from the porch.

She filled a basket with sandwiches and jars of iced tea and pickled beets. Olive made her way slowly over the uneven plowed ground and saw Jacob and the boys ahead.

* * *

"There's Aunt Olive," Luke said as he straightened from the straw he bundled.

Jacob whoaed the horse and stood straight. His back was sore, his face and chest sunburned and his hands raw from holding the reins. Two weeks of gut-wrenching labor had left him wrung out. His mind often drifted to Olive as he drove the horse, tired as well, one more row southward, one more row northward in a seemingly unending battle.

"What's she doing here?" he asked Luke.

"I dunna know."

Jacob watched his son look away. He was angry this morning when Luke came through the fields with John in tow and they had argued.

"Jacob," Olive called, "I brought lunch."

They met in the shade of an oak tree, and Olive pulled supper from the basket. "Did Luke tell you to come over here?" Jacob asked.

Olive looked at Luke's wide eyes and shook her head. "No. I haven't seen the children for awhile and decided to visit."

The boys shoved ham and beets in their mouth and chugged down iced tea. Soon their eyes were closing as they sat side-by-side against the trunk of the tree.

"Peg burnt her finger this morning, Jacob. I'm not sure she should be home all these days alone with Mark," Olive said.

"Is she alright?" Jacob asked.

"She's fine. But the children seem tired and out of sorts. Why didn't you ask me to help you with them while you brought your crops in?"

"We'll be fine."

"No, I don't think you will be fine. I thought we were friends, Jacob," Olive said.

"We are friends."

"And you're too proud to ask me for help. You helped me and Mary and John. Why wouldn't you let me help you?"

Jacob looked at Olive's angry face. She was wrong. It wasn't pride that stopped him from asking her help. He lay in bed too many nights and fell asleep to a vision of Olive telling him she loved him. And if she was near that sentiment would be right smacked dab between them, making him feel his heart threatening to break yet again and Mary's accusations too true. He didn't want to face them, didn't have the time or energy to deal with them, only knew that if Olive wasn't within sight, he could forget his fears momentarily.

"I didn't want to bother you," Jacob said.

Olive's eyes opened wide. "Of all the stupid things I've heard you say, that takes the cake. Never mind," she continued to Jacob's open mouth, "that these children bear the brunt of your stupidity. I'm going back to the house, now and fix dinner and help Mary with laundry. Come on, boys. You've had enough for one day. I think you two should go fishing."

Jacob watched her stomp away and mutter, a boy on each side clinging to her hands. Here she was again, in his life, full of sass and deciding that the day's work was done for the boys.

"Now wait a second, Olive. If I have Luke out here, I can get this field done," Jacob called out.

She turned to him, and Jacob stepped back from the look on her face.

"These boys are tired and are going with me. Don't you dare say another word, Jacob Butler. I mean it."

His mouth closed as Olive's head whipped back in the direction of his house, and John and Luke skipped along beside her. *Damn her,* he thought. But a smile wrinkled his face at the toss of her hair as she challenged him to speak. He missed her so goddamned much. He missed how she guided the children and smiled and spoke her mind. He let out a hoarse laugh, thinking how much he loved arguing with Olive. And loved Olive. His face fell as the sentiment strung along naturally in his thoughts. But I can't. I won't. I won't love someone like that ever again, he thought. What if she got sick, what if she died. Jacob let all the "what if's" work on his mind as he gathered the horses reins and steeled his resolve. "I don't love her. I can't love her," he chanted to himself and threw his weary body into the mind numbing tasks before him.

* * *

Over the next few days, Olive arrived shortly after Jacob left his house and left as she saw him coming through the fields. His house was clean, bread was baked, and his children, happy. He sent John and Luke home every day at noontime, and someone would deliver his meal in kind. The constant worry over Peg and Mark alone was gone, and Luke's sullen attitude had disappeared. Jacob pushed himself hard in the fields, knowing his work there was near done and happy with what he produced. He stepped into the house, full of chatter, and the smell of dinner on the stove. He was surprised to see Olive's wagon still there.

* * *

"Jacob, I want you to bring the children over to my house every Tuesday and Thursday to begin with studies again. Luke told me you were near done with the fields, and I won't be coming over during the day," Olive said as she folded her hands at her waist.

"Alright," Jacob said and plopped down in a chair.

Olive's head tilted in surprise. She had expected an argument from him and was prepared for battle. "I don't want the children to have a long lapse in their school work."

"Fine," Jacob said and poured tea from the crockery pitcher on the table. Peg and Luke kissed him and ran outside with Mary and John already in the wagon.

"These children, every one of them, are bright, and continuity is important especially in their reading skills," Olive continued.

"Olive, I said fine. I'll have the children over there every Tuesday and Thursday for lessons."

Olive snorted and stumbled. "Well, fine, then."

As she neared the door, she stopped when Jacob spoke.

"Thank you, Olive."

"You're welcome," she said. She wanted to throw herself into his arms and take what he offered, but she knew she could not. She longed for his kisses and touch, but knew she could not give herself to a man who didn't love her. Her mind ached for his conversation and opinions, but she knew she was not entitled to them. She longed for his heart and knew it would never be hers.

* * *

Olive decided fall was her favorite season. Children back to routine, trees with a symphony of colors and cool nights. She sat on her porch one such evening watching fireflies after the children had gone to bed. She was planning a lesson for the following day and now closed her book and leaned back. Olive's eyes were near closed in the quiet of the evening when she heard the sound of a horse. The beat of hooves was not from the direction of Jacob's, and she jumped up and flew into the house. Olive threw the bar over the door with shaking hands and climbed onto the hearth to retrieve the shotgun. The shells rolled in her sweaty palms as she struggled to load and heard a banging at the door.

"Who's there?" Olive shouted.

"I'm here for the boy and the girl both. Git em up and out here, or you'll be sorry, girlie."

Olive's eyes widened with fear, and she saw Mary peeking around her door. "Get John, Mary." Olive's stomach rolled as she peeked out her front window and saw Sophie's father swaying on his feet. She saw only one horse. "Take John and climb out your bedroom window, Mary. Get behind the barn, and then make your way to Jacob's"

John and Mary's faces were white with fear, and Olive was afraid John would begin to cry. Mary pulled him along to her bedroom and closed the door. "They're not here. Now get off my property."

Olive jumped, and the rifle clattered to the floor as Jeb Davis threw himself at her front door time and again. The hinges heaved, and the man stumbled into her house.

"Where are them kids?" he growled.

Olive watched the spittle drip from the corner of the man's mouth and saw the drunken, wild look in his eyes. Her breaths were short, and she knew fear as she had never known before.

"They're gone," she whispered.

Jeb Davis flew forward, faster than Olive could have imagined, and slapped her, open-handed across the face. She flew into a heap on the floor, in the moment of no pain before an injury takes hold. When she looked up, she watched Mary leaping at her grandfather, beating him with her fists, around his face and chest. Olive's heart fell, knowing they were now both at this wild man's mercy. Please, dear God, let John be gone, she mumbled and tasted blood on her lip. But her prayers went unanswered as she watched John stare white-faced and wide-eyed at the milieu. Mary screamed as her grandfather pulled her hair sharply, and her head snapped around.

Mary spotted John and screamed, "Run, John."

Mary's face contorted with pain, and Olive grabbed her from Jeb Davis' hold. The shotgun lay between them. Mary watched him eye the weapon and dove for it. But the old man was faster, and he chuckled as he stood, rifle in hand. Olive's heart was racing, and Mary shook wildly in her arms.

"I ain't going with you," Mary spat at him. "You'll hafta kill me first."

An evil grin split the man's lips, and he replied. "Yer gonna wish you were dead, when I git ya home."

Olive and Mary uniformly backed up until their legs hit the chair. But Mary's courage in the face of this man made Olive's back straighten. *By damn, we'll go down fighting,* she thought.

"You'll never get these children. They are mine. John's on his way for help this minute. Soon you'll have no choice but to leave," Olive said.

He stepped forward and pulled Mary out of Olive's arms. With a rope he pulled from his jacket, he began to tie her wrists. Olive watched blood bubble where the rope dug the girl's flesh, but Mary never took her eyes from her grandfather's face.

"Keep your mouths shut, and I won't stuff 'em," he muttered.

Davis yanked Olive up and out of her seat, and she was sure her arm nearly came out of her shoulder. Olive flinched as he pulled her arms around her back, and Mary stepped forward and spit in his face. The child's grim countenance did not change when the man slapped her, and she fell, hitting her head on the rocker. Jeb Davis slowly pulled a filthy bandana from his pocket and wiped the spittle from his cheek.

"Get up," he shouted.

Olive's eyes widened as she saw blood dripping from Mary's forehead. She shook her head in a vehement warning. Mary looked back at her grandfather as she stood.

"Get outside," he growled.

Once on the porch with the two prisoners in front of him, he lifted his leg and kicked Olive in the backside. She tumbled down the steps unable to catch herself, and her head rang. Rolling around in the dirt, spitting dust, Olive felt Jeb Davis pull her upright. He leaned close to her ear and said, "That's for taking what's rightfully mine."

Olive smelled liquor and body odor, and her vision swam.

"You two start walking. I'll be right behind ya. And if ya try anything funny, girl," he said as he turned to Mary, "I'll blow your auntie's brains all over this here field."

Olive hurried to Mary and whispered, "Come on, Mary. Do as he says."

Olive and Mary walked and stumbled down the road in the moonlight, until the man on the horse shouted. "Here, turn in here. We'll cut through Butler's land."

The bottom of Olive's dress was soon heavy and covered with mud, and she stumbled stepping over the rows of cut corn. She prayed John could make it to Jacob's. Afraid and alone, she imagined, poor John, he'll never recover from this whatever the outcome.

"Where are we going, Mary?" Olive asked.

"I don't know," the girl whispered back. "They'd know where to look for us if we were going to his homestead but we're going the other way."

The moon came through the clouds on Mary's words, and Olive saw stark terror on her niece's face.

* * *

Jacob had trouble falling asleep that evening as he checked on his children for the tenth time. Everyone's fine, he said to himself, even as felt a wave of panic arise in his chest. He lay back down and finally gave into the long day and closed his eyes.

Jacob awoke slowly from a fitful dream that would not surface nor release him. He rolled to his back and felt compelled to turn his head to the side. A small shadow shaking and heaving stood before him in the darkness. He sat up and said, "Luke?"

The head twisted in the darkness from side-to-side. Jacob scrambled from his bed and lit the lamp with a suddenly shaking hand. He turned back to the form as light crept into the shadows and saw John barefoot in his nightshirt before him. Fear writhed down his back as he knelt in front of the boy and put his hands on the small arms. The nightshirt was filthy, and John's feet bloody and caked with mud. Jacob swallowed when he saw the look in John's eyes.

"What John? What happened?" Jacob asked.

John trembled and flinched and Peg and Luke woke up. Jacob wanted to shout and shake the mute boy, but he knew the child was close to hysteria. "Luke, he tells you things, sometimes, somehow. See if you can find out what happened."

Jacob pulled on his pants and a shirt over his shoulders as he listened to Luke beg the other boy to speak. But John stood numbly and Jacob saw him begin to shake violently.

"Was there a fire?" Jacob asked.

John shook his head.

Then Jacob asked the question to which he knew he did not want an answer. "Are Mary and Olive alright?"

John's head shook from side to side and tears rolled down his face.

Jacob loaded his gun with shaking hands, wishing he knew what or whom he faced and turned back to John. "I'm going there, right now. I'll help them."

John's mouth opened as if to speak and closed.

"Please, John, tell Daddy what happened!" Peg cried.

The boy swallowed and took nervous breaths as Jacob continued to ready himself. Jacob checked the bullets in his pistol, ready to tuck it into his pants when he heard a grating word emerge in a voice that did not come from either of his children.

"He... he," John struggled and fought to say.

Jacob flew to his knees in front of the boy and held his shoulders. "Who John? Tell me who."

If Jacob had been able to will the boy the courage or composure to complete the sentence he would have, but he could only watch as the small-frightened child formed letters with his mouth, unable to voice them as words.

"It's alright, John. You did good. You got here on your own at night, and I know you're afraid. I'll go to Olive and your sister. You stay here with Peg and Luke."

John's lips pulled together and he closed his eyes. "He... he took 'em."

Jacob knew real fear now and nodded slowly to John to continue.

"Ma's pa," John grated out and coughed.

Jacob pulled the boy close and hugged and kissed him. John had spoken, and Jacob knew it had taken all he had in his small heart to say the words. But knowing Jeb Davis was the culprit spurned Jacob's fear higher.

"Come on, children. Luke, get your brother. I'm going to take you down to the fruit cellar. Here, Peg, carry the lamp."

Jacob hurried and carried and dragged the crying children to the cellar with some blankets and put the lamp on a high shelf. "When I leave, Luke, I want you to bar the door. Don't open it for anyone but me. Do you understand?"

Jacob settled the children as best and fast as he could and began up the steps. He looked back down to three ashen faces and Mark sleeping in Luke's arms. "I'm going now. Don't worry, children. Everything will be fine. Luke, don't forget the door." He wanted to hold them and kiss them as he watched them nod bravely. "I love you all."

Jacob waited until he heard the bar cross and began to run in the direction of Olive's. Now knowing what he faced and not occupied with hiding the children or arming himself, Jacob's mind wandered. What had that madman done to Olive and Mary? How could he live with himself if the worst came true? He should have killed Jeb Davis the first time he bothered Olive. He would surely kill the man now. "But what if I am too late," he said aloud as he panted in the cool night air. If she's gone, I won't be able to go on, he thought, and tears came to the back of eyes.

Jacob's mind was suddenly filled with Margaret's face as she told him she loved him and lay dying. His lips quivered as he felt Margaret's limp, clammy hand caress his face for the last time. And with that thought, the moon cleared the clouds, and a cool breeze swept across his now sweat-soaked back. He saw the shadows of barren corn stocks sway in the breeze and an unearthly chill sweep down his spine. The wind sang the eerie song of drying, dying leaves and Jacob heard and felt a voice call to him.

"Jacob."

He looked from one side of the dark road to other and felt drops of sweat fly from his hair. But the voice that came to Jacob's mind was not of this world. And he knew.

"Margaret," he whispered.

Fearing there was not a moment to spare, Jacob kept up his pace, even as he wondered of his own sanity. "Help me, Margaret," he heaved.

Moments elapsed and he thought surely he dreamed but the wind whipped again and the voice he now often struggled to recall filled his head. "Love her, Jacob."

"Love who, Margaret? Love who?" he panted and shouted. "Love who?"

The wind died as quickly as it came, and he heard nothing but the night frogs and steady sure beat of his own feet on the mud packed road. Olive is alive. He knew now with surety. For there was certainly only one woman alive that he loved. Jacob's head cleared of fear and mystery, and he calmed and quieted even as the quick clip of his heartbeat raced in his ears.

"Give me the strength, dear God, to be fast enough. Make my aim true."

On his prayer he stopped running and bent waist down to catch his breath. Jacob gulped air and closed his eyes. When he opened them, he was staring at muddy footprints in the road. With a horse following. He turned to the cornfield, his own property and saw a path through the rows of dead stalks.

* * *

Olive and Mary trudged through the field towards the line of trees that marked the end of Jacob's property. Olive's stomach rolled as the sweat poured from her face. She was terrified. Not as much for herself, she decided, but for Mary, walking stone-faced beside her.

"I love you, Mary," Olive whispered.

"Quit gabbing," Jeb Davis said and pulled his horse to a stop. "Stand still, the both of you."

Olive heard him dismount and watched Mary look at her grandfather out of the corner of her eye. Olive's eyes closed as she realized he stood beside the horse and relieved himself. Mary inched back slowly behind the man's turned back. She slipped to the rump of the nag and beat the horse with her bound hands. "Yaw," the girl shouted.

The horse bolted and knocked Jeb Davis to his knees. Mary and Olive's head snapped to each other as they watched the man curse and wriggle in the mud. Mary took off first, with Olive close behind, for the dim cover of the trees. They grunted and struggled, but neither looked back as they ran. Olive heard the man shouting and gaining and stepped up her pace. Olive saw Mary pull the rope on her hands and finally free herself. "Hurry, Mary!"

"Split up when we hit the trees," Mary cried.

"Untie me," Olive said. Mary yanked the knot on Olive's wrist, and she squeezed her hand through.

With the first footfall under leaves, Mary darted to the left, and Olive ran straight ahead into the snapping low branches. She could see nothing in the black of the forest and soon tripped, sending her flying into a pile of rotting leaves. Olive curled into a ball heaving for breath yet too terrified to breath. She heard the crunch of heavy footsteps and saw the back shadow of a man not ten yards away.

"I'll find you, don't make no mistake. Then I'll beat ya sound."

Olive heard the threat as if the speaker was but inches away and wondered where Mary was hiding. The sound of the rifle cocking opened Olive's eyes wide, followed by the rustle of leaves. The shot blast drew a young female shout and Olive jumped. She pulled herself up and watched as Jeb Davis drew Mary to her knees and slapped her soundly. The crack of the hand to Mary's face and her frightened cry after forced Olive to her feet.

"I'll make you sorry you was ever born," Jeb Davis said and kicked the girl on the ground.

"Leave her alone," Olive cried and stumbled through roots and downed branches.

"I ought a kill you as you stand," Jeb Davis turned and said to Olive.

Olive watched Mary struggle to her feet as she turned the stone she carried over and over in her palm. "Let me see to Mary, and we'll come along quietly." Olive forced all fears and distractions from her head and concentrated on saving Mary's life. She walked, head high and clear, in her torn dirty dress in the direction of the girl. Olive felt the distance closing between herself and Jeb Davis and now willed the seconds to pass quickly. Three more steps, two more steps, she chanted to herself and clenched the cool moss covered rock in her hand. She prayed the cover of night would conceal her swing and that Mary would have the strength to run. Olive smelled damp earth and the stench of Jeb Davis and swung with all her might.

"Run, Mary, run," Olive shouted.

The sound of stone meeting bone wrung through Olive's head, and she heard the clatter of the rifle. Jeb Davis roared in pain and turned swaying and swinging for Olive. She swung again with the rock to soft flesh, and the man dropped to his knees.

"I won't leave you," Mary cried.

"Run, Mary, go to Jacob," Olive screamed and saw the now growling man lurch towards her.

Olive's back hit the forest floor and something dug deeply into her side. Davis was atop of her sweating and dripping, slapping her, half-crazed.

Mary stood rooted to her spot as her aunt gave her life to save her. She heard the crack of bone and a pained whimper, and her lip trembled. Mary stopped and turned, shouting. "I'll get Jacob. I love you, Aunt Olive. I'll be back."

Mary ran into the clearing and saw a shadow ahead running to her. Her first instinct was to drop to the ground but a shout from the man stopped her.

* * *

"Olive!"

"Jacob!" Mary shouted, crying and stumbling to him.

Jacob raced for her. "Mary, thank God. Are you all right? Where's Olive?"

Mary's face twitched and tears rolled through grime in stripes to her chin. She shook wildly and held Jacob' forearms. "He's got her, Jacob. He's goin' ta beat her to death."

Jacob's head came up to look to the stand of trees. He looked back down to Mary. "I'll get her, Mary. Lie down between the rows in this field. There might be gunfire and I don't want you caught in it."

The girl nodded, wild-eyed.

"Now listen to me, Mary. If something should happen, and I can't help you..."

"No, Jacob, no..."

He shook the hysterical girl's shoulders. "Listen to me, Mary. If I can't help you... you head south to this other band of trees. There's a falling down house there. You hide til morning and then get to the sheriff. Your brother and my children are in the fruit cellar at my house."

Mary nodded. "Please, Jacob. Save Aunt Olive."

"That's what I aim to do, Mary. Now lie down," Jacob said.

Mary lay down straight between turned rows of earth and looked up to Jacob with lips white from fear and tension. "Kill him."

Jacob nodded, knowing full well whom the girl meant. He turned to the direction Mary came from and began to run. He stopped knowing he was a prime target in the moon light but unable to control the anger rising in him.

"Jeb Davis, you lousy piece of shit. Come out here and fight a man. Leave the women and little girl alone."

Rattling and rustling from the brush revealed Jeb Davis dragging and pushing a limp Olive in front of him. Her head hung and rolled, and Jacob's breath drew on a hitch as he looked at her.

"Olive," he said reverently. "Olive," he shouted trying to lure her beaten body back to consciousness. "Let her go, and I won't kill you, Davis."

"Nobody takes what's mine, Butler."

He watched Jeb Davis sway on his feet and struggle to hold Olive. He's hurt, Jacob thought. My girls gave him a fight. The man snarled and growled and yanked Olive hard where his arm lay under her breasts. Olive's eyes opened.

"Mary," she shouted wildly.

"I'm here, Olive. I'm coming for you," Jacob shouted.

"Jacob," Olive wheezed.

Jeb Davis aimed his shotgun and fired.

Jacob saw the glint of the metal in the moonlight as it came up to him and did not move. The shot went wild, and Davis threw the now spent weapon to the ground. Jacob watched the man as he unsheathed a hunting knife and brought it to Olive's throat.

"I'll gut her like a pig 'fore yer anywhere's near."

Jacob began to slowly walk forward, knowing now his only chance to save Olive was to get within range for his pistol. Jacob heard a whimpered cry from behind and kept moving. One foot ahead, another, twenty feet, now. Now fifteen.

"Let her go, Davis."

His pistol gripped tightly in his hand, Jacob did not move his gaze from the face of his enemy, his target of Jeb Davis. The man's eyes were feral, and he spit and sputtered as Olive struggled against his chest.

"Be still now, Olive." Jacob raised his arm slowly, breathing deep and holding his breath. The barrel pointed at the man's forehead, inches from Olive's face.

* * *

Olive's eyes opened wide as she realized Jacob's intent. She drew a great gulp of breath and stood stone still. Olive watched the knife pull from her throat briefly and saw the force of its return begin when she heard the shot. Her hand loosened from the man's grip, and she clenched the wrist, wielding the knife. She stared at the blade as it shook and willed all her strength to hold it at bay. The man's arm suddenly went limp, and she felt him fall away. Her head rolled from back to side, and Olive pooled to the ground in a heap.

Chapter Twelve

JACOB WATCHED HIS ADVERSARY FALL, AND OLIVE crumble in the sight of his pistol. His solemn walk gave way to a panicked run, and when he reached Olive, his gaze went to Jeb Davis, now unstirring, with a small hole between his eyes, gushing blood. Jacob's hands dropped to his side as he fell to his knees beside Olive. Her face, her beautiful face was battered and bruised, and blood soiled her dress around her waist. As Jacob lifted her limp hand, he saw raw gashes on her wrist and a tear, his own, fell on his hand. He sniffed and laid two fingers on her neck. His head dropped in prayer when he felt a steady beat, and his lip trembled as fat tears rolled down his face and off his chin.

* * *

Olive's eyes fluttered open. Kneeling beside her was Jacob, his head bowed, massive shoulders quivering.

"Is he dead?" she asked.

Jacob's head flew up, and she was witness to his raw pain and suffering. Tears stuck in the thick stubble of his beard, and he sniffed and wiped his hand across his nose. Jacob nodded and picked her hand up in his.

"Mary, is Mary alright?"

Jacob nodded again, eyes downward.

Olive watched this man, so proud, so strong, so sure, struggle fitfully for composure. Jacob blinked away tears and swallowed. She lifted a trembling hand to his face and cradled his cheek. Jacob's eyes closed and he pressed into her hand. She smiled. "Jacob," she said.

His head came up, and his eyes opened in worry.

"Jacob, I'll be fine. Help me up." Olive struggled to get her feet under her when she felt Jacob's arms lift her. She let her head rest on his wide shoulder and tried to ignore the coming pain.

His head turned to hers and he lightly touched his lips to her forehead. "Never again, Olive. No one will ever hurt you again."

Her breath let go on a sigh and she wearily sank into Jacob's strong hold and his promise. Olive could see Mary coming to her and Jacob

"Is he dead?" the girl asked.

Jacob nodded.

Olive held her hand out to Mary and cried all her unshed tears. "It's over."

Mary sobbed. "I'm not crying for that crazy man. I'm glad he's dead. I'm just, I'm just... crying."

Olive struggled from Jacob's hold and swayed on her feet. She pulled Mary into her arms, and the two cried and clung to each other. "I love you, Mary. You were so brave."

Mary pulled back from her aunt with wide eyes. "Yeah, but you. You...woulda ...you were going to let him kill you."

"But he didn't, did he? We made it, Mary." The girl nodded, and Olive pulled her close for a kiss.

Mary mumbled into her aunt's torn and dirty dress. "I love you."

Olive's eyes met Jacob's and tears welled again.

"Do you think you can walk, Mary?" Jacob asked. "I want to carry your aunt."

"I can walk, Jacob," Olive said as she swayed on her feet. The night light grew dim to Olive and she felt her world roll away.

* * *

Jacob caught Olive as her body gave into injuries, pain, and the absence of fear. He carried her stoically, assuring Mary she had fainted. They trudged together in the moonlight, and Mary's feet dragged.

"Come on, Mary. You can make it. I see the light of the house around those trees," Jacob said.

Jacob laid Olive gently in his bed, while Mary freed the children. They raced to him and held tightly. When John saw Olive, beaten, his eyes grew wide, and he ran to his sister.

"I'm going for the doctor, children. Bar the door, Mary. I think everything's fine now, but don't take any chances," Jacob said.

Jacob saddled his horse, dragged his weary body up and faced the sunrise sky.

* * *

The children gathered around Jacob's feet on the porch, while Doc Burns examined Olive. When the door opened, all heads snapped to attention.

"Three broken ribs, an ugly gash in her back, and too many assorted bruises to count." The doctor said as faces lined with worry and lips trembled. "But nothing that won't heal with bed rest. Now let me take a look at you, Mary."

Mary complied sullenly as the doctor led her into the house. Jacob's eyes were dry and sandy when the doctor emerged again.

"She's fine, Jacob. I'm going over to Beth and Jack's and fetch some help for you." He ignored Jacob's shaking head and climbed into his buggy. "I think Olive's coming around. Better go see to her."

Jacob sat down beside Olive on his bed and saw through the curtain, Mary fast asleep.

"Olive?" he said.

* * *

Her eyes opened slowly, and she smiled at him. He was here. Here beside her. Steadfast. And exhausted. "Jacob, lie down. I don't remember how I got home, but I know you had something to do with it."

"Doc Burns went for Beth," Jacob said and sat elbows on his knees, holding Olive's hands.

"Lie down, then. Beth will be here."

Jacob's head came up slowly, and he met Olive's gaze. "Never again, Olive."

She remembered his words as he lifted her from the field and she smiled. "I don't think I have other enemies of Jeb Davis's caliber. I'll be fine."

"How could you have enemies, Olive?" Jacob said and ran his hands through his hair. "Not a sweeter, kinder more wonderful woman on the face of this earth."

"Thank you," Olive whispered.

Minutes passed quietly, and Jacob clung to her hand. "I've been a fool."

Olive's head tilted. "A fool, Jacob? No."

"Yeah. A fool. I thought, well, I thought, that if I didn't say the words they wouldn't be true. I was scared of losing you, like

Margaret and…"

Olive shook her head and smiled. "We were scared today. All of us. Don't say something you don't want to, Jacob."

Jacob knelt down beside Olive's bed and clutched her hand to his chest and spoke quickly. "Margaret came to me, Olive. She came to me as I was running for you and Mary. She said, 'love her,' and it was you she was talking about. And when I, well, Olive, I know I love you. Not saying the words don't make a bit of difference."

Tears formed in Olive's eyes, and her lip trembled.

Jacob stared at her intensely. "I don't love you 'cause Margaret told me to, Olive. I love you because you're a wonderful mother and brave and beautiful. I will love you forever."

Olive inched over on the mattress. "Lie down, Jacob."

He smiled tentatively and stretched out beside her. She snuggled under his arm and laid her head on his shoulder. "I love you, Jacob," she said softly as her eyes closed.

One month later

What a strange dream she had awoken from. She was to be a bride today. At thirty-six, feeling the years creep up on her mind as those same years pulled her body downward. She was to marry a handsome, young man, a prince who saved her from evil and they would live out the years God gave her, together.

But this was no dream. Peg and Mary helped her dress and fixed her long hair in a crown. She had lovingly sewed a cream, brocade gown. The one of her dreams as a girl, altered to fit and cover a woman near forty. Olive stood in front of the oval mirror, turning sideways, hoping the corset Beth had strung her into didn't fray. She turned slowly around the room, seeing the furniture from her parent's home and hoping they could see her this day and be proud. Proud of the path she had chosen and the man at the end of this road.

Peg and Mary had hunched secretively over the sewing machine days ago and now presented her with a lace-edged blue hanky for her to carry. The girl's stitches hadn't picked up all of the lace and some hung on precariously but Olive had plopped down, bleary-eyed on the bed, when they gave it to her. They stood and smiled at her and each other and told of their travels for the fabrics. She looked up to them, her daughters, and thanked them. Olive told them she needed nothing new, for her dress was just finished and for the old part, well, she would serve that purpose.

He stood, awaiting her with Luke and John by his side, in the November light that streamed through the window that warm winter day. Jacob was nervous, she could tell. Oddly, she was not. Nothing felt more natural, more right, more meant to be, than walking towards him at the altar. Their eyes had met when she turned the corner from the vestibule of the church and held true as he reached his hand out to hers. She watched his lip tremble and smiled calmly at him.

* * *

I am now Mrs. Jacob Butler and the mother of five children, Olive thought as Jacob swung her around for a dance. She stared at him as he smiled proudly and nodded to those who watched. Would she bear the load of being a wife? A mother? Would she be the one he craved and talked to? Was she up to the task of filling those shoes? Would he always want her?

But the deed was done, Olive said calmly to herself. She was that mother, that wife and if love, real love, was the yeast to this bread of marriage than she would rise to the demands. Because loving Jacob was what she knew she was intended to do. By design, from a God of wisdom and mercy, brought together to love.

* * *

"Why do you have the lights all out?" Jacob asked as he stuck his head in her bedroom door. "I'm going to trip, and you'll be a widow before your wedding night."

Olive stared at him in the shadows of the moon from over the edge of her blanket just under her nose. She watched him pad around her room, their room now, and hang his suit in the chiffarobe. The shadow of his body turned to her, and he came to sit on the bed.

"Olive, why are you hiding?" Jacob asked. " Don't be afraid."

"I'm not afraid."

Jacob chuckled. "Then why are you hiding?"

Olive's head tilted and she looked out the window to the full moon. "I'm not hiding from you, Jacob. I'm not afraid of you."

"Then what?" he asked and turned her face gently.

Her lashes dropped. "I'm not eighteen, Jacob."

"Thank God."

Olive pulled her face from his hand. "Don't tease me. Please."

Jacob knelt on the bed, over her. "Look at me, Olive. I want you. No one else."

Olive looked up at him as he loomed over her and saw the truth in his eyes.

"You are more beautiful with each passing day and never more so than when you said, 'I do.' And I want you now, more than ever."

"I want you as well, Jacob. I love you."

He stretched out beside her and pulled her into his arms. He kissed her softly and whispered into her ear. "Let me love you, then and show you. This isn't about our bodies, Olive. It's about our hearts."

She closed her eyes and sunk into his words and his touch. He worshipped every inch of her as she slowly revealed herself to him. And as he loomed above her, poised and impatient, she let the sensations reel her away.

This man was meant to be inside her, he designed for her, she for him. What in her imagination, had been unnatural and odd, felt right. Was wonderful. Olive pulled Jacob further into her, and her head reeled with power on the ache of his sigh.

And he brought her slowly to pleasure. When Jacob's back arched, Olive watched his eyes flutter as he gave into the demands of his body and his dead weight upon her, heaved for breath, sweat glistened in the moonlight. His love words in her hair brought her hands to his face.

Olive's limbs were lazy, and her eyes barely open. Their passion sated, she voiced in a half-breath the sum of her thoughts.

"Fiddle-dee-dee."

I hope you enjoyed Olive and Jacob's story. Please share your thoughts about *Romancing Olive* with your friends and family, leave a review where you purchased the book, or share on social media sites like Facebook.

Please visit hollybushbooks.com to read excerpts from my two other Prairie Romances, *Train Station Bride* and *Reconstructing Jackson*. You'll also find Victorian Romances *Cross the Ocean* and *Charming the Duke,* both set in London. My newest book is a Contemporary Romance titled, *Red, White & Screwed,* about middle-aged divorcee, Glenda Nelson and the comic trials and tribulations of aging parents, arguing teenagers, and a rekindled love life.

Drop by my website and leave me a note on the guestbook. I love to hear from readers!

Printed in Great Britain
by Amazon.co.uk, Ltd.,
Marston Gate.